Rip Van Winkle

and Other Stories

by

Washington Irving

illustrated by Susanne Suba

JUNIOR DELUXE EDITIONS   Garden City, New York

CONTENTS

Contents

RIP VAN WINKLE
and Other Stories

Rip Van Winkle

A POSTHUMOUS WRITING OF
DIEDRICH KNICKERBOCKER
BY WASHINGTON IRVING

By Woden, God of Saxons,
From whence comes Wensday, that is Wodensday,
Truth is a thing that ever I will keep
Unto thylke day in which I creep into
My sepulchre——
CARTWRIGHT

Whoever has made a voyage up the Hudson must remember the Kaatskill Mountains. They are a dismembered branch of the great Appalachian family, and are seen away to the west of the river, swelling up to a noble height, and lording it over the surrounding country. Every change of season, every change of weather, indeed, every hour of the day, produces some change in the magical hues and shapes of these mountains, and they are regarded by all the good wives, far and near, as perfect barometers. When the weather is fair and settled, they are clothed in blue and purple, and print their bold outlines on the clear evening sky; but, sometimes, when the rest of the landscape is cloudless, they will gather a hood of gray vapors about their summits, which, in the last rays of the setting sun, will glow and light up like a crown of glory.

At the foot of these fairy mountains, the voyager may have descried the light smoke curling up from a village, whose shingle-roofs gleam among the trees, just where the blue tints of the upland melt away into the fresh green of the nearer landscape. It is a little village of great antiquity, having been founded by some of the Dutch colonists, in the early times of the province, just about the beginning of the government of the good Peter Stuyvesant, (may he rest in peace!) and there were some of the houses of the original settlers standing within a few years, built of small yellow bricks brought from Holland, having latticed windows and gable fronts, surmounted with weather-cocks.

In that same village, and in one of these very houses (which, to tell the precise truth, was sadly time-worn and weather-beaten), there lived many years since, while the country was yet a province of Great Britain, a simple good-natured fellow of the name of Rip Van Winkle. He was a descendant of the Van Winkles who figured so gallantly in the chivalrous days of Peter Stuyvesant, and accompanied him to the siege of Fort Christina. He inherited, however, but little of the martial character of his ancestors. I have observed that he was a simple, good-natured man; he was, moreover, a kind neighbor, and an obedient, hen-pecked husband. Indeed, to the latter circumstance might be owing that meekness of spirit which gained him such universal popularity; for those men are most apt to be obsequious and conciliating abroad, who are under the discipline of shrews at home. Their tempers, doubtless, are rendered pliant and malleable in the fiery furnace of domestic tribulation; and a curtain lecture is worth all the sermons in the world for teaching the virtues of patience and long-suffering. A termagant wife may, therefore, in some respects, he considered a tolerable blessing; and if so, Rip Van Winkle was thrice blessed.

Certain it is, that he was a great favorite among all the good wives of the village, who, as usual, with the amiable sex, took his part in all family squabbles; and never failed, whenever they talked those matters over in their evening gossipings, to lay all the blame on Dame Van Winkle. The children of the village, too, would shout with joy whenever he approached. He assisted at their sports, made their playthings, taught them to fly kites and shoot marbles, and told them long stories of ghosts, witches, and Indians. Whenever he went dodging about the village, he was surrounded by a troop of them, hanging on his skirts, clambering on his back, and playing a thousand tricks on him with impunity; and not a dog would bark at him throughout the neighborhood.

The great error in Rip's composition was an insuperable aversion to all kinds of profitable labor. It could not be from the want of assiduity or perseverance; for he would sit on a wet rock, with a rod as long and heavy as a Tartar's lance, and fish all day without a murmur, even though he should not be encouraged by a single nibble. He would carry a fowling-piece on his shoulder for hours together, trudging through woods and swamps, and up hill and down dale, to shoot a few squirrels or wild pigeons. He would never refuse to assist a neighbor even in the roughest toil, and was a foremost man at all country frolics for husking Indian corn, or building stone fences; the women of the village, too, used to employ him to run their errands, and to do such little odd jobs as their less obliging husbands would not do for them. In a word Rip was ready to attend to anybody's business but his own; but as to doing family duty, and keeping his farm in order, he found it impossible.

In fact, he declared it was of no use to work on his farm; it was the most pestilent little piece of ground in the whole country; everything about it went wrong, and would go wrong, in spite of him. His fences were continually falling to pieces; his cow would either go astray, or get among the cabbages; weeds were sure to grow quicker in his fields than anywhere else; the rain always made a point of setting in just as he had some out-door work to do; so that though his patrimonial estate had dwindled away under his management, acre by acre, until there was little more left than a mere patch of Indian corn and potatoes, yet it was the worst conditioned farm in the neighborhood.

His children, too, were as ragged and wild as if they belonged to nobody. His son Rip, an urchin begotten in his own likeness, promised to inherit the habits, with the old clothes of his father. He was generally seen trooping like a colt at his mother's heels, equipped in a pair of his father's cast-off galligaskins, which he had much ado to hold up with one hand, as a fine lady does her train in bad weather.

Rip Van Winkle, however, was one of those happy mortals, of foolish, well-oiled dispositions, who take the world easy, eat white bread or brown, whichever can be got with least thought or trouble, and would rather starve on a penny than work for a pound. If left to himself, he would have whistled life away in perfect contentment; but his wife kept continually dinning in his ears about his idleness, his carelessness, and the ruin he was bringing on his family. Morning, noon, and night, her tongue was incessantly going, and everything he said or did was sure to produce a torrent of household eloquence. Rip had but one way of replying to all lectures of the kind, and that, by frequent use, had grown into a habit. He shrugged his shoulders, shook his head, cast up his eyes, but said nothing. This, however, always provoked a fresh volley from his wife; so that he was fain to draw off his forces, and take to the outside of the house—the only side which, in truth, belongs to a hen-pecked husband.

Rip's sole domestic adherent was his dog Wolf, who was as much hen-pecked as his master; for Dame Van Winkle regarded them as companions in idleness, and even looked upon Wolf with an evil eye, as the cause of his master's going so often astray. True it is, in all points of spirit befitting an honorable dog, he was as courageous an animal as ever scoured the woods—but what courage can withstand the ever-during and all-besetting terrors of a woman's tongue? The moment Wolf entered the house his crest fell, his tail drooped to the ground, or curled between his legs, he sneaked about with a gallows air, casting many a sidelong glance at Dame Van Winkle, and at the least flourish of a broomstick or ladle, he would fly to the door with yelping precipitation.

Times grew worse and worse with Rip Van Winkle as years of matrimony rolled on; a tart temper never mellows with age, and a sharp tongue is the only edged tool that grows keener with constant use. For a long while he used to console himself, when driven from home, by frequenting a kind of perpetual club of the sages, philosophers, and other idle personages of the village; which held its sessions on a bench before a small inn, designated by a rubicund portrait of His Majesty George the Third. Here they used to sit in the shade through a long lazy summer's day, talking listlessly over village gossip, or telling endless sleepy stories about nothing. But it would have been worth any statesman's money to have heard the profound discussions that sometimes took place, when by chance an old newspaper fell into their hands from some passing traveller. How solemnly they would listen to the contents, as drawled out by Derrick Van Bummel, the schoolmaster, a dapper learned little man, who was not to be daunted by the most gigantic word in the dictionary; and how sagely they would deliberate upon the public events some months after they had taken place.

The opinions of this junto were completely controlled by Nicholas Vedder, a patriarch of the village, and landlord of the inn, at the door of which he took his seat from morning till night, just moving sufficiently to avoid the sun and keep in the shade of a large tree; so that the neighbors could tell the hour by his movements as accurately as by a sun-dial. It is true he was rarely heard to speak, but smoked his pipe incessantly. His adherents, however (for every great man has his adherents), perfectly understood him, and knew how to gather his opinions. When anything that was read or related displeased him, he was observed to smoke his pipe vehemently, and to send forth short, frequent and angry puffs; but when pleased, he would inhale the smoke slowly and tranquilly, and emit it in light and placid clouds; and sometimes, taking the pipe from his mouth, and letting the fragrant vapor curl about his nose, would gravely nod his head in token of perfect approbation.

From even this stronghold the unlucky Rip was at length routed by his termagant wife, who would suddenly break in upon the tranquillity of the assemblage and call the members all to naught; nor was that august personage, Nicholas Vedder himself, sacred from the daring tongue of this terrible virago, who charged him outright with encouraging her husband in habits of idleness.

Poor Rip was at last reduced almost to despair; and his only alternative, to escape from the labor of the farm and clamor of his wife, was to take gun in hand and stroll away into the woods. Here he would sometimes seat himself at the foot of a tree, and share the contents of his wallet with Wolf, with whom he sympathized as a fellow-sufferer in persecution. "Poor Wolf," he would say, "thy mistress leads thee a dog's life of it; but never mind, my lad, whilst I live thou shalt never want a friend to stand by thee!" Wolf would wag his tail, look wistfully in his master's face, and if dogs can feel pity I verily believe he reciprocated the sentiment with all his heart.

In a long ramble of the kind on a fine autumnal day, Rip had unconsciously scrambled to one of the highest parts of the Kaatskill Mountains. He was after his favorite sport of squirrel shooting, and the still solitudes had echoed and re-echoed with the reports of his gun. Panting and fatigued, he threw himself, late in the afternoon, on a green knoll, covered with mountain herbage, that crowned the brow of a precipice. From an opening between the trees he could overlook all the lower country for many a mile of rich woodland. He saw at a distance the

lordly Hudson, far, far below him, moving on its silent but majestic course, with the reflection of a purple cloud, or the sail of a lagging bark, here and there sleeping on its glassy bosom, and at last losing itself in the blue highlands.

On the other side he looked down into a deep mountain glen, wild, lonely, and shagged, the bottom filled with fragments from the impending cliffs, and scarcely lighted by the reflected rays of the setting sun. For some time Rip lay musing on this scene; evening was gradually advancing; the mountains began to throw their long blue shadows over the valleys; he saw that it would be dark long before he could reach the village, and he heaved a heavy sigh when he thought of encountering the terrors of Dame Van Winkle.

As he was about to descend, he heard a voice from a distance, hallooing, "Rip Van Winkle! Rip Van Winkle!" He looked round, but could see nothing but a crow winging its solitary flight across the mountain. He thought his fancy must have deceived him, and turned again to descend, when he heard the same cry ring through the still evening air: "Rip Van Winkle! Rip Van Winkle!" At the same time Wolf bristled up his back, and giving a low growl, skulked to his master's side, looking fearfully down into the glen. Rip now felt a vague apprehension stealing over him; he looked anxiously in the same direction, and perceived a strange figure slowly toiling up the rocks, and bending under the weight of something he carried on his back. He was surprised to see any human being in this lonely and unfrequented place, but supposing it to be someone of the neighborhood in need of his assistance, he hastened down to yield it.

On nearer approach he was still more surprised at the

singularity of the stranger's appearance. He was a short square-built old fellow, with thick bushy hair, and a grizzled beard. His dress was of the antique Dutch fashion—a cloth jerkin strapped round the waist—several pair of breeches, the outer one of ample volume, decorated with rows of buttons down the sides, and bunches at the knees. He bore on his shoulder a stout keg, that seemed full of liquor, and made signs for Rip to approach and assist him with the load. Though rather shy and distrustful of this new acquaintance, Rip complied with his usual alacrity; and mutually relieving one another, they clambered up a narrow gully, apparently the dry bed of a mountain torrent. As they ascended, Rip every now and then heard long rolling peals, like distant thunder, that seemed to issue out of a deep ravine, or rather cleft, between lofty rocks, toward which their rugged path conducted. He paused for an instant, but supposing it to be the muttering of one of those transient thunder-showers which often take place in mountain heights, he proceeded. Passing through the ravine, they came to a hollow, like a small amphitheatre, surrounded by perpendicular precipices, over the brinks of which impending trees shot their branches, so that you only caught glimpses of the azure sky and the bright evening cloud. During the whole time Rip and his companion had labored on in silence; for though the former marvelled greatly what could be the object of carrying a keg of liquor up this wild mountain, yet there was something strange and incomprehensible about the unknown, that inspired awe and checked familiarity.

On entering the amphitheatre, new objects of wonder presented themselves. On a level spot in the centre was a company of odd-looking personages playing at ninepins. They were

dressed in a quaint outlandish fashion; some wore short doublets, other jerkins, with long knives in their belts, and most of them had enormous breeches, of similar style with that of the guide's. Their visages, too, were peculiar: one had a large beard, broad face, and small piggish eyes; the face of another seemed to consist entirely of nose, and was surmounted by a white sugar-loaf hat set off with a little red cock's tail. They all had beards, of various shapes and colors. There was one who seemed to be the commander. He was a stout old gentleman, with a weather-beaten countenance; he wore a laced doublet, broad belt and hanger, high-crowned hat and feather, red stockings, and high-heeled shoes, with roses in them. The whole group reminded Rip of the figures in an old Flemish painting, in the parlor of Dominie Van Shaick, the village parson, and which had been brought over from Holland at the time of the settlement.

What seemed particularly odd to Rip was, that though these folks were evidently amusing themselves, yet they maintained the gravest faces, the most mysterious silence, and were, withal, the most melancholy party of pleasure he had ever witnessed. Nothing interrupted the stillness of the scene but the noise of the balls, which, whenever they were rolled, echoed along the mountains like rumbling peals of thunder.

As Rip and his companion approached them, they suddenly desisted from their play, and stared at him with such fixed statue-like gaze, and such strange, uncouth, lack-lustre countenances, that his heart turned within him, and his knees smote together. His companion now emptied the contents of the keg into large flagons, and made signs to him to wait upon the company. He obeyed with fear and trembling; they quaffed the liquor in profound silence, and then returned to their game.

By degrees Rip's awe and apprehension subsided. He even ventured, when no eye was fixed upon him, to taste the beverage, which he found had much of the flavor of excellent Hollands. He was naturally a thirsty soul, and was soon tempted to repeat the draught. One taste provoked another; and he reiterated his visits to the flagon so often that at length his senses were overpowered, his eyes swam in his head, his head gradually declined, and he fell into a deep sleep.

On waking, he found himself on the green knoll whence he had first seen the old man of the glen. He rubbed his eyes—it was a bright sunny morning. The birds were hopping and twittering among the bushes, and the eagle was wheeling aloft, and breasting the pure mountain breeze. "Surely," thought Rip, "I have not slept here all night." He recalled the occurrences before he fell asleep. The strange man with a keg of liquor—the mountain ravine—the wild retreat among the rocks—the woe-begone party at ninepins—the flagon—"Oh! That flagon! That wicked flagon!" thought Rip. "What excuse shall I make to Dame Van Winkle!"

He looked round for his gun, but in place of the clean well-oiled fowling-piece, he found an old firelock lying by him, the barrel incrusted with rust, the lock falling off, and the stock worm-eaten. He now suspected that the grave roysters of the mountain had put a trick upon him, and, having dosed him with liquor, had robbed him of his gun. Wolf, too, had disappeared, but he might have strayed away after a squirrel or partridge. He whistled after him and shouted his name, but all in vain; the echoes repeated his whistle and shout, but no dog was to be seen.

He determined to revisit the scene of the last evening's gambol, and if he met with any of the party, to demand his dog and gun. As he rose to walk, he found himself stiff in the joints, and wanting in his usual activity. "These mountain beds do not agree with me," thought Rip, "and if this frolic should lay me up with a fit of the rheumatism, I shall have a blessed time with Dame Van Winkle." With some difficulty he got down into the glen: he found the gully up which he and his companion had ascended the preceding evening; but to his astonishment a mountain stream was now foaming down it, leaping from rock to rock, and filling the glen with babbling murmurs. He, however, made shift to scramble up its sides, working his toilsome way through thickets of birch, sassafrass, and witch-hazel, and sometimes tripped up or entangled by the wild grapevines that twisted their coils or tendrils from tree to tree, and spread a kind of network in his path.

At length he reached to where the ravine had opened through the cliffs to the amphitheatre; but no traces of such opening remained. The rocks presented a high impenetrable wall, over which the torrent came tumbling in a sheet of feathery foam, and fell into a broad deep basin, black from the shadows of the surrounding forest. Here, then, poor Rip was brought to a stand. He again called and whistled after his dog; he was only answered by the cawing of a flock of idle crows, sporting high in air about a dry tree that overhung a sunny precipice; and who, secure in their elevation, seemed to look down and scoff at the poor man's perplexities. What was to be done? The morning was passing away, and Rip felt famished for want of his breakfast. He grieved to give up his

dog and gun; he dreaded to meet his wife; but it would not do
to starve among the mountains. He shook his head, shouldered
the rusty firelock, and, with a heart full of trouble and anxiety,
turned his steps homeward.

As he approached the village he met a number of people,
but none whom he knew, which somewhat surprised him, for
he had thought himself acquainted with everyone in the
country round. Their dress, too, was of a different fashion
from that to which he was accustomed. They all stared at him
with equal marks of surprise, and whenever they cast their
eyes upon him, invariably stroked their chins. The constant
recurrence of this gesture induced Rip, involuntarily, to do the
same, when, to his astonishment, he found his beard had
grown a foot long!

He had now entered the skirts of the village. A troop of
strange children ran at his heels, hooting after him, and point-
ing at his gray beard. The dogs, too, not one of which he
recognized for an old acquaintance, barked at him as he passed.
The very village was altered; it was larger and more populous.
There were rows of houses which he had never seen before,
and those which had been his familiar haunts had disappeared.
Strange names were over the doors—strange faces at the windows—everything was strange. His mind now misgave him;
he began to doubt whether both he and the world around him
were not bewitched. Surely this was his native village, which
he had left but the day before. There stood the Kaatskill
Mountains—there ran the silver Hudson at a distance—there
was every hill and dale precisely as it had always been. Rip
was sorely perplexed—"That flagon last night," thought he,
"has addled my poor head sadly!"

It was with some difficulty that he found the way to his own house, which he approached with silent awe, expecting every moment to hear the shrill voice of Dame Van Winkle. He found the house gone to decay—the roof fallen in, the windows shattered, and the doors off the hinges. A half-starved dog that looked like Wolf was skulking about it. Rip called him by name, but the cur snarled, showed his teeth, and passed on. This was an unkind cut indeed—"My very dog," sighed poor Rip, "has forgotten me!"

He entered the house, which, to tell the truth, Dame Van Winkle had always kept in neat order. It was empty, forlorn, and apparently abandoned. This desolateness overcame all his connubial fears—he called loudly for his wife and children— the lonely chambers rang for a moment with his voice, and then all again was silence.

He now hurried forth, and hastened to his old resort, the village inn—but it too was gone. A large rickety wooden building stood in its place, with great gaping windows, some of them broken and mended with old hats and petticoats, and over the door was painted, "the Union Hotel, by Jonathan Doolittle." Instead of the great tree that used to shelter the quiet little Dutch inn of yore, there now was reared a tall naked pole, with something on the top that looked like a red night-cap, and from it was fluttering a flag, on which was a singular assemblage of stars and stripes—all this was strange and incomprehensible. He recognized on the sign, however, the ruby face of King George, under which he had smoked so many a peaceful pipe; but even this was singularly metamorphosed. The red coat was changed for one of blue and buff, a sword was held in the hand instead of a sceptre, the head was decorated with a cocked hat, and underneath, was painted in large characters, GENERAL WASHINGTON.

There was, as usual, a crowd of folk about the door, but none that Rip recollected. The very character of the people seemed changed. There was a busy, bustling, disputatious tone about it, instead of the accustomed phlegm and drowsy tranquillity. He looked in vain for the sage Nicholas Vedder, with his broad face, double chin, and fair long pipe, uttering clouds of tobacco-smoke instead of idle speeches; or Van Bummel, the schoolmaster, doling forth the contents of an ancient newspaper. In place of these, a lean, bilious-looking fellow, with his pockets full of handbills, was haranguing vehemently about rights of citizens—elections—members of Congress—liberty— Bunker's Hill—heroes of seventy-six—and other words, which were a perfect Babylonish jargon to the bewildered Van Winkle.

The appearance of Rip, with his long grizzled beard, his rusty fowling-piece, his uncouth dress, and an army of women and children at his heels, soon attracted the attention of the tavern politicians. They crowded round him, eying him from head to foot with great curiosity. The orator bustled up to him, and, drawing him partly aside, inquired "On which side he voted?" Rip stared in vacant stupidity. Another short but busy little fellow pulled him by the arm, and, rising on tiptoe, inquired in his ear, "Whether he was Federal or Democrat?" Rip was equally at a loss to comprehend the question; when a knowing, self-important old gentleman, in a sharp cocked hat, made his way through the crowd, putting them to the right and left with his elbows as he passed, and planting himself before Van Winkle, with one arm akimbo, the other rest-

ing on his cane, his keen eyes and sharp hat penetrating, as it were, into his very soul, demanded in an austere tone, "What brought him to the election with a gun on his shoulder, and a mob at his heels, and whether he meant to breed a riot in the village?"—"Alas! Gentlemen," cried Rip, somewhat dismayed, "I am a poor quiet man, a native of the place, and a loyal subject of the king, God bless him!"

Here a general shout burst from the bystanders—"A tory! A tory! A spy! A refugee! Hustle him! Away with him!" It was with great difficulty that the self-important man in the cocked hat restored order; and, having assumed a tenfold austerity of brow, demanded again of the unknown culprit, what he came there for, and whom he was seeking? The poor man humbly assured him that he meant no harm, but merely came there in search of some of his neighbors, who used to keep about the tavern.

"Well—who are they? Name them."

Rip bethought himself a moment, and inquired, "Where's Nicholas Vedder?"

There was a silence for a little while, when an old man replied in a thin piping voice, "Nicholas Vedder! Why, he is dead and gone these eighteen years! There was a wooden tombstone in the church-yard that used to tell all about him, but that's rotten and gone too."

"Where's Brom Dutcher?"

"Oh, he went off to the army in the beginning of the war; some say he was killed at the storming of Stony Point—others say he was drowned in a squall at the foot of Antony's Nose. I don't know—he never came back again."

"Where's Van Bummel, the schoolmaster?"

"He went off to the wars too, was a great militia general, and is now in Congress."

Rip's heart died away at hearing of these sad changes in his home and friends, and finding himself thus alone in the world. Every answer puzzled him too, by treating of such enormous lapses of time, and of matters which he could not understand: war—congress—Stony Point; he had no courage to ask after any more friends, but cried out in despair, "Does nobody here know Rip Van Winkle?"

"Oh, Rip Van Winkle!" exclaimed two or three, "Oh, to be sure! That's Rip Van Winkle yonder, leaning against the tree."

Rip looked, and beheld a precise counterpart of himself, as he went up the mountain: apparently as lazy, and certainly as ragged. The poor fellow was now completely confounded. He doubted his own identity, and whether he was himself or another man. In the midst of his bewilderment, the man in the cocked hat demanded who he was, and what was his name?

"God knows," exclaimed he, at his wit's end; "I'm not myself—I'm somebody else—that's me yonder—no—that's somebody else got into my shoes—I was myself last night, but I fell asleep on the mountain, and they've changed my gun, and everything's changed, and I'm changed, and I can't tell my name, or who I am!"

The bystanders began now to look at each other, nod, wink significantly, and tap their fingers against their foreheads. There was a whisper, also, about securing the gun, and keeping the old fellow from doing mischief, at the very suggestion of which the self-important man in the cocked hat retired with some precipitation. At this critical moment a fresh, comely woman pressed through the throng to get a peep at the gray-bearded man. She had a chubby child in her arms, which, frightened at his looks, began to cry. "Hush, Rip," cried she, "Hush, you little fool; the old man won't hurt you." The name of the child, the air of the mother, the tone of her voice, all awakened a train of recollections in his mind. "What is your name, my good woman?" asked he.

"Judith Gardenier."

"And your father's name?"

"Ah, poor man, Rip Van Winkle was his name, but it's twenty years since he went away from home with his gun, and never has been heard of since—his dog came home without him; but whether he shot himself, or was carried away by the Indians, nobody can tell. I was then but a little girl."

Rip had but one question more to ask; but he put it with a faltering voice:

"Where's your mother?"

"Oh, she too had died but a short time since; she broke a blood-vessel in a fit of passion at a New England peddler."

There was a drop of comfort, at least, in this intelligence. The honest man could contain himself no longer. He caught his daughter and her child in his arms. "I am your father!" cried he, "Young Rip Van Winkle once—old Rip Van Winkle now! Does nobody know poor Rip Van Winkle?"

All stood amazed, until an old woman, tottering out from among the crowd, put her hand to her brow, and peering under it in his face for a moment, exclaimed, "Sure enough! It is Rip Van Winkle—it is himself! Welcome home again, old neighbor. Why, where have you been these twenty long years?"

Rip's story was soon told, for the whole twenty years had

been to him but as one night. The neighbors stared when they heard it; some were seen to wink at each other, and put their tongues in their cheeks; and the self-important man in the cocked hat, who, when the alarm was over, had returned to the field, screwed down the corners of his mouth, and shook his head—upon which there was a general shaking of the head throughout the assemblage.

It was determined, however, to take the opinion of old Peter Vanderdonk, who was seen slowly advancing up the road. He was a descendant of the historian of that name, who wrote one of the earliest accounts of the province. Peter was the most ancient inhabitant of the village, and well versed in all the wonderful events and traditions of the neighborhood. He recollected Rip at once, and corroborated his story in the most satisfactory manner. He assured the company that it was a fact, handed down from his ancestor the historian, that the Kaatskill Mountains had always been haunted by strange beings. That it was affirmed that the great Hendrick Hudson, the first discoverer of the river and country, kept a kind of vigil there every twenty years, with his crew of the *Half-Moon*; being permitted in this way to revisit the scenes of his enterprise, and keep a guardian eye upon the river, and the great city called by his name. That his father had once seen them in their old Dutch dresses playing at ninepins in a hollow of the mountain; and that he himself had heard one summer afternoon, the sound of their balls, like distant peals of thunder.

To make a long story short, the company broke up, and returned to the more important concerns of the election. Rip's daughter took him home to live with her; she had a snug, well-furnished house, and a stout cheery farmer for a husband, whom Rip recollected for one of the urchins that used to climb upon his back. As to Rip's son and heir, who was the ditto of himself, seen leaning against the tree, he was employed to work on the farm; but evinced an hereditary disposition to attend to anything else but his business.

Rip now resumed his old walks and habits; he soon found many of his former cronies, though all rather the worse for the wear and tear of time, and preferred making friends among the rising generation, with whom he soon grew into great favor.

Having nothing to do at home, and being arrived at that happy age when a man can be idle with impunity, he took his place once more on the bench at the inn door, and was reverenced as one of the patriarchs of the village, and a chronicle of the old times "before the war." It was some time before he could get into the regular track of gossip, or could be made to comprehend the strange events that had taken place during his torpor. How that there had been a revolutionary war—that the country had thrown off the yoke of old England —and that, instead of being a subject of his Majesty George the Third, he was now a free citizen of the United States. Rip, in fact, was no politician; the changes of states and empires made but little impression on him; but there was one species of despotism under which he had long groaned, and that was —petticoat government. Happily that was at an end; he had got his neck out of the yoke of matrimony, and could go in and out whenever he pleased, without dreading the tyranny of Dame Van Winkle. Whenever her name was mentioned, however, he shook his head, shrugged his shoulders, and cast up his eyes; which might pass either for an expression of resignation to his fate, or joy of his deliverance.

He used to tell his story to every stranger that arrived at Mr. Doolittle's hotel. He was observed, at first, to vary on some points every time he told it, which was, doubtless, owing to his having so recently awaked. It at last settled down precisely to the tale I have related, and not a man, woman, or child in the neighborhood, but knew it by heart. Some always pretended to doubt the reality of it, and insisted that Rip had been out of his head, and that this was one point on which he always remained flighty. The old Dutch inhabitants, however, almost universally gave it full credit. Even to this day they never hear a thunderstorm of a summer afternoon about the Kaatskill, but they say Hendrick Hudson and his crew are at their game of ninepins; and it is a common wish of all henpecked husbands in the neighborhood, when life hangs heavy on their hands, that they might have a quieting draught out of Rip Van Winkle's flagon.

The Legend
of
Sleepy Hollow

FOUND AMONG THE PAPERS OF
THE LATE DIEDRICH KNICKERBOCKER
BY WASHINGTON IRVING

A pleasing land of drowsy head it was,
Of dreams that wave before the half-shut eye;
And of gay castles in the clouds that pass,
For ever flushing round a summer sky.

CASTLE OF INDOLENCE

In the bosom of one of those spacious coves which indent the eastern shore of the Hudson, at that broad expansion of the river denominated by the ancient Dutch navigators the Tappaan Zee, and where they always prudently shortened sail, and implored the protection of St. Nicholas when they crossed, there lies a small market-town or rural port, which by some is called Greensburgh, but which is more generally and properly known by the name of Tarrytown. This name was given, we are told, in former days, by the good housewives of the adjacent country, from the inveterate propensity of their husbands to linger about the tavern on market days. Be that as it may, I do not vouch for the fact, but merely advert to it, for the sake of being precise and authentic. Not far from this village, perhaps about two miles, there is a little valley, or rather lap of land, among high hills, which is one of the quietest places in the whole world. A small brook glides through it, with just murmur enough to lull one to repose; and the occasional whistle of a quail, or tapping of a woodpecker, is almost the only sound that ever breaks in upon the uniform tranquillity.

I recollect that, when a stripling, my first exploit in squirrel-shooting was in a grove of tall walnut-trees that shades one side of the valley. I had wandered into it at noon time, when all nature is peculiarly quiet, and was startled by the roar of my own gun, as it broke the Sabbath stillness around, and was prolonged and reverberated by the angry echoes. If ever I should wish for a retreat, whither I might steal from the world and its distractions, and dream quietly away the remnant of a troubled life, I know of none more promising than this little valley.

From the listless repose of the place, and the peculiar character of its inhabitants, who are descendants from the original Dutch settlers, this sequestered glen has long been known by the name of SLEEPY HOLLOW, and its rustic lads are called the Sleepy Hollow Boys throughout all the neighboring country. A drowsy, dreamy influence seems to hang over the land, and to pervade the very atmosphere. Some say that the place was bewitched by a high German doctor, during the early days of the settlement; others, that an old Indian chief, the prophet or wizard of his tribe, held his powwows there before the country was discovered by Master Hendrick Hudson. Certain it is, the place still continues under the sway of some witching power, that holds a spell over the minds of the good people, causing them to walk in a continual reverie. They are given to all kinds of marvellous beliefs; are subject to trances and visions; and frequently see strange sights, and hear music and voices in the air. The whole neighborhood abounds with local tales, haunted spots, and twilight superstitions; stars shoot and meteors glare oftener across the valley than any other part of the country, and the nightmare, with her whole ninefold, seems to make it the favorite scene of her gambols.

The dominant spirit, however, that haunts this enchanted region, and seems to be commander-in-chief of all the powers of the air, is the apparition of a figure on horseback without a head. It is said by some to be the ghost of a Hessian trooper, whose head had been carried away by a cannonball, in some nameless battle during the revolutionary war; and who is ever and anon seen by the country folk, hurrying along in the gloom of night as if on the wings of the wind. His haunts are not confined to the valley, but extend at times to the adjacent roads, and especially to the vicinity of a church at no great distance. Indeed, certain of the most authentic historians of those parts, who have been careful in collecting and collating the floating facts concerning this spectre, allege that the body of the trooper, having been buried in the churchyard, the ghost rides forth to the scene of battle in nightly quest of his head; and that the rushing speed with which he sometimes passes along the Hollow, like a midnight blast, is owing to his being belated, and in a hurry to get back to the churchyard before daybreak.

Such is the general purport of this legendary superstition, which has furnished materials for many a wild story in that region of shadows; and the spectre is known, at all the country firesides, by the name of the Headless Horseman of Sleepy Hollow.

It is remarkable that the visionary propensity I have mentioned is not confined to the native inhabitants of the valley, but is unconsciously imbibed by everyone who resides there for a time. However wide awake they may have been before they entered that sleepy region, they are sure, in a little time, to inhale the witching influence of the air, and begin to grow imaginative—to dream dreams, and see apparitions.

I mention this peaceful spot with all possible laud; for it is in such little retired Dutch valleys, found here and there embosomed in the great State of New York, that population, manners, and customs, remain fixed; while the great torrent of migration and improvement, which is making such incessant changes in other parts of this restless country, sweeps by them unobserved. They are like those little nooks of still water which border a rapid stream; where we may see the straw and bubble riding quietly at anchor, or slowly revolving in their mimic harbor, undisturbed by the rush of the passing current. Though many years have elapsed since I trod the drowsy shades of Sleepy Hollow, yet I question whether I should not still find the same trees and the same families vegetating in its sheltered bosom.

In this by-place of nature, there abode, in a remote period of American history, that is to say, some thirty years since, a worthy wight of the name of Ichabod Crane; who sojourned, or, as he expressed it, "tarried," in Sleepy Hollow, for the purpose of instructing the children of the vicinity. He was a native of Connecticut; a State which supplies the Union with pioneers for the mind as well as for the forest, and sends forth yearly its legions of frontier woodsmen and country schoolmasters. The cognomen of Crane was not inapplicable to his person. He was tall, but exceedingly lank, with narrow shoulders, long arms and legs, hands that dangled a mile out of his sleeves, feet that might have served for shovels, and his whole frame most loosely hung together. His head was small, and flat at top, with huge ears, large green glassy eyes, and a long snipe nose, so that it looked like a weathercock, perched upon his spindle neck, to tell which way the wind blew. To see him striding along the profile of a hill on a windy day, with his clothes bagging and fluttering about him, one might have mistaken him for the genius of famine descending upon the earth, or some scarecrow eloped from a cornfield.

His schoolhouse was a low building of one large room, rudely constructed of logs; the windows partly glazed, and partly patched with leaves of old copy-books. It was most ingeniously secured at vacant hours, by a withe twisted in the handle of the door, and stakes set against the window shutters; so that, though a thief might get in with perfect ease, he would find some embarrassment in getting out; an idea most probably borrowed by the architect, Yost Van Houten, from the mystery of an eel-pot. The schoolhouse stood in a rather lonely but pleasant situation, just at the foot of a woody hill, with a brook running close by, and a formidable birch tree growing at one end of it. From hence the low murmur of his pupils' voices, conning over their lessons, might be heard in a drowsy summer's day, like the hum of a bee-hive; interrupted now and then by the authoritative voice of the master, in the tone of menace or command; or, peradventure, by the appalling sound of the birch, as he urged some tardy loiterer along the flowery path of knowledge. Truth to say, he was a conscientious man, and ever bore in mind the golden maxim, "Spare the rod and spoil the child." Ichabod Crane's scholars certainly were not spoiled.

I would not have it imagined, however, that he was one of those cruel potentates of the school, who joy in the smart of their subjects; on the contrary, he administered justice with discrimination rather than severity; taking the burthen off the backs of the weak, and laying it on those of the strong. Your mere puny stripling, that winced at the least flourish of the rod, was passed by with indulgence; but the claims of justice were satisfied by inflicting a double portion on some little, tough, wrong-headed, broad-skirted Dutch urchin, who sulked and swelled and grew dogged and sullen beneath the birch. All this he called "doing his duty by their parents"; and he never inflicted a chastisement without following it by the assurance, so consolatory to the smarting urchin, that "he would remember it, and thank him for it the longest day he had to live."

When school hours were over, he was even the companion and playmate of the larger boys; and on holiday afternoons would convoy some of the smaller ones home, who happened to have pretty sisters, or good housewives for mothers, noted for the comforts of the cupboard. Indeed, it behooved him to keep on good terms with his pupils. The revenue arising from his school was small, and would have been scarcely sufficient to furnish him with daily bread, for he was a huge feeder, and though lank, had the dilating powers of an anaconda; but to help out his maintenance, he was, according to country custom in those parts, boarded and lodged at the houses of the farmers, whose children he instructed. With these he lived successively a week at a time; thus going the rounds of the neighborhood, with all his worldly effects tied up in a cotton handkerchief.

That all this might not be too onerous on the purses of his rustic patrons, who are apt to consider the costs of schooling a grievous burden, and schoolmasters as mere drones, he had various ways of rendering himself both useful and agreeable. He assisted the farmers occasionally in the lighter labors of their farms; helped to make hay; mended the fences; took the horses to water; drove the cows from pasture; and cut wood for the winter fire. He laid aside, too, all the dominant dignity and absolute sway with which he lorded it in his little empire, the school, and became wonderfully gentle and ingratiating. He found favor in the eyes of the mothers, by petting the children, particularly the youngest; and like the lion bold, which whilom so magnanimously the lamb did hold, he would sit with a child on one knee, and rock a cradle with his foot for whole hours together.

In addition to his other vocations, he was the singing-master of the neighborhood, and picked up many bright shillings by instructing the young folks in psalmody. It was a matter of no little vanity to him, on Sundays, to take his station in front of the church gallery, with a band of chosen singers; where, in his own mind, he completely carried away the palm from the parson. Certain it is, his voice resounded far above all the rest of the congregation; and there are peculiar quavers still to be heard in that church, and which may be heard half a mile off, quite to the opposite side of the mill-pond, on a still Sunday morning, which are said to be legitimately descended from the nose of Ichabod Crane. Thus, by divers little makeshifts in that ingenious way which is commonly denominated "by hook and by crook," the worthy pedagogue got on tolerably enough, and was thought, by all who understood nothing of the labor of headwork, to have a wonderfully easy life of it.

The schoolmaster is generally a man of some importance in the female circle of a rural neighborhood; being considered a kind of idle gentlemanlike personage, of vastly superior taste and accomplishments to the rough country swains, and indeed, inferior in learning only to the parson. His appearance, therefore, is apt to occasion some little stir at the tea-table of a farmhouse, and the addition of a supernumerary dish of cakes or sweetmeats, or, peradventure, the parade of a silver tea-pot. Our man of letters, therefore, was peculiarly happy in the smiles of all the country damsels. How he would figure among them in the churchyard, between services on Sundays gathering grapes for them from the wild vines that overran the surrounding trees; reciting for their amusement all the epitaphs on the tombstones; or sauntering, with a whole bevy of them, along the banks of the adjacent mill-pond; while the more bashful country bumpkins hung sheepishly back, envying his superior elegance and address.

From his half itinerant life, also, he was a kind of travelling gazette, carrying the whole budget of local gossip from house to house; so that his appearance was always greeted with satisfaction. He was, moreover, esteemed by the women as a man of great erudition, for he had read several books quite through,

and was a perfect master of Cotton Mather's history of New England Witchcraft, in which, by the way, he most firmly and potently believed.

He was, in fact, an odd mixture of small shrewdness and simple credulity. His appetite for the marvellous, and his powers of digesting it, were equally extraordinary; and both had been increased by his residence in this spellbound region. No tale was too gross or monstrous for his capacious swallow. It was often his delight, after his school was dismissed in the afternoon, to stretch himself on the rich bed of clover, bordering the little brook that whimpered by his schoolhouse, and there con over old Mather's direful tales, until the gathering dusk of the evening made the printed page a mere mist before his eyes. Then, as he wended his way, by swamp and stream and awful woodland, to the farmhouse where he happened to be quartered, every sound of nature, at that witching hour, fluttered his excited imagination: the moan of the whip-poor-will[1] from the hillside; the boding cry of the tree-toad, that harbinger of storm; the dreary hooting of the screech-owl, or the sudden rustling in the thicket of birds frightened from their roost. The fireflies, too, which sparkled most vividly in the darkest places, now and then startled him, as one of uncommon brightness would stream across his path; and if, by chance, a huge blockhead of a beetle came winging his blundering flight against him, the poor varlet was ready to give up the ghost, with the idea that he was struck with a witch's token. His only resource on such occasions, either to drown thought, or drive away evil spirits, was to sing psalm tunes—

[1] The whip-poor-will is a bird which is only heard at night. It receives its name from its note, which is thought to resemble those words.

and the good people of Sleepy Hollow, as they sat by their doors of an evening, were often filled with awe, at hearing his nasal melody, "in linked sweetness long drawn out," floating from the distant hill, or along the dusky road.

Another of his sources of fearful pleasure was, to pass long winter evenings with the old Dutch wives, as they sat spinning by the fire, with a row of apples roasting and spluttering along the hearth, and listen to their marvellous tales of ghosts and goblins, and haunted fields, and haunted brooks, and haunted bridges, and haunted houses, and particularly of the headless horseman, or galloping Hessian of the Hollow, as they sometimes called him. He would delight them equally by his anecdotes of witchcraft, and of the direful omens and portentous sights and sounds in the air, which prevailed in the earlier times of Connecticut; and would frighten them wofully with speculations upon comets and shooting stars; and with the alarming fact that the world did absolutely turn round, and that they were half the time topsy-turvy!

But if there was a pleasure in all this, while snugly cuddling in the chimney corner of a chamber that was all of a ruddy glow from the crackling wood fire, and where, of course, no spectre dared to show his face, it was dearly purchased by the terrors of his subsequent walk homewards. What fearful shapes and shadows beset his path amidst the dim and ghastly glare of a snowy night! With what wistful look did he eye every trembling ray of light streaming across the waste fields from some distant window! How often was he appalled by some shrub covered with snow, which, like a sheeted spectre, beset his very path! How often did he shrink with curdling awe at the sound of his own steps on the frosty crust beneath his feet; and dreaded to look over his shoulder, lest he should behold some uncouth being tramping close behind him! And how often was he thrown into complete dismay by some rushing blast, howling among the trees, in the idea that it was the Galloping Hessian on one of his nightly scourings!

All these, however, were mere terrors of the night, phantoms of the mind that walked in darkness; and though he had seen many spectres in his time, and been more than once beset by Satan in divers shapes, in his lonely perambulations, yet daylight put an end to all these evils; and he would have passed a pleasant life of it, in despite of the devil and all his works, if his path had not been crossed by a being that causes more perplexity to mortal man than ghosts, goblins, and the whole race of witches put together, and that was—a woman.

Among the musical disciples who assembled, one evening in each week, to receive his instructions in psalmody, was Katrina Van Tassel, the daughter and only child of a substantial Dutch farmer. She was a blooming lass of fresh eighteen; plump as a partridge; ripe and melting and rosy cheeked as one of her father's peaches, and universally famed, not merely for her beauty, but her vast expectations. She was withal a little of a coquette, as might be perceived even in her dress, which was a mixture of ancient and modern fashions, as most suited to set off her charms. She wore the ornaments of pure yellow gold, which her great-great-grandmother had brought over from Saardam; the tempting stomacher of the olden time; and withal a provokingly short petticoat, to display the prettiest foot and ankle in the country round.

Ichabod Crane had a soft and foolish heart towards the sex; and it is not to be wondered at, that so tempting a morsel soon found favor in his eyes; more especially after he had visited her in her paternal mansion. Old Baltus Van Tassel was a perfect picture of a thriving, contented, liberal-hearted farmer. He seldom, it is true, sent either his eyes or his thoughts beyond the boundaries of his own farm; but within those everything was snug, happy, and well-conditioned. He was satisfied with his wealth, but not proud of it; and piqued himself upon the hearty abundance, rather than the style in which he lived. His stronghold was situated on the banks of the Hudson, in one of those green, sheltered, fertile nooks, in which Dutch farmers are so fond of nestling. A great elm-tree spread its broad branches over it; at the foot of which bubbled up a spring of the softest and sweetest water, in a little well, formed of a barrel; and then stole sparkling away through the grass, to a neighboring brook, that bubbled along among alders and dwarf willows. Hard by the farmhouse was a vast barn, that might have served for a church; every window and crevice of which seemed bursting forth with the treasures of the farm. The flail was busily resounding within it from morning to night; swallows and martins skimmed twittering about the eaves; and rows of pigeons, some with one eye turned up, as if watching the weather, some with their heads under their wings, or buried in their bosoms, and others swelling, and cooing, and bowing about their dames, were enjoying the sunshine on the roof. Sleek unwieldy porkers were grunting in the repose and abundance of their pens; whence sallied forth, now and then, troops of sucking pigs, as if to snuff the air. A stately squadron of snowy geese were riding in an adjoining pond, convoying whole fleets of ducks; regiments of turkeys were gobbling through the farmyard, and guinea fowls fretting

46

about it, like ill-tempered housewives, with their peevish, discontented cry. Before the barn door strutted the gallant cock, that pattern of a husband, a warrior, and a fine gentleman, clapping his burnished wings, and crowing in the pride and gladness of his heart—sometimes tearing up the earth with his feet, and then generously calling his ever-hungry family of wives and children to enjoy the rich morsel which he had discovered.

The pedagogue's mouth watered, as he looked upon this sumptuous promise of luxurious winter fare. In his devouring mind's eye, he pictured to himself every roasting-pig running about with a pudding in his belly, and an apple in his mouth; the pigeons were snugly put to bed in a comfortable pie, and tucked in with a coverlet of crust; the geese were swimming in their own gravy; and the ducks pairing cosily in dishes, like snug married couples, with a decent competency of onion sauce. In the porkers he saw carved out the future sleek side of bacon, and juicy relishing ham; not a turkey but he beheld daintily trussed up, with its gizzard under its wing, and, peradventure, a necklace of savory sausages; and even bright chanticleer himself lay sprawling on his back, in a side dish, with uplifted claws, as if craving that quarter which his chivalrous spirit disdained to ask while living.

As the enraptured Ichabod fancied all this, and as he rolled his great green eyes over the fat meadow-lands, the rich fields of wheat, of rye, of buckwheat, and Indian corn, and the orchards burdened with ruddy fruit, which surrounded the warm tenement of Van Tassel, his heart yearned after the damsel who was to inherit these domains, and his imagination expanded with the idea, how they might be readily turned into cash, and the money invested in immense tracts of wild land, and shingle palaces in the wilderness. Nay, his busy fancy already realized his hopes, and presented to him the blooming Katrina, with a whole family of children, mounted on the top of a wagon loaded with household trumpery, with pots and kettles dangling beneath; and he behind himself bestriding a pacing mare, with a colt at her heels, setting out for Kentucky, Tennessee, or the Lord knows where.

When he entered the house the conquest of his heart was complete. It was one of those spacious farmhouses, with high-ridged, but lowly-sloping roofs, built in the style handed down from the first Dutch settlers, the low projecting eaves forming a piazza along the front, capable of being closed up in bad weather. Under this were hung flails, harness, various utensils of husbandry, and nets for fishing in the neighboring river. Benches were built along the sides for summer use; and a great spinning-wheel at one end, and a churn at the other, showed the various uses to which this important porch might be devoted. From this piazza the wondering Ichabod entered the hall, which formed the centre of the mansion and the place of usual residence. Here, rows of resplendent pewter, ranged on a long dresser, dazzled his eyes. In one corner stood a huge bag of wool ready to be spun; in another a quantity of linsey-woolsey just from the loom; ears of Indian corn, and strings of dried apples and peaches, hung in gay festoons along the walls, mingled with the gaud of red peppers, and a door left ajar gave him a peep into the best parlor, where the claw-footed chairs, and dark mahogany tables, shone like mirrors. And irons, with their accompanying shovel and tongs, glistened from their covert of asparagus tops; mock-oranges and conch-shells decorated the mantel-piece; strings of various colored birds' eggs were suspended above it. A great ostrich egg was hung from the centre of the room, and a corner cupboard, knowingly left open, displayed immense treasures of old silver and well-mended china.

From the moment Ichabod laid his eyes upon these regions of delight, the peace of his mind was at an end, and his only study was how to gain the affections of the peerless daughter of Van Tassel. In this enterprise, however, he had more real difficulties than generally fell to the lot of a knight-errant of yore, who seldom had anything but giants, enchanters, fiery dragons, and such like easily conquered adversaries, to contend with; and had to make his way merely through gates of iron and brass, and walls of adamant, to the castle keep, where the lady of his heart was confined, all of which he achieved as easily as a man would carve his way to the centre of a Christmas pie, and then the lady gave him her hand as a matter of course. Ichabod, on the contrary, had to win his way to the heart of a country coquette, beset with a labyrinth of whims and caprices, which were forever presenting new difficulties and impediments; and he had to encounter a host of fearful adversaries of real flesh and blood, the numerous rustic admirers, who beset every portal to her heart, keeping a watchful and angry eye upon each other, but ready to fly out in the common cause against any new competitor.

Among these the most formidable was a burly, roaring, roystering blade, of the name of Abraham, or, according to the Dutch abbreviation, Brom Van Brunt, the hero of the country round, which rang with his feats of strength and hardihood. He was broad-shouldered and double-jointed, with short curly black hair, and a bluff, but not unpleasant countenance, having a mingled air of fun and arrogance. From his Herculean frame and great powers of limb, he had received the nickname of BROM BONES, by which he was universally known. He was famed for great knowledge and skill in horsemanship, being as dexterous on horseback as a Tartar. He was foremost at all races and cock-fights; and, with the ascendency which bodily strength acquires in rustic life, was the umpire in all disputes, setting his hat on one side, and giving his decisions with an air and tone admitting of no gainsay or appeal. He was always ready for either a fight or a frolic; but had more mischief than ill-will in his composition; and, with all his overbearing roughness, there was a strong dash of waggish good humor at bottom. He had three or four boon companions, who regarded him as their model, and at the head of whom he scoured the country, attending every scene of feud or merriment for miles round. In cold weather he was distinguished by a fur cap, surmounted with a flaunting fox's tail; and when the folks at a country gathering descried this well-known crest at a distance, whisking about among a squad of hard riders, they always stood by for a squall. Sometimes his crew would be heard dashing along past the farmhouses at midnight, with whoop and halloo, like a troop of Don Cossacks; and the old dames, startled out of their sleep, would listen for a moment till the hurry-scurry had clattered by, and then exclaim, "Ay, there goes Brom Bones and his gang!" The neighbors looked upon him with a mixture of awe, admiration, and good will; and when any madcap prank or rustic brawl occurred in the vicinity, always shook their heads, and warranted Brom Bones was at the bottom of it.

This rantipole hero had for some time singled out the blooming Katrina for the object of his uncouth gallantries, and though his amorous toyings were something like the gentle caresses and endearments of a bear, yet it was whispered that she did not altogether discourage his hopes. Certain it is, his advances were signals for rival candidates to retire, who felt no inclination to cross a lion in his amours; insomuch, that when his horse was seen tied to Van Tassel's paling, on a Sunday night, a sure sign that his master was courting, or, as it is termed, "sparking," within, all other suitors passed by in despair, and carried the war into other quarters.

Such was the formidable rival with whom Ichabod Crane had to contend, and, considering all things, a stouter man than he would have shrunk from the competition, and a wiser man would have despaired. He had however, a happy mixture of pliability and perseverance in his nature; he was in form and spirit like a supple-jack—yielding, but tough; though he bent, he never broke; and though he bowed beneath the slightest pressure, yet, the moment it was away—jerk! he was as erect, and carried his head as high as ever.

To have taken the field openly against his rival would have been madness; for he was not a man to be thwarted in his amours, any more than that stormy lover, Achilles. Ichabod, therefore, made his advances in a quiet and gently-insinuating manner. Under cover of his character of singing-master, he made frequent visits at the farmhouse; not that he had anything to apprehend from the meddlesome interference of parents, which is so often a stumbling-block in the path of lovers. Balt Van Tassel was an easy, indulgent soul; he loved his daughter better even than his pipe, and like a reasonable man and an excellent father, let her have her way in everything. His notable little wife, too, had enough to do to attend to her housekeeping and manage her poultry; for, as she sagely observed, ducks and geese are foolish things, and must be looked after, but girls can take care of themselves. Thus while the busy dame bustled about the house, or plied her spinning-wheel at one end of the piazza, honest Balt would sit smoking his evening pipe at the other, watching the achievements of a little wooden warrior, who, armed with a sword in each hand, was most valiantly fighting the wind on the pinnacle of the barn. In the meantime, Ichabod would carry on his suit with the daughter by the side of the spring under the great elm, or sauntering along in the twilight, that hour so favorable to the lover's eloquence.

I profess not to know how women's hearts are wooed and won. To me they have always been matters of riddle and admiration. Some seem to have but one vulnerable point, or door of access; while others have a thousand avenues, and may be captured in a thousand different ways. It is a great triumph of skill to gain the former, but a still greater proof of generalship to maintain possession of the latter, for the man must battle for his fortress at every door and window. He who wins a thousand common hearts is therefore entitled to some renown; but he who keeps undisputed sway over the heart of a coquette, is indeed a hero. Certain it is, this was not the case with the redoubtable Brom Bones; and from the moment Ichabod Crane made his advances, the interests of the former evidently declined; his horse was no longer seen tied at the palings on Sunday nights, and a deadly feud gradually arose between him and the preceptor of Sleepy Hollow.

Brom, who had a degree of rough chivalry in his nature, would fain have carried matters to open warfare, and have settled their pretensions to the lady, according to the mode of those most concise and simple reasoners, the knights-errant of yore—by single combat; but Ichabod was too conscious of the superior might of his adversary to enter the lists against him: he had overheard a boast of Bones, that he would "double the schoolmaster up, and lay him on a shelf of his own schoolhouse"; and he was too wary to give him an opportunity. There was something extremely provoking in this obstinately pacific system; it left Brom no alternative but to draw upon the funds of rustic waggery in his disposition, and to play off boorish practical jokes upon his rival. Ichabod became the object of whimsical persecution to Bones, and his gang of rough riders. They harried his hitherto peaceful domains; smoked out his singing-school, by stopping up the chimney; broke into the schoolhouse at night, in spite of its formidable fastenings of withe and window stakes, and turned everything topsy-turvy: so that the poor schoolmaster began to think all the witches in the country held their meetings there. But what was still more annoying, Brom took all opportunities of turning him into ridicule in presence of his mistress, and had a scoundrel dog whom he taught to whine in the most ludicrous manner, and introduced as a rival of Ichabod's to instruct her in psalmody.

In this way matters went on for some time, without producing any material effect on the relative situation of the contending powers. On a fine autumnal afternoon, Ichabod, in pensive mood, sat enthroned on the lofty stool whence he usually watched all the concerns of his little literary realm. In his hand he swayed a ferule, that sceptre of despotic power;

the birch of justice reposed on three nails, behind the throne, a constant terror to evil doers; while on the desk before him might be seen sundry contraband articles and prohibited weapons, detected upon the persons of idle urchins; such as half-munched apples, popguns, whirligigs, fly-cages, and whole legions of rampant little paper game-cocks. Apparently there had been some appalling act of justice recently inflicted, for his scholars were all busily intent upon their books, or slyly whispering behind them with one eye kept upon the master; and a kind of buzzing stillness reigned throughout the school-room. It was suddenly interrupted by the appearance of a Negro, in tow-cloth jacket and trowsers, a round-crowned fragment of a hat, like a cap of Mercury, and mounted on the back of a ragged, wild, half-broken colt, which he managed with a rope by way of halter. He came clattering up to the school door with an invitation to Ichabod to attend a merry-making or "quilting frolic," to be held that evening at Mynheer Van Tassel's; and having delivered his message with that air of importance, and effort at fine language, which a Negro is apt to display on petty embassies of the kind, he dashed over the brook, and was seen scampering away up the hollow, full of the importance and hurry of his mission.

All was now bustle and hubbub in the late quiet school-room. The scholars were hurried through their lessons, without stopping at trifles; those who were nimble skipped over half with impunity, and those who were tardy, had a smart application now and then in the rear, to quicken their speed, or help them over a tall word. Books were flung aside without being put away on the shelves, inkstands were overturned, benches thrown down, and the whole school was turned loose an hour before the usual time, bursting forth like a legion of young imps, yelping and racketing about the green, in joy at their early emancipation.

The gallant Ichabod now spent at least an extra half-hour at his toilet, brushing and furbishing up his best, and indeed only suit of rusty black, and arranging his locks by a bit of broken looking-glass, that hung up in the schoolhouse. That he might make his appearance before his mistress in the true style of a cavalier, he borrowed a horse from the farmer with whom he was domiciliated, a choleric old Dutchman, of the name of Hans Van Ripper, and, thus gallantly mounted, issued forth, like a knight-errant in quest of adventures. But it is meet I should, in the true spirit of romantic story, give some account of the looks and equipments of my hero and his steed. The animal he bestrode was a broken-down plough-horse, that had outlived almost everything but his viciousness. He was gaunt and shagged, with a ewe neck and a head like a hammer; his rusty mane and tail were tangled and knotted with burrs; one eye had lost its pupil, and was glaring and spectral; but the other had the gleam of a genuine devil in it. Still he must have had fire and mettle in his day, if we may judge from the name he bore of Gunpowder. He had, in fact, been a favorite steed of his master's, the choleric Van Ripper, who was a furious rider, and had infused, very probably, some of his own spirit into the animal; for, old and broken-down as he looked, there was more of the lurking devil in him than in any young filly in the country.

Ichabod was a suitable figure for such a steed. He rode with short stirrups, which brought his knees nearly up to the pommel of the saddle; his sharp elbows stuck out like grasshoppers';

he carried his whip perpendicularly in his hand, like a sceptre, and, as his horse jogged on, the motion of his arms was not unlike the flapping of a pair of wings. A small wool hat rested on the top of his nose, for so his scanty strip of forehead might be called; and the skirts of his black coat fluttered out almost to the horse's tail. Such was the appearance of Ichabod and his steed, as they shambled out of the gate of Hans Van Ripper, and it was altogether such an apparition as is seldom to be met with in broad daylight.

It was, as I have said, a fine autumnal day, the sky was clear and serene, and nature wore that rich and golden livery which we always associate with the idea of abundance. The forests had put on their sober brown and yellow, while some trees of the tenderer kind had been nipped by the frosts into brilliant dyes of orange, purple, and scarlet. Streaming files of wild ducks began to make their appearance high in the air; the bark of the squirrel might be heard from the groves of beech and hickory nuts, and the pensive whistle of the quail at intervals from the neighboring stubble-field.

The small birds were taking their farewell banquets. In the fulness of their revelry, they fluttered, chirping and frolicking, from bush to bush, and tree to tree, capricious from the very profusion and variety around them. There was the honest cock-robin, the favorite game of stripling sportsmen, with its loud querulous note; and the twittering blackbirds flying in sable clouds; and the golden-winged woodpecker, with his crimson crest, his broad black gorget, and splendid plumage; and the cedar-bird, with its red-tipt wings and yellow-tipt tail, and its little monteiro cap of feathers; and the blue-jay, that noisy coxcomb, in his gay light-blue coat and white underclothes;

screaming and chattering, nodding and bobbing and bowing, and pretending to be on good terms with every songster of the grove.

As Ichabod jogged slowly on his way, his eye, ever open to every symptom of culinary abundance, ranged with delight over the treasures of jolly autumn. On all sides he beheld vast stores of apples; some hanging in oppressive opulence on the trees; some gathered into baskets and barrels for the market; others heaped up in rich piles for the cider-press. Farther on he beheld great fields of Indian corn, with its golden ears peeping from their leafy coverts, and holding out the promise of cakes and hasty-pudding; and the yellow pumpkins lying beneath them, turning up their fair round bellies to the sun, and giving ample prospects of the most luxurious of pies; and anon he passed the fragrant buckwheat fields, breathing the odor of the bee-hive, and as he beheld them, soft anticipations stole over his mind of dainty slapjacks, well buttered, and garnished with honey or treacle, by the delicate little dimpled hand of Katrina Van Tassel.

Thus feeding his mind with many sweet thoughts and "sugared suppositions," he journeyed along the sides of a range of hills which look out upon some of the goodliest scenes of the mighty Hudson. The sun gradually wheeled his broad disk down into the west. The wide bosom of the Tappaan Zee lay motionless and glassy, excepting that here and there a gentle undulation waved and prolonged the blue shadow of the distant mountain. A few amber clouds floated in the sky, without a breath of air to move them. The horizon was of a fine golden tint, changing gradually into a pure apple green, and from that into the deep blue of the mid-heaven. A slanting ray lingered

on the woody crests of the precipices that overhung some parts of the river, giving greater depth to the dark-gray and purple of their rocky sides. A sloop was loitering in the distance, dropping slowly down with the tide, her sail hanging uselessly against the mast; and as the reflection of the sky gleamed along the still water, it seemed as if the vessel was suspended in the air.

It was towards evening that Ichabod arrived at the castle of the Heer Van Tassel, which he found thronged with the pride and flower of the adjacent country. Old farmers, a spare leathern-faced race, in homespun coats and breeches, blue stockings, huge shoes, and magnificent pewter buckles. Their brisk withered little dames, in close crimped caps, long-waisted short-gowns, homespun petticoats, with scissors and pincushions, and gay calico pockets hanging on the outside. Buxom lasses, almost as antiquated as their mothers, excepting where a straw hat, a fine ribbon, or perhaps a white frock gave symptoms of city innovation. The sons, in short square-skirted coats with rows of stupendous brass buttons, and their hair generally queued in the fashion of the times, especially if they could procure an eel-skin for the purpose, it being esteemed, throughout the country, as a potent nourisher and strengthener of the hair.

Brom Bones, however, was the hero of the scene, having come to the gathering on his favorite steed Daredevil, a creature, like himself, full of mettle and mischief, and which no one but himself could manage. He was, in fact, noted for preferring vicious animals, given to all kinds of tricks, which kept the rider in constant risk of his neck, for he held a tractable well-broken horse as unworthy of a lad of spirit.

Fain would I pause to dwell upon the world of charms that burst upon the enraptured gaze of my hero, as he entered the state parlor of Van Tassel's mansion. Not those of the bevy of buxom lasses, with their luxurious display of red and white; but the ample charms of a genuine Dutch country tea-table, in the sumptuous time of autumn. Such heaped-up platters of cakes of various and almost indescribable kinds, known only to experienced Dutch housewives! There was the doughty doughnut, the tenderer oly koek, and the crisp and crumbling cruller; sweet cakes and short cakes, ginger cakes and honey cakes, and the whole family of cakes. And then there were apple pies and peach pies and pumpkin pies; besides slices of ham and smoked beef; and moreover delectable dishes of preserved plums, and peaches, and pears, and quinces; not to mention broiled shad and roasted chickens; together with bowls of milk and cream, all mingled higgledy-piggledy, pretty much as I have enumerated them, with the motherly tea-pot sending up its clouds of vapor from the midst—Heaven bless the mark! I want breath and time to discuss this banquet as it deserves, and am too eager to get on with my story. Happily, Ichabod Crane was not in so great a hurry as his historian, but did ample justice to every dainty.

He was a kind and thankful creature, whose heart dilated in proportion as his skin was filled with good cheer; and whose spirits rose with eating as some men's do with drink. He could not help, too, rolling his large eyes round him as he ate, and chuckling with the possibility that he might one day be lord of all this scene of almost unimaginable luxury and splendor. Then, he thought, how soon he'd turn his back upon the old schoolhouse, snap his fingers in the face of Hans Van Ripper,

and every other niggardly patron, and kick any itinerant pedagogue out of doors that should dare to call him comrade!

Old Baltus Van Tassel moved about among his guests with
a face dilated with content and good humor, round and jolly
as the harvest moon. His hospitable attentions were brief, but
expressive, being confined to a shake of the hand, a slap on the
shoulder, a loud laugh, and a pressing invitation to "fall to,
and help themselves."

And now the sound of the music from the common room,
or hall, summoned to the dance. The musician was an old
gray-headed Negro, who had been the itinerant orchestra of
the neighborhood for more than half a century. His instru-
ment was as old and battered as himself. The greater part of
the time he scraped on two or three strings, accompanying
every movement of the bow with a motion of the head, bowing
almost to the ground, and stamping with his foot whenever a
fresh couple were to start.

Ichabod prided himself upon his dancing as much as upon
his vocal powers. Not a limb, not a fibre about him was idle;
and to have seen his loosely hung frame in full motion, and
clattering about the room, you would have thought Saint
Vitus himself, that blessed patron of the dance, was figuring
before you in person. He was the admiration of all the Negroes; who, having gathered, of all ages and sizes, from the
farm and the neighborhood, stood forming a pyramid of shining black faces at every door and window, gazing with delight
at the scene, rolling their white eyeballs, and showing grin-
ning rows of ivory from ear to ear. How could the flogger of
urchins be otherwise than animated and joyous—the lady of
his heart was his partner in the dance, and smiling graciously

in reply to all his amorous oglings; while Brom Bones, sorely smitten with love and jealousy, sat brooding by himself in one corner.

When the dance was at an end, Ichabod was attracted to a knot of the sager folks, who, with old Van Tassel, sat smoking at one end of the piazza, gossiping over former times, and drawing out long stories about the war.

This neighborhood, at the time of which I am speaking, was one of those highly-favored places which abound with chronicle and great men. The British and American line had run near it during the war; it had, therefore, been the scene of marauding, and infested with refugees, cow-boys, and all kinds of border chivalry. Just sufficient time had elapsed to enable each story-teller to dress up his tale with a little becoming fiction, and, in the indistinctness of his recollection, to make himself the hero of every exploit.

There was the story of Doffue Martling, a large, blue-bearded Dutchman, who had nearly taken a British frigate with an old iron nine-pounder from a mud breastwork, only that his gun burst at the sixth discharge. And there was an old gentleman who shall be nameless, being too rich a mynheer to be lightly mentioned, who, in the battle of Whiteplains, being an excellent master of defence, parried a musket ball with a small sword, insomuch that he absolutely felt it whiz round the blade, and glance off at the hilt; in proof of which, he was ready at any time to show the sword, with the hilt a little bent. There were several more that had been equally great in the field, not one of whom but was persuaded that he had a considerable hand in bringing the war to a happy termination.

But all these were nothing to the tales of ghosts and apparitions that succeeded. The neighborhood is rich in legendary treasures of the kind. Local tales and superstitions thrive best in these sheltered, long-settled retreats; but are trampled under foot by the shifting throng that forms the population of most of our country places. Besides, there is no encouragement for ghosts in most of our villages, for they have scarcely had time to finish their first nap, and turn themselves in their graves, before their surviving friends have travelled away from the neighborhood; so that when they turn out at night to walk their rounds, they have no acquaintance left to call upon. This is perhaps the reason why we so seldom hear of ghosts except in our long-established Dutch communities.

The immediate cause, however, of the prevalence of supernatural stories in these parts, was doubtless owing to the vicinity of Sleepy Hollow. There was a contagion in the very air that blew from that haunted region; it breathed forth an atmosphere of dreams and fancies infecting all the land. Several of the Sleepy Hollow people were present at Van Tassel's, and, as usual, were doling out their wild and wonderful legends. Many dismal tales were told about funeral trains, and mourning cries and wailings heard and seen about the great tree where the unfortunate Major André was taken, and which stood in the neighborhood. Some mention was made also of the woman in white, that haunted the dark glen at Raven Rock, and was often heard to shriek on winter nights before a storm, having perished there in the snow. The chief part of the stories, however, turned upon the favorite spectre of Sleepy Hollow, the headless horseman, who had been heard several times of late, patrolling the country; and, it was said, tethered his horse nightly among the graves in the churchyard.

The sequestered situation of this church seems always to have made it a favorite haunt of troubled spirits. It stands on a knoll, surrounded by locust-trees and lofty elms, from among which its decent whitewashed walls shine modestly forth, like Christian purity beaming through the shades of retirement. A gentle slope descends from it to a silver sheet of water, bordered by high trees, between which, peeps may be caught at the blue hills of the Hudson. To look upon its grass-grown yard, where the sunbeams seem to sleep so quietly, one would think that there at least the dead might rest in peace. On one side of the church extends a wide woody dell, along which raves a large brook among broken rocks and trunks of fallen trees. Over a deep black part of the stream, not far from the church, was formerly thrown a wooden bridge; the road that led to it, and the bridge itself, were thickly shaded by overhanging trees, which cast a gloom about it, even in the daytime; but occasioned a fearful darkness at night. This was one of the favorite haunts of the headless horseman; and the place where he was most frequently encountered. The tale was told of old Brouwer, a most heretical disbeliever in ghosts, how he met the horseman returning from his foray into Sleepy Hollow, and was obliged to get up behind him; how they galloped over bush and brake, over hill and swamp, until they reached the bridge; when the horseman suddenly turned into a skeleton, threw old Brouwer into the brook, and sprang away over the tree-tops with a clap of thunder.

This story was immediately matched by a thrice marvellous

adventure of Brom Bones, who made light of the galloping Hessian as an arrant jockey. He affirmed that, on returning one night from the neighboring village of Sing-Sing, he had been overtaken by this midnight trooper; that he had offered to race with him for a bowl of punch, and should have won it too, for Daredevil beat the goblin horse all hollow, but, just as they came to the church bridge, the Hessian bolted, and vanished in a flash of fire.

All these tales, told in that drowsy undertone with which men talk in the dark, the countenances of the listeners only now and then receiving a casual gleam from the glare of a pipe, sank deep in the mind of Ichabod. He repaid them in kind with large extracts from his invaluable author, Cotton Mather, and added many marvellous events that had taken place in his native State of Connecticut, and fearful sights which he had seen in his nightly walks about Sleepy Hollow.

The revel now gradually broke up. The old farmers gathered together their families in their wagons, and were heard for some time rattling along the hollow roads, and over the distant hills. Some of the damsels mounted on pillions behind their favorite swains, and their light-hearted laughter, mingling with the clatter of hoofs, echoed along the silent woodlands, sounding fainter and fainter until they gradually died away—and the late scene of noise and frolic was all silent and deserted. Ichabod only lingered behind, according to the custom of country lovers, to have a tête-à-tête with the heiress, fully convinced that he was now on the high road to success. What passed at this interview I will not pretend to say, for in fact I do not know. Something, however, I fear me, must have gone wrong, for he certainly sallied forth, after no great interval, with an air quite desolate and chop-fallen.—Oh these women! These women! Could that girl have been playing off any of her coquettish tricks?—Was her encouragement of the poor pedagogue all a mere sham to secure her conquest of his rival? —Heaven only knows, not I!—Let it suffice to say, Ichabod stole forth with the air of one who had been sacking a hen-roost, rather than a fair lady's heart. Without looking to the right or left to notice the scene of rural wealth, on which he had so often gloated, he went straight to the stable, and with several hearty cuffs and kicks, roused his steed most uncourteously from the comfortable quarters in which he was soundly sleeping, dreaming of mountains of corn and oats, and whole valleys of timothy and clover.

It was the very witching time of night that Ichabod, heavy-hearted and crest-fallen, pursued his travel homewards, along the sides of the lofty hills which rise above Tarrytown, and which he had traversed so cheerily in the afternoon. The hour was as dismal as himself. Far below him, the Tappaan Zee spread its dusky and indistinct waste of waters, with here and there the tall mast of a sloop, riding quietly at anchor under the land. In the dead hush of midnight, he could even hear the barking of the watch-dog from the opposite shore of the Hudson; but it was so vague and faint as only to give an idea of his distance from this faithful companion of man. Now and then, too, the long-drawn crowing of a cock, accidentally awakened, would sound far, far off, from some farmhouse away among the hills—but it was like a dreaming sound in his ear. No signs of life occurred near him, but occasionally the melancholy chirp of a cricket, or perhaps the guttural twang of a bull-frog, from a neighboring marsh, as if sleeping uncomfortably, and turning suddenly in his bed.

All the stories of ghosts and goblins that he had heard in the afternoon, now came crowding upon his recollection. The night grew darker and darker; the stars seemed to sink deeper in the sky, and driving clouds occasionally hid them from his sight. He had never felt so lonely and dismal. He was, moreover, approaching the very place where many of the scenes of the ghost stories had been laid. In the centre of the road stood an enormous tulip-tree, which towered like a giant above all the other trees of the neighborhood, and formed a kind of landmark. Its limbs were gnarled, and fantastic, large enough to form trunks for ordinary trees, twisting down almost to the earth, and rising again into the air. It was connected with the tragical story of the unfortunate André, who had been taken prisoner hard by; and was universally known by the name of Major André's tree. The common people regarded it with a mixture of respect and superstition, partly out of sympathy for the fate of its ill-starred namesake, and partly from the tales of strange sights and doleful lamentations told concerning it.

As Ichabod approached this fearful tree, he began to whistle: he thought his whistle was answered—it was but a blast sweeping sharply through the dry branches. As he approached a little nearer, he thought he saw something white hanging in the midst of the tree—he paused and ceased whistling; but on looking more narrowly, perceived that it was a place where the tree had been scathed by lightning, and the white wood laid bare. Suddenly he heard a groan—his teeth chattered and his knees smote against the saddle: it was but the rubbing of one

huge bough upon another, as they were swayed about by the breeze. He passed the tree in safety, but new perils lay before him.

About two hundred yards from the tree a small brook crossed the road, and ran into a marshy and thickly-wooded glen, known by the name of Wiley's swamp. A few rough logs, laid side by side, served for a bridge over this stream. On that side of the road where the brook entered the wood, a group of oaks and chestnuts, matted thick with wild grapevines, threw a cavernous gloom over it. To pass this bridge was the severest trial. It was at this identical spot that the unfortunate André was captured, and under the covert of those chestnuts and vines were the sturdy yeomen concealed who surprised him. This has ever since been considered a haunted stream, and fearful are the feelings of the schoolboy who has to pass it alone after dark.

As he approached the stream his heart began to thump; he summoned up, however, all his resolution, gave his horse half a score of kicks in the ribs, and attempted to dash briskly across the bridge; but instead of starting forward, the perverse old animal made a lateral movement, and ran broadside against the fence. Ichabod, whose fears increased with the delay, jerked the reins on the other side, and kicked lustily with the contrary foot: it was all in vain; his steed started, it is true, but it was only to plunge to the opposite side of the road into a thicket of brambles and alder bushes. The schoolmaster now bestowed both whip and heel upon the starveling ribs of old Gunpowder, who dashed forward, snuffling and snorting, but came to a stand just by the bridge, with a suddenness that had nearly sent his rider sprawling over his head. Just at this moment a plashy tramp by the side of the bridge caught the sensitive ear of Ichabod. In the dark shadow of the grove, on the margin of the brook, he beheld something huge, misshapen, black and towering. It stirred not, but seemed gathered up in the gloom, like some gigantic monster ready to spring upon the traveller.

The hair of the affrighted pedagogue rose upon his head with terror. What was to be done? To turn and fly was now too late; and besides, what chance was there of escaping ghost or goblin, if such it was, which could ride upon the wings of the wind? Summoning up, therefore, a show of courage, he demanded in stammering accents—"Who are you?" He received no reply. He repeated his demand in a still more agitated voice. Still there was no answer. Once more he cudgelled the sides of the inflexible Gunpowder, and, shutting his eyes, broke forth with involuntary fervor into a psalm tune. Just then the shadowy object of alarm put itself in motion, and, with a scramble and a bound, stood at once in the middle of the road. Though the night was dark and dismal, yet the form of the unknown might now in some degree be ascertained. He appeared to be a horseman of large dimensions, and mounted on a black horse of powerful frame. He made no offer of molestation or sociability, but kept aloof on one side of the road, jogging along on the blind side of old Gunpowder, who had now got over his fright and waywardness.

Ichabod, who had no relish for this strange midnight companion, and bethought himself of the adventure of Brom Bones with the Galloping Hessian, now quickened his steed, in hopes of leaving him behind. The stranger, however, quickened his horse to an equal pace. Ichabod pulled up, and fell into a walk, thinking to lag behind—the other did the same. His heart began to sink within him; he endeavored to resume his psalm tune, but his parched tongue clove to the roof of his mouth, and he could not utter a stave. There was something in the moody and dogged silence of this pertinacious companion, that was mysterious and appalling. It was soon fearfully accounted for. On mounting a rising ground, which brought the figure of his fellow-traveller in relief against the sky, gigantic in height, and muffled in a cloak, Ichabod was horror-struck, on perceiving that he was headless!—but his horror was still more increased, on observing that the head, which should have rested on his shoulders, was carried before him on the pommel of the saddle. His terror rose to desperation; he rained a shower of kicks and blows upon Gunpowder, hoping, by a sudden movement, to give his companion the slip—but the spectre started full jump with him. Away then they dashed, through thick and thin; stones flying, and sparks flashing at every bound. Ichabod's flimsy garments fluttered in the air, as he stretched his long lank body away over his horse's head, in the eagerness of his flight.

They had now reached the road which turns off to Sleepy Hollow; but Gunpowder, who seemed possessed with a demon, instead of keeping up it, made an opposite turn, and plunged headlong down hill to the left. This road leads through a sandy hollow, shaded by trees for about a quarter of a mile, where it crosses the bridge famous in goblin story, and just beyond swells the green knoll on which stands the white-washed church.

As yet the panic of the steed had given his unskilful rider an apparent advantage in the chase; but just as he had got half way through the hollow, the girths of the saddle gave way, and he felt it slipping from under him. He seized it by the pommel, and endeavored to hold it firm, but in vain; and had just time to save himself by clasping old Gunpowder round the neck, when the saddle fell to the earth, and he heard it trampled under foot by his pursuer. For a moment the terror of Hans Van Ripper's wrath passed across his mind—for it was his Sunday saddle; but this was no time for petty fears; the goblin was hard on his haunches; and (unskilful rider that he was!) he had much ado to maintain his seat; sometimes slipping on one side, sometimes on another, and sometimes jolted on the high ridge of his horse's backbone, with a violence that he verily feared would cleave him asunder.

An opening in the trees now cheered him with the hopes that the church bridge was at hand. The wavering reflection of a silver star in the bosom of the brook told him that he was not mistaken. He saw the walls of the church dimly glaring under the trees beyond. He recollected the place where Brom Bones's ghostly competitor had disappeared. "If I can but reach that bridge," thought Ichabod, "I am safe." Just then he heard the black steed panting and blowing close behind him; he even fancied that he felt his hot breath. Another convulsive kick in the ribs, and old Gunpowder sprang upon the bridge; he thundered over the resounding planks; he gained the opposite side; and now Ichabod cast a look behind to see if his pursuer should vanish, according to rule, in a flash of fire and brimstone. Just then he saw the goblin rising in his stirrups, and in the very act of hurling his head at him. Ichabod endeavored to dodge the horrible missile, but too late. It encountered his cranium with a tremendous crash—he was tumbled headlong into the dust, and Gunpowder, the black steed, and the goblin rider, passed by like a whirlwind.

The next morning the old horse was found without his saddle, and with the bridle under his feet, soberly cropping the grass at his master's gate. Ichabod did not make his appearance at breakfast—dinner-hour came, but no Ichabod. The boys assembled at the schoolhouse, and strolled idly about the banks of the brook; but no schoolmaster. Hans Van Ripper now began to feel some uneasiness about the fate of poor Ichabod, and his saddle. An inquiry was set on foot, and after diligent investigation they came upon his traces. In one part of the road leading to the church was found the saddle trampled in the dirt; the tracks of horses' hoofs deeply dented in the road, and evidently at furious speed, were traced to the bridge, beyond which, on the bank of a broad part of the brook, where the water ran deep and black, was found the hat of the unfortunate Ichabod, and close beside it a shattered pumpkin.

The brook was searched, but the body of the schoolmaster was not to be discovered. Hans Van Ripper, as executor of his estate, examined the bundle which contained all his worldly effects. They consisted of two shirts and a half; two stocks for the neck; a pair or two of worsted stockings; an old pair of corduroy smallclothes; a rusty razor; a book of psalm tunes, full of dogs' ears; and a broken pitchpipe. As to the books and furniture of the schoolhouse, they belonged to the community, excepting Cotton Mather's History of Witchcraft, a New England Almanac, and a book of dreams and fortune-telling; in which last was a sheet of foolscap much scribbled and blotted in several fruitless attempts to make a copy of verses in honor of the heiress of Van Tassel. These magic books and the poetic scrawl were forthwith consigned to the flames by Hans Van Ripper; who from that time forward determined to send his children no more to school; observing, that he never knew any good to come of this same reading and writing. Whatever money the schoolmaster possessed, and he had received his quarter's pay but a day or two before, he must have had about his person at the time of his disappearance.

The mysterious event caused much speculation at the church on the following Sunday. Knots of gazers and gossips were collected in the churchyard, at the bridge, and at the spot where the hat and pumpkin had been found. The stories of Brouwer, of Bones, and a whole budget of others, were called to mind; and when they had diligently considered them all, and compared them with the symptoms of the present case, they shook their heads, and came to the conclusion that Ichabod had been carried off by the Galloping Hessian. As he was a bachelor, and in nobody's debt, nobody troubled his head any more about him. The school was removed to a different quarter of the hollow, and another pedagogue reigned in his stead.

It is true, an old farmer, who had been down to New York on a visit several years after, and from whom this account of the ghostly adventure was received, brought home the intelligence that Ichabod Crane was still alive; that he had left the neighborhood, partly through fear of the goblin and Hans Van Ripper, and partly in mortification at having been suddenly dismissed by the heiress; that he had changed his quarters to a distant part of the country; had kept school and studied law at the same time, had been admitted to the bar, turned politician, electioneered, written for the newspapers, and finally had been made a justice of the Ten Pound Court. Brom Bones too, who shortly after his rival's disappearance conducted the blooming Katrina in triumph to the altar, was observed to look exceedingly knowing whenever the story of Ichabod was related, and always burst into a hearty laugh at the mention of the pumpkin; which led some to suspect that he knew more about the matter than he chose to tell.

The old country wives, however, who are the best judges of these matters, maintain to this day that Ichabod was spirited away by supernatural means; and it is a favorite story often told about the neighborhood round the winter evening fire. The bridge became more than ever an object of superstitious awe, and that may be the reason why the road has been altered of late years, so as to approach the church by the border of the mill-pond. The schoolhouse being deserted, soon fell to decay, and was reported to be haunted by the ghost of the unfortunate pedagogue; and the ploughboy, loitering homeward of a still summer evening, has often fancied his voice at a distance, chanting a melancholy psalm tune among the tranquil solitudes of Sleepy Hollow.

Dolph Heyliger

I take the town of concord, where I dwell,
All Kilborn be my witness, if I were not
Begot in bashfulness, brought up in shamefacedness.
Let 'un bring a dog but to my vace that can
Zay I have beat 'un, and without a vault;
Or but a cat will swear upon a book,
I have as much as zet a vire her tail,
And I'll give him or her a crown for 'mends.

TALE OF A TUB

In the early time of the province of New York, while it groaned under the tyranny of the English governor, Lord Cornbury, who carried his cruelties towards the Dutch inhabitants so far as to allow no Dominie, or schoolmaster, to officiate in their language without his special license; about this time there lives in the jolly little old city of the Manhattoes a kind motherly dame, known by the name of Dame Heyliger. She was the widow of a Dutch sea-captain, who died suddenly of a fever, in consequence of working too hard, and eating too heartily, at the time when all the inhabitants turned out in a panic, to fortify the place against the invasion of a small

79

French privateer.[1] He left her with very little money, and one infant son, the only survivor of several children. The good woman had need of much management to make both ends meet, and keep up a decent appearance. However, as her husband had fallen a victim to his zeal for the public safety, it was universally agreed that "something ought to be done for the widow"; and on the hopes of this "something" she lived tolerably for some years; in the meantime everybody pitied and spoke well of her, and that helped along.

She lived in a small house, in a small street called Garden Street, very probably from a garden which may have flourished there some time or other. As her necessities every year grew greater, and the talk of the public about doing "something for her" grew less, she had to cast about for some mode of doing something for herself, by way of helping out her slender means, and maintaining her independence, of which she was somewhat tenacious.

Living in a mercantile town, she had caught something of the spirit, and determined to venture a little in the great lottery of commerce. On a sudden, therefore, to the great surprise of the street, there appeared at her window a grand array of gingerbread kings and queens, with their arms stuck akimbo, after the invariable royal manner. There were also several broken tumblers, some filled with sugar-plums, some with marbles; there were, moreover, cakes of various kinds, and barley-sugar, and Holland dolls, and wooden horses, with here and there gilt-covered picture-books, and now and then a skein of thread, or a dangling pound of candles. At the door of the house sat the good old dame's cat, a decent demure-looking

[1] 1705.

personage, who seemed to scan everybody that passed, to criticize their dress, and now and then to stretch her neck, and to look out with sudden curiosity, to see what was going on at the other end of the street; but if by chance any idle vagabond dog came by, and offered to be uncivil—hoity-toity!—how she would bristle up, and growl, and spit, and strike out her paws! She was as indignant as ever was an ancient and ugly spinster on the approach of some graceless profligate.

But though the good woman had to come down to those humble means of subsistence, yet she still kept up a feeling of family pride, being descended from the Vanderspiegels, of Amsterdam; and she had the family arms painted and framed, and hung over her mantelpiece. She was, in truth, much respected by all the poorer people of the place; her house was quite a resort of the old wives of the neighborhood; they would drop in there of a winter's afternoon, as she sat knitting on one side of her fireplace, her cat purring on the other, and the tea-kettle singing before it; and they would gossip with her until late in the evening. There was always an arm-chair for Peter de Groodt, sometimes called Long Peter, and sometimes Peter Longlegs, the clerk and sexton of the little Lutheran church, who was her great crony, and indeed the oracle of her fireside. Nay, the Dominie himself did not disdain, now and then, to step in, converse about the state of her mind, and take a glass of her special good cherry-brandy. Indeed, he never failed to call on New-Year's day, and wish her a happy New Year; and the good dame, who was a little vain on some points, always piqued herself on giving him as large a cake as anyone in town.

"I have said that she had one son. He was the child of her

81

old age; but could hardly be called the comfort, for, of all unlucky urchins, Dolph Heyliger was the most mischievous. Not that the whipster was really vicious; he was only full of fun and frolic, and had that daring, gamesome spirit which is extolled in a rich man's child, but execrated in a poor man's. He was continually getting into scrapes; his mother was incessantly harassed with complaints of some waggish pranks which he had played off; bills were sent in for windows that he had broken; in a word, he had not reached his fourteenth year before he was pronounced, by all the neighborhood, to be a "wicked dog, the wickedest dog in the street!" Nay, one old gentleman, in a claret-colored coat, with a thin red face, and ferret eyes, went so far as to assure Dame Heyliger, that her son would, one day or other, come to the gallows!

Yet, notwithstanding all this, the poor old soul loved her boy. It seemed as though she loved him the better the worse he behaved, and that he grew more in her favor the more he grew out of favor with the world. Mothers are foolish, fond-hearted beings; there's no reasoning them out of their dotage; and, indeed, this poor woman's child was all that was left to love her in this world—so we must not think it hard that she turned a deaf ear to her good friends, who sought to prove to her that Dolph would come to a halter.

To do the varlet justice, too, he was strongly attached to his parent. He would not willingly have given her pain on any account; and when he had been doing wrong, it was but for him to catch his poor mother's eye fixed wistfully and sorrowfully upon him, to fill his heart with bitterness and contrition. But he was a heedless youngster, and could not, for the life of him, resist any new temptation to fun and mischief. Though quick at his learning, whenever he could be brought to apply himself, he was always prone to be led away by idle company, and would play truant to hunt after birds'-nests, to rob orchards, or to swim in the Hudson.

In this way he grew up, a tall, lubberly boy; and his mother began to be greatly perplexed what to do with him, or how to put him in a way to do for himself; for he had acquired such an unlucky reputation, that no one seemed willing to employ him.

Many were the consultations, that she held with Peter de Groodt, the clerk and sexton, who was her prime counsellor. Peter was as much perplexed as herself, for he had no great opinion of the boy, and thought he would never come to good. He at once advised her to send him to sea: a piece of advice only given in the most desperate cases; but Dame Heyliger would not listen to such an idea; she could not think of letting Dolph go out of her sight. She was sitting one day knitting by her fireside, in great perplexity, when the sexton entered with an air of unusual vivacity and briskness. He had just come from a funeral. It had been that of a boy of Dolph's years, who had been apprentice to a famous German doctor, and had died of a consumption. It is true, there had been a whisper that the deceased had been brought to his end by being made a subject of the doctor's experiments, on which he was apt to try the effects of a new compound, or a quieting draught. This, however, it is likely, was a mere scandal; at any rate, Peter de Groodt did not think it worth mentioning; though, had we time to philosophize, it would be a curious matter for speculation, why a doctor's family is apt to be so lean and cadaverous, and a butcher's so jolly and rubicund.

Peter de Groodt, as I said before, entered the house of Dame Heyliger with unusual alacrity. A bright idea had popped into his head at the funeral, over which he had chuckled as he shovelled the earth into the grave of the doctor's disciple. It had occurred to him, that, as the situation of the deceased was vacant at the doctor's, it would be the very place for Dolph. The boy had parts, and could pound a pestle, and run an errand with any boy in the town; and what more was wanted in a student?

The suggestion of the sage Peter was a vision of glory to the mother. She already saw Dolph, in her mind's eye, with a cane at his nose, a knocker at his door, and an M.D. at the end of his name—one of the established dignitaries of the town.

The matter, once undertaken, was soon effected; the sexton had some influence with the doctor, they having had much dealing together in the way of their separate professions; and the very next morning he called and conducted the urchin, clad in his Sunday clothes, to undergo the inspection of Dr. Karl Lodovick Knipperhausen.

They found the doctor seated in an elbow-chair, in one corner of his study, or laboratory, with a large volume, in German print, before him. He was a short fat man, with a dark square face, rendered more dark by a black velvet cap. He had a little nobbed nose, not unlike the ace of spades, with a pair of spectacles gleaming on each side of his dusky countenance, like a couple of bow-windows.

Dolph felt struck with awe on entering into the presence of this learned man; and gazed about him with boyish wonder at the furniture of this chamber of knowledge; which appeared to

84

him almost as the den of a magician. In the centre stood a claw-footed table, with pestle and mortar, phials and gallipots, and a pair of small burnished scales. At one end was a heavy clothes-press, turned into a receptacle for drugs and compounds; against which hung the doctor's hat and cloak, and gold-headed cane, and on the top grinned a human skull. Along the mantelpiece were glass vessels, in which were snakes and lizards, and a human fœtus preserved in spirits. A closet, the doors of which were taken off, contained three whole shelves of books, and some, too, of mighty folio dimensions—a collection the like of which Dolph had never before beheld. As, however, the library did not take up the whole of the closet, the doctor's thrifty housekeeper had occupied the rest with pots of pickles and preserves; and had hung about the room, among awful implements of the healing art, strings of red pepper and corpulent cucumbers, carefully preserved for seed.

Peter de Groodt and his protégé were received with great gravity and stateliness by the doctor, who was a very wise, dignified little man, and never smiled. He surveyed Dolph from head to foot, above, and under, and through his spectacles, and the poor lad's heart quailed as these great glasses glared on him like two full moons. The doctor heard all that Peter de Groodt had to say in favor of the youthful candidate; and then wetting his thumb with the end of his tongue, he began deliberately to turn over page after page of the great black volume before him. At length, after many hums and haws, and strokings of the chin, and all that hesitation and deliberation with which a wise man proceeds to do what he intended to do from the very first, the doctor agreed to take the lad as a disciple; to give him bed, board, and clothing, and to instruct him in the healing art; in return for which he was to have his services until his twenty-first year.

Behold, then, our hero, all at once transformed from an unlucky urchin running wild about the streets, to a student of medicine, diligently pounding a pestle, under the auspices of the learned Doctor Karl Lodovick Knipperhausen. It was a happy transition for his fond old mother. She was delighted with the idea of her boy's being brought up worthy of his ancestors; and anticipated the day when he would be able to hold up his head with the lawyer, that lived in the large house opposite; or, peradventure, with the Dominie himself.

Doctor Knipperhausen was a native of the Palatinate in Germany; whence, in company with many of his countrymen, he had taken refuge in England, on account of religious persecution. He was one of nearly three thousand Palatines, who came over from England in 1710, under the protection of Governor Hunter. Where the doctor had studied, how he had acquired his medical knowledge, and where he had received his diploma, it is hard at present to say, for nobody knew at the time; yet it is certain that his profound skill and abstruse knowledge were the talk and wonder of the common people, far and near.

His practice was totally different from that of any other physician—consisting in mysterious compounds, known only to himself, in the preparing and administering of which, it was said, he always consulted the stars. So high an opinion was entertained of his skill, particularly by the German and Dutch inhabitants, that they always resorted to him in desperate cases. He was one of those infallible doctors that are always effecting sudden and surprising cures, when the patient has been given up by all the regular physicians; unless, as is shrewdly observed, the case has been left too long before it was put into their hands. The doctor's library was the talk and marvel of the neighborhood, I might almost say of the entire burgh. The good people looked with reverence at a man who had read three whole shelves full of books, and some of them, too, as large as a family Bible. There were many disputes among the members of the little Lutheran church, as to which was the wisest man, the doctor or the Dominie. Some of his admirers even went so far as to say, that he knew more than the governor himself—in a word, it was thought that there was no end to his knowledge!

No sooner was Dolph received into the doctor's family, than he was put in possession of the lodging of his predecessor. It was a garret-room of a steep-roofed Dutch house, where the rain had pattered on the shingles, and the lightning gleamed, and the wind piped through the crannies in stormy weather; and where whole troops of hungry rats, like Don Cossacks, galloped about, in defiance of traps and ratsbane.

He was soon up to his ears in medical studies, being employed, morning, noon, and night, in rolling pills, filtering tinctures, or pounding the pestle and mortar in one corner of the laboratory; while the doctor would take his seat in another corner, when he had nothing else to do, or expected visitors, and arrayed in his morning-gown and velvet cap, would pore over the contents of some folio volume. It is true, that the regular thumping of Dolph's pestle, or, perhaps, the drowsy buzzing of the summer-flies, would now and then lull the little man into a slumber; but then his spectacles were always wide awake, and studiously regarding the book.

There was another personage in the house, however, to whom Dolph was obliged to pay allegiance. Though a bachelor, and a man of such great dignity and importance, the doctor was, like many other wise men, subject to petticoat government. He was completely under the sway of his housekeeper—a spare, busy, fretting housewife, in a little, round, quilted German cap, with a huge bunch of keys jingling at the girdle of an exceedingly long waist. Frau Ilsé (or Frow Ilsy, as it was pronounced) had accompanied him in his various migrations from Germany to England, and from England to the province; managing his establishment and himself too: ruling him, it is true, with a gentle hand, but carrying a high hand with all the world beside. How she had acquired such ascendancy I do not pretend to say. People, it is true, did talk—but have not people been prone to talk ever since the world began? Who can tell how women generally contrive to get the upper hand? A husband, it is true, may now and then be master in his own house; but who ever knew a bachelor that was not managed by his housekeeper?

Indeed, Frau Ilsy's power was not confined to the doctor's household. She was one of those prying gossips who know everyone's business better than they do themselves; and whose all-seeing eyes, and all-telling tongues, are terrors through a neighborhood.

Nothing of any moment transpired in the world of scandal of this little burgh, but it was known to Frau Ilsy. She had her crew of cronies, that were perpetually hurrying to her little parlor with some precious bit of news; nay, she would sometimes discuss a whole volume of secret history, as she held the street-door ajar, and gossiped with one of these garrulous cronies in the very teeth of a December blast.

Between the doctor and the housekeeper it may easily be supposed that Dolph had a busy life of it. As Frau Ilsy kept the keys, and literally ruled the roast, it was starvation to offend her, though he found the study of her temper more perplexing even than that of medicine. When not busy in the laboratory, she kept him running hither and thither on her errands; and on Sundays he was obliged to accompany her to and from church, and carry her Bible. Many a time has the poor varlet stood shivering and blowing his fingers, or holding his frost-bitten nose, in the church-yard, while Ilsy and her cronies were huddled together, wagging their heads, and tearing some unlucky character to pieces.

With all his advantages, however, Dolph made very slow progress in his art. This was no fault of the doctor's, certainly, for he took unwearied pains with the lad, keeping him close to the pestle and mortar, or on the trot about the town with phials and pill-boxes; and if he ever flagged in his industry, which he was rather apt to do, the doctor would fly into a passion, and ask him if he ever expected to learn his profession, unless he applied himself closer to the study. The fact is, he still retained the fondness for sport and mischief that had marked his childhood; the habit, indeed, had strengthened with his years, and gained force from being thwarted and constrained. He daily grew more and more untractable, and lost favor in the eyes, both of the doctor and the housekeeper.

In the meantime the doctor went on, waxing wealthy and renowned. He was famous for his skill in managing cases not laid down in the books. He had cured several old women and young girls of witchcraft—a terrible complaint, and nearly as prevalent in the province in those days as hydrophobia is at present. He had even restored one strapping country-girl to perfect health, who had gone so far as to vomit crooked pins and needles; which is considered a desperate stage of the malady. It was whispered, also, that he was possessed of the art of preparing love-powders; and many applications had he in consequence from love-sick patients of both sexes. But all these cases formed the mysterious part of his practice, in which, according to the cant phrase, "secrecy and honor might be depended on." Dolph, therefore, was obliged to turn out of the study whenever such consultations occurred, though it is said he learnt more of the secrets of the art at the key-hole than by all the rest of his studies put together.

As the doctor increased in wealth, he began to extend his possessions, and to look forward, like other great men, to the time when he should retire to the repose of a country-seat. For this purpose he had purchased a farm, or, as the Dutch settlers called it, a *bowerie*, a few miles from town. It had been the residence of a wealthy family, that had returned some time since to Holland. A large mansion-house stood in the centre of it, very much out of repair, and which, in consequence of certain reports, had received the appellation of the Haunted House. Either from these reports, or from its actual dreariness, the doctor found it impossible to get a tenant; and that the place might not fall to ruin before he could reside in it himself, he placed a country boor, with his family, in one wing, with the privilege of cultivating the farm on shares.

The doctor now felt all the dignity of a landholder rising within him. He had a little of the German pride of territory in his composition, and almost looked upon himself as owner of a principality. He began to complain of the fatigue of business; and was fond of riding out "to look at his estate." His little expeditions to his lands were attended with a bustle and parade that created a sensation throughout the neighborhood. His wall-eyed horse stood, stamping and whisking off the flies, for a full hour before the house. Then the doctor's saddle-bags would be brought out and adjusted; then, after a little while, his cloak would be rolled up and strapped to the saddle; then his umbrella would be buttoned to the cloak; while, in the meantime, a group of ragged boys, that observant class of beings, would gather before the door. At length the doctor would issue forth, in a pair of jack-boots that reached above his knees, and a cocked hat flapped down in front. As he was a short, fat man, he took some time to mount into the saddle; and when there, he took some time to have the saddle and stirrups properly adjusted, enjoying the wonder and admiration of the urchin crowd. Even after he had set off, he would pause in the middle of the street, or trot back two or three times to give some parting orders; which were answered by the housekeeper from the door, or Dolph from the study, or the black cook from the cellar, or the chambermaid from the garret-window; and there were generally some last words bawled after him, just as he was turning the corner.

The whole neighborhood would be aroused by this pomp and circumstance. The cobbler would leave his last; the barber would thrust out his frizzled head, with a comb sticking in it; a knot would collect at the grocer's door, and the word would be buzzed from one end of the street to the other, "The Doctor's riding out to his country-seat!"

These were golden moments for Dolph. No sooner was the doctor out of sight, than pestle and mortar were abandoned; the laboratory was left to take care of itself, and the student was off on some madcap frolic.

Indeed, it must be confessed, the youngster, as he grew up, seemed in a fair way to fulfil the prediction of the old claret-colored gentleman. He was the ringleader of all holiday sports and midnight gambols; ready for all kinds of mischievous pranks and hair-brained adventures.

There is nothing so troublesome as a hero on a small scale, or rather, a hero in a small town. Dolph soon became the abhorrence of all drowsy, housekeeping old citizens, who hated noise, and had no relish for waggery. The good dames, too, considered him as little better than a reprobate, gathered their daughters under their wings whenever he approached, and pointed him out as a warning to their sons. No one seemed to hold him in much regard except the wild striplings of the place, who were captivated by his open-hearted, daring manners— and the Negroes, who always looked upon every idle, do-nothing youngster as a kind of gentleman. Even the good Peter de Groodt, who had considered himself a kind of patron of the lad, began to despair of him; and would shake his head dubiously, as he listened to a long complaint from the housekeeper, and sipped a glass of her raspberry brandy.

Still his mother was not to be wearied out of her affection by all the waywardness of her boy; nor disheartened by the stories of his misdeeds, with which her good friends were continually regaling her. She had, it is true, very little of the pleasure which rich people enjoy, in always hearing their children praised; but she considered all this ill-will as a kind of persecution which he suffered, and she liked him the better on that account. She saw him growing up a fine, tall, good-looking youngster, and she looked at him with the secret pride of a mother's heart. It was her great desire that Dolph should appear like a gentleman, and all the money she could save went towards helping out his pocket and his wardrobe. She would look out of the window after him, as he sallied forth in his best array, and her heart would yearn with delight: and once, when Peter de Groodt, struck with the youngster's gallant appearance on a bright Sunday morning, observed, "Well, after all, Dolph does grow a comely fellow!" the tear of pride started into the mother's eye. "Ah, neighbor! Neighbor!" exclaimed she. "They may say what they please; poor Dolph will yet hold up his head with the best of them!"

Dolph Heyliger had now nearly attained his one-and-twentieth year, and the term of his medical studies was just expiring; yet it must be confessed that he knew little more of the profession than when he first entered the doctor's doors. This, however, could not be from any want of quickness of parts, for he showed amazing aptness in mastering other branches of knowledge, which he could only have studied at intervals. He was, for instance, a sure marksman, and won all the geese and turkeys at Christmas holidays. He was a bold rider; he was famous for leaping and wrestling; he played tolerably on the fiddle; could swim like a fish; and was the best hand in the whole place at fives and ninepins.

All these accomplishments, however, procured him no favor in the eyes of the doctor, who grew more and more crabbed and intolerant the nearer the term of apprenticeship approached. Frau Ilsy, too, was forever finding some occasion to raise a windy tempest about his ears, and seldom encountered him about the house without a clatter of the tongue; so that at length the jingling of her keys, as she approached, was to Dolph like the ringing of the prompter's bell, that gives notice of a theatrical thunder-storm. Nothing but the infinite good humor of the heedless youngster enabled him to bear all this domestic tyranny without open rebellion. It was evident that the doctor and his housekeeper were preparing to beat the poor youth out of the nest, the moment his term should have expired—a short-hand mode which the doctor had of providing for useless disciples.

Indeed the little man had been rendered more than usually irritable lately in consequence of various cares and vexations which his country estate had brought upon him. The doctor had been repeatedly annoyed by the rumors and tales which prevailed concerning the old mansion, and found it difficult to prevail even upon the country-man and his family to remain there rent-free. Every time he rode out to the farm he was teased by some fresh complaint of strange noises and fearful sights, with which the tenants were disturbed at night; and the doctor would come home fretting and fuming, and vent his spleen upon the whole household. It was indeed a sore grievance that affected him both in pride and purse. He was threatened with an absolute loss of the profits of his property; and then, what a blow to his territorial consequence, to be the landlord of a haunted house!

It was observed, however, that with all his vexation, the doctor never proposed to sleep in the house himself; nay, he could never be prevailed upon to remain on the premises after dark, but made the best of his way for town as soon as the bats began to flit about in the twilight. The fact was, the doctor had a secret belief in ghosts, having passed the early part of his life in a country where they particularly abound; and indeed the story went, that, when a boy, he had once seen the devil upon the Hartz Mountains in Germany.

At length the doctor's vexations on this head were brought to a crisis. One morning as he sat dozing over a volume in his study, he was suddenly startled from his slumbers by the bustling in of the housekeeper.

"Here's a fine to do!" cried she, as she entered the room. "Here's Claus Hopper come in, bag and baggage, from the farm, and swears he'll have nothing more to do with it. The whole family have been frightened out of their wits; for there's such racketing and rummaging about the old house, that they can't sleep quiet in their beds!"

"Donner and blitzen!" cried the doctor, impatiently. "Will they never have done chattering about that house? What a pack of fools, to let a few rats and mice frighten them out of good quarters!"

"Nay, nay," said the housekeeper, wagging her head knowingly, and piqued at having a good ghost-story doubted, "there's more in it than rats and mice. All the neighborhood talks about the house; and then such sights as have been seen in it! Peter de Groodt tells me, that the family that sold you the house, and went to Holland, dropped several strange hints about it, and said, 'they wished you joy of your bargain'; and you know yourself there's no getting any family to live in it."

"Peter de Groodt's a ninny—an old woman," said the doctor, peevishly. "I'll warrant he's been filling these people's heads full of stories. It's just like his nonsense about the ghost that haunted the church-belfry, as an excuse for not ringing the bell that cold night when Harmanus Brinkerhoff's house was on fire. Send Claus to me."

Claus Hopper now made his appearance; a simple country lout, full of awe at finding himself in the very study of Dr. Knipperhausen, and too much embarrassed to enter in much detail of the matters that had caused his alarm. He stood twirling his hat in one hand, resting sometimes on one leg, sometimes on the other, looking occasionally at the doctor, and now and then stealing a fearful glance at the death's-head that seemed ogling him from the top of the clothes-press.

The doctor tried every means to persuade him to return to the farm, but all in vain; he maintained a dogged determination on the subject; and at the close of every argument or solicitation would make the same brief, inflexible reply, "Ich kan nicht, mynheer." The doctor was a "little pot, and soon hot"; his patience was exhausted by these continual vexations about his estate. The stubborn refusal of Claus Hopper seemed to him like flat rebellion; his temper suddenly boiled over, and Claus was glad to make a rapid retreat to escape scalding.

When the bumpkin got to the housekeeper's room, he found Peter de Groodt, and several other true believers, ready to receive him. Here he indemnified himself for the restraint he had suffered in the study, and opened a budget of stories about the haunted house that astonished all his hearers. The house-keeper believed them all, if it was only to spite the doctor for having received her intelligence so uncourteously. Peter de Groodt matched them with many a wonderful legend of the times of the Dutch dynasty, and of the Devil's Stepping-stones; and of the pirate hanged at Gibbet Island, that continued to swing there at night long after the gallows was taken down; and of the ghost of the unfortunate Governor Leisler, hanged for treason, which haunted the old fort and the government-house. The gossiping knot dispersed, each charged with direful intelligence. The sexton disburdened himself at a vestry meeting that was held that very day, and the black cook forsook her kitchen, and spent half the day at the street-pump, that gossiping-place for servants, dealing forth the news to all that came for water. In a little time the whole town was in a buzz with tales about the haunted house. Some said that Claus Hopper had seen the devil, while others hinted that the house was haunted by the ghosts of some of the patients whom the doctor had physicked out of the world, and that was the reason why he did not venture to live in it himself.

All this put the little doctor in a terrible fume. He threatened vengeance on anyone who should affect the value of his property by exciting popular prejudices. He complained loudly of thus being in a manner dispossessed of his territories by mere bugbears; but he secretly determined to have the house exorcised by the Dominie. Great was his relief, therefore, when in the midst of his perplexities, Dolph stepped forward and undertook to garrison the haunted house. The youngster had been listening to all the stories of Claus Hopper and Peter de Groodt: he was fond of adventure, he loved the marvellous, and his imagination had become quite excited by these tales of wonder. Besides, he had led such an uncomfortable life at the doctor's, being subjected to the intolerable thraldom of early hours, that he was delighted at the prospect of having a house to himself, even though it should be a haunted one. His offer was eagerly accepted, and it was determined he should mount guard that very night. His only stipulation was, that the enterprise should be kept secret from his mother; for he knew the poor soul would not sleep a wink if she knew her son was waging war with the powers of darkness.

When night came on he set out on his perilous expedition. The old black cook, his only friend in the household, had provided him with a little mess for supper, and a rush-light; and she tied round his neck an amulet, given her by an African conjurer, as a charm against evil spirits. Dolph was escorted on his way by the doctor and Peter de Groodt, who had agreed to accompany him to the house, and to see him safe lodged. The night was overcast, and it was very dark when they arrived at the grounds which surrounded the mansion. The sexton led the way with the lantern. As they walked along the avenue of acacias, the fitful light, catching from bush to bush, and tree to tree, often startled the doughty Peter and made him fall back upon his followers; and the doctor grappled still closer hold of Dolph's arm, observing that the ground was very slippery and uneven. At one time they were nearly put to total rout by a bat, which came flitting about the lantern; and the notes of the insects from the trees, and the frogs from a neighboring pond, formed a most drowsy and doleful concert. The front door of the mansion opened with a grating sound that made the doctor turn pale. They entered a tolerably large hall, such as is common in American country-houses, and which serves for a sitting-room in warm weather. From this they went up a wide staircase, that groaned and creaked as they trod, every step making its particular note, like the key of a harpsichord. This led to another hall on the second story, whence they entered the room where Dolph was to sleep. It was large, and scantily furnished; the shutters were closed; but as they were much broken, there was no want of a circulation of air. It appeared to have been that sacred chamber, known among Dutch housewives by the name of "the best bedroom"; which is the best furnished room in the house, but in which scarce anybody is ever permitted to sleep. Its splendor, however, was all at an end. There were a few broken articles of furniture about the room, and in the centre stood a heavy deal table and a large arm-chair, both of which had the look of being coeval with the mansion. The fireplace was wide, and had been faced with Dutch tiles, representing Scripture stories; but some of them had fallen out of their places, and lay scattered about the hearth. The sexton lit the rush-light; and the doctor, looking fearfully about the room, was just exhorting Dolph to be of good cheer, and to pluck up a stout heart, when a noise in the chimney, like voices and struggling, struck a sudden panic into the sexton. He took to his heels with the lantern; the doctor followed hard after him; the stairs groaned and creaked as they hurried down, increasing their agitation and speed by its noise. The front door slammed after them; and Dolph heard them scrabbling down the avenue, till the sound of their feet was lost in the distance. That he did not join in this precipitate retreat might have been owing to his possessing a little more courage than his companions, or perhaps that he had caught a glimpse of the cause of their dismay, in a nest of chimney-swallows, that came tumbling down into the fireplace.

Being now left to himself, he secured the front door by a strong bolt and bar; and having seen that the other entrances were fastened, returned to his desolate chamber. Having made his supper from the basket which the good old cook had provided, he locked the chamber-door, and retired to rest on a mattress in one corner. The night was calm and still; and nothing broke upon the profound quiet but the lonely chirping of a cricket from the chimney of a distant chamber. The rushlight, which stood in the centre of the deal table, shed a feeble yellow ray, dimly illumining the chamber and making uncouth shapes and shadows on the walls, from the clothes which Dolph had thrown over a chair.

With all his boldness of heart, there was something subduing in this desolate scene; and he felt his spirits flag within him, as he lay on his hard bed and gazed about the room. He was turning over in his mind his idle habits, his doubtful prospects, and now and then heaving a heavy sigh as he thought on his poor old mother; for there is nothing like the silence and loneliness of night to bring dark shadows over the brightest mind. By and by he thought he heard a sound as of someone walking below stairs. He listened, and distinctly heard a step on the great staircase. It approached solemnly and slowly, tramp—tramp—tramp! It was evidently the tread of some heavy personage; and yet how could he have got into the house without making a noise? He had examined all the fastenings, and was certain that every entrance was secure. Still the steps advanced, tramp—tramp—tramp! It was evident that the person approaching could not be a robber, the step was too loud and deliberate; a robber would either be stealthy or precipitate. And now the footsteps had ascended the staircase; they were slowly advancing along the passage, resounding through the silent and empty apartments. The very cricket had ceased its melancholy note, and nothing interrupted their awful distinctness. The door, which had been locked on the inside, slowly swung open, as if self-moved. The footsteps entered the room: but no one was to be seen. They passed slowly and audibly across it, tramp—tramp—tramp! But whatever made the sound was invisible. Dolph rubbed his eyes, and stared about him; he could see to every part of the dimly-lighted chamber; all was vacant; yet he still heard those mysterious footsteps, solemnly walking about the chamber. They ceased, and all was dead silence. There was something more appalling in this invisible visitation than there would have been in anything that addressed itself to the eyesight. It was awfully vague and indefinite. He felt his heart beat against his ribs; a cold sweat broke out upon his forehead; he lay for some time in a state of violent agitation; nothing, however, occurred to increase his alarm. His light gradually burnt down into the socket, and he fell asleep. When he awoke it was broad daylight; the sun was peering through the cracks of the window-shutters, and the birds were merrily singing about the house. The bright cheery day soon put to flight all the terrors of the preceding night. Dolph laughed, or rather tried to laugh, at all that had passed, and endeavored to persuade himself that it was a mere freak of the imagination, conjured up by the stories he had heard; but he was a little puzzled to find the door of his room locked on the inside, notwithstanding that he had positively seen it swing open as the footsteps had entered. He returned to town in a state of considerable perplexity; but he determined to say nothing on the subject, until his doubts were either confirmed or removed by another night's watching. His silence was a grievous disappointment to the gossips who had gathered at the doctor's mansion. They had prepared their minds to hear direful tales, and were almost in a rage at being assured he had nothing to relate.

The next night, then, Dolph repeated his vigil. He now entered the house with some trepidation. He was particular in examining the fastenings of all the doors, and securing them well. He locked the door of his chamber, and placed a chair against it; then having dispatched his supper, he threw himself on his mattress and endeavored to sleep. It was all in vain; a thousand crowding fancies kept him waking. The time slowly dragged on, as if minutes were spinning themselves out into hours. As the night advanced, he grew more and more nervous; and he almost started from his couch when he heard the mysterious footstep again on the staircase. Up it came, as before, solemnly and slowly, tramp—tramp—tramp! It approached along the passage; the door again swung open, as if there had been neither lock nor impediment, and a strange-looking figure stalked into the room. It was an elderly man, large and robust, clothed in the old Flemish fashion. He had on a kind of short cloak, with a garment under it, belted round the waist; trunk-hose, with great bunches or bows at the knees; and a pair of russet boots, very large at top, and standing widely from his legs. His hat was broad and slouched, with a feather trailing over one side. His iron-gray hair hung in thick masses on his neck; and he had a short grizzled beard. He walked slowly round the room, as if examining that all was safe; then, hanging his hat on a peg beside the door, he sat down in the elbow-chair, and, leaning his elbow on the table, fixed his eyes on Dolph with an unmoving and deadening stare.

Dolph was not naturally a coward; but he had been brought up in an implicit belief in ghosts and goblins. A thousand stories came swarming to his mind that he had heard about this building; and as he looked at this strange personage, with his uncouth garb, his pale visage, his grizzly beard, and his fixed, staring, fishlike eye, his teeth began to chatter, his hair to rise on his head, and a cold sweat to break out all over his body. How long he remained in this situation he could not tell, for he was like one fascinated. He could not take his gaze off from the spectre; but lay staring at him, with his whole intellect absorbed in the contemplation. The old man remained seated behind the table, without stirring, or turning an eye, always keeping a dead steady glare upon Dolph. At length the household cock, from a neighboring farm, clapped his wings, and gave a loud cheerful crow that rung over the fields. At the sound the old man slowly rose, and took down his hat from the peg; the door opened, and closed after him; he was heard to go slowly down the staircase, tramp—tramp—tramp!—and when he had got to the bottom, all was again silent. Dolph lay and listened earnestly; counted every footfall; listened, and listened, if the steps should return, until, exhausted by watching and agitation, he fell into a troubled sleep.

Daylight again brought fresh courage and assurance. He would fain have considered all that had passed as a mere dream; yet there stood the chair in which the unknown had seated himself; there was the table on which he had leaned; there was the peg on which he had hung his hat; and there was the door, locked precisely as he himself had locked it, with the chair placed against it. He hastened downstairs, and examined the doors and windows; all were exactly in the same state in which he had left them, and there was no apparent way by which any being could have entered and left the house, without leaving some trace behind. "Pooh!" said Dolph to himself. "It was all a dream." But it would not do; the more he endeavored to shake the scene off from his mind, the more it haunted him.

Though he persisted in a strict silence as to all that he had seen or heard, yet his looks betrayed the uncomfortable night that he had passed. It was evident that there was something wonderful hidden under this mysterious reserve. The doctor took him into the study, locked the door, and sought to have a full and confidential communication; but he could get nothing out of him. Frau Ilsy took him aside into the pantry, but to as little purpose; and Peter de Groodt held him by the button for a full hour, in the church-yard, the very place to get at the bottom of a ghost-story, but came off not a whit wiser than the rest. It is always the case, however, that one truth concealed makes a dozen current lies. It is like a guinea locked up in a bank, that has a dozen paper representatives. Before the day was over, the neighborhood was full of reports. Some said that Dolph Heyliger watched in the haunted house, with pistols loaded with silver bullets; others, that he had a long talk with a spectre without a head; others, that Doctor Knipperhausen and the sexton had been hunted down the Bowery lane, and quite into town, by a legion of ghosts of their customers. Some shook their heads, and thought it a shame the doctor should put Dolph to pass the night alone in that dismal house, where he might be spirited away no one knew whither; while others observed, with a shrug, that if the devil did carry off the youngster, it would be but taking his own.

These rumors at length reached the ears of the good Dame Heyliger, and, as may be supposed, threw her into a terrible alarm. For her son to have exposed himself to danger from living foes, would have been nothing so dreadful in her eyes, as to dare alone the terrors of the haunted house. She hastened to the doctor's, and passed a great part of the day in attempting to dissuade Dolph from repeating his vigil; she told him a score of tales, which her gossiping friends had just related to her, of persons who had been carried off, when watching alone in old ruinous houses. It was all to no effect. Dolph's pride, as well as curiosity, was piqued. He endeavored to calm the apprehensions of his mother, and to assure her that there was no truth in all the rumors she had heard; she looked at him dubiously and shook her head; but finding his determination was not to be shaken, she brought him a little thick Dutch Bible, with brass clasps, to take with him, as a sword wherewith to fight the powers of darkness; and, lest that might not be sufficient, the housekeeper gave him the Heidelberg catechism by way of dagger.

The next night, therefore, Dolph took up his quarters for the third time in the old mansion. Whether dream or not, the same thing was repeated. Towards midnight, when everything was still, the same sound echoed through the empty halls, tramp—tramp—tramp! The stairs were again ascended; the door again swung open; the old man entered; walked round the room; hung up his hat, and seated himself by the table. The same fear and trembling came over poor Dolph, though not in so violent a degree. He lay in the same way, motionless and fascinated, staring at the figure, which regarded him as before with a dead, fixed, chilling gaze. In this way they remained for a long time, till, by degrees, Dolph's courage began gradually to revive. Whether alive or dead, this being had certainly some object in his visitation; and he recollected to have heard it said, spirits have no power to speak until spoken to. Summoning up resolution, therefore, and making two or three attempts, before he could get his parched tongue in motion, he addressed the unknown in the most solemn form of adjuration, and demanded to know what was the motive of his visit.

No sooner had he finished, than the old man rose, took down his hat, the door opened, and he went out, looking back upon Dolph just as he crossed the threshold, as if expecting him to follow. The youngster did not hesitate an instant. He took the candle in his hand, and the Bible under his arm, and obeyed the tacit invitation. The candle emitted a feeble, uncertain ray, but still he could see the figure before him slowly descend the stairs. He followed trembling. When it had reached the bottom of the stairs, it turned through the hall towards the back door of the mansion. Dolph held the light over the balustrades; but, in his eagerness to catch a sight of the unknown, he flared his feeble taper so suddenly, that it went out. Still there was sufficient light from the pale moonbeams, that fell through a narrow window, to give him an indistinct view of the figure, near the door. He followed, therefore, downstairs, and turned towards the place; but when he arrived there, the unknown had disappeared. The door remained fast barred and bolted; there was no other mode of exit; yet the being, whatever he might be, was gone. He unfastened the door, and looked out into the fields. It was a hazy, moonlight night, so that the eye could distinguish objects at some distance. He thought he saw the unknown in a footpath which led from the door. He was not mistaken; but how had he got out of the house? He did not pause to think, but followed on. The old man proceeded at a measured pace, without looking about him, his footsteps sounding on the hard ground. He passed through the orchard of apple-trees, always keeping the footpath. It led to a well, situated in a little hollow, which had supplied the farm with water. Just at this well Dolph lost sight of him. He rubbed his eyes and looked again; but nothing was to be seen of the unknown. He reached the well, but nobody was there. All the surrounding ground was open and clear; there was no bush nor hiding-place. He looked down the well, and saw, at a great depth, the reflection of the sky in the still water. After remaining here for some time, without seeing or hearing anything more of his mysterious conductor, he returned to the house, full of awe and wonder. He bolted the door, groped his way back to bed, and it was long before he could compose himself to sleep.

His dreams were strange and troubled. He thought he was following the old man along the side of a great river, until they came to a vessel on the point of sailing; and that his conductor led him on board and vanished. He remembered the commander of the vessel, a short swarthy man, with crisped black hair, blind of one eye, and lame of one leg; but the rest of his dream was very confused. Sometimes he was sailing; sometimes on shore; now amidst storms and tempests, and now wandering quietly in unknown streets. The figure of the old man was strangely mingled up with the incidents of the dream, and the whole distinctly wound up by his finding himself on board of the vessel again, returning home, with a great bag of money!

When he woke, the gray, cool light of dawn was streaking the horizon, and the cocks passing the reveille from farm to farm throughout the country. He rose more harassed and perplexed than ever. He was singularly confounded by all that he had seen and dreamt, and began to doubt whether his mind was not affected, and whether all that passing in his thoughts might not be mere feverish fantasy. In his present state of mind, he did not feel disposed to return immediately to the doctor's, and undergo the cross-questioning of the household. He made a scanty breakfast, therefore, on the remains of the last night's provisions, and then wandered out into the fields to meditate on all that had befallen him. Lost in thought, he rambled about, gradually approaching the town, until the morning was far advanced, when he was aroused by a hurry and bustle around him. He found himself near the water's edge, in a throng of people, hurrying to a pier, where was a vessel ready to make sail. He was unconsciously carried along by the impulse of the crowd, and found that it was a sloop, on the point of sailing up the Hudson to Albany. There was much leave-taking, and kissing of old women and children, and great activity in carrying on board baskets of bread and cakes, and provisions of all kinds, notwithstanding the mighty joints of meat that dangled over the stern; for a voyage to Albany was an expedition of great moment in those days. The commander of the sloop was hurrying about, and giving a world of orders, which were not very strictly attended to; one man being busy in lighting his pipe, and another in sharpening his snickersnee.

The appearance of the commander suddenly caught Dolph's attention. He was short and swarthy, with crisped black hair; blind of one eye and lame of one leg—the very commander that he had seen in his dream! Surprised and aroused, he considered the scene more attentively, and recalled still further traces of his dream: the appearance of the vessel, of the river, and of images, a variety of other objects accorded with the imperfect vaguely rising to recollection.

As he stood musing on these circumstances, the captain suddenly called out to him in Dutch, "Step on board, young man, or you'll be left behind!" He was startled by the summons; he saw that the sloop was cast loose, and was actually moving from the pier; it seemed as if he was actuated by some irresistible impulse; he sprang upon the deck, and the next moment the sloop was hurried off by the wind and tide. Dolph's thoughts and feelings were all in tumult and confusion. He had been strongly worked upon by the events which had recently befallen him, and could not but think there was some connection between his present situation and his last night's dream. He felt as if under supernatural influence; and tried to assure himself with an old and favorite maxim of his, that "one way or other all would turn out for the best." For a moment, the indignation of the doctor at his departure, without leave, passed across his mind, but that was matter of little moment; then he thought of the distress of his mother at his strange disappearance, and the idea gave him a sudden pang; he would have entreated to be put on shore; but he knew with such wind and tide the entreaty would have been in vain. Then the inspiring love of novelty and adventure came rushing in full tide through his bosom; he felt himself launched strangely and suddenly on the world, and under full way to explore the regions of wonder that lay up this mighty river, and beyond those blue mountains which had bounded his horizon since childhood. While he was lost in this whirl of thought, the sails strained to the breeze; the shores seemed to hurry away

behind him; and before he perfectly recovered his self-posses-
sion, the sloop was ploughing her way past Spiking-devil and
Yonkers, and the tallest chimney of the Manhattoes had
faded from his sight.

I have said that a voyage up the Hudson in those days was
an undertaking of some moment; indeed, it was as much
thought of as a voyage to Europe is at present. The sloops
were often many days on the way; the cautious navigators taking in sail when it blew fresh, and coming to anchor at night;
and stopping to send the boat ashore for milk for tea; without
which it was impossible for the worthy old lady passengers
to subsist. And there were the much-talked-of perils of the
Tappaan Zee, and the highlands. In short, a prudent Dutch
burgher would talk of such a voyage for months, and even
years, beforehand; and never undertook it without putting his
affairs in order, making his will, and having prayers said for
him in the Low Dutch churches.

In the course of such a voyage, therefore, Dolph was satisfied
he would have time enough to reflect, and to make up his
mind as to what he should do when he arrived at Albany.
The captain with his blind eye, and lame leg, would, it is
true, bring his strange dream to mind, and perplex him sadly
for a few moments; but of late his life had been made up so
much of dreams and realities, his nights and days had been so
jumbled together, that he seemed to be moving continually in
a delusion. There is always, however, a kind of vagabond consolation in a man's having nothing in this world to lose; with
this Dolph comforted his heart, and determined to make the
most of the present enjoyment.

In the second day of the voyage they came to the highlands.

It was the latter part of a calm, sultry day, that they floated gently with the tide between these stern mountains. There was that perfect quiet which prevails over nature in the languor of summer heat; the turning of a plank, or the accidental falling of an oar on deck, was echoed from the mountain-side, and reverberated along the shores; and if by chance the captain gave a shout of command, there were airy tongues which mocked it from every cliff.

Dolph gazed about him in mute delight and wonder at these scenes of nature's magnificence. To the left the Dunderberg reared its woody precipices, height over height, forest over forest, away into the deep summer sky. To the right, strutted forth the bold promontory of Antony's Nose, with a solitary eagle wheeling about it; while beyond, mountain succeeded to mountain, until they seemed to lock their arms together, and confine this mighty river in their embraces. There was a feeling of quiet luxury in gazing at the broad green bosoms here and there scooped out among the precipices; or at woodlands high in air, nodding over the edge of some beetling bluff, and their foliage all transparent in the yellow sunshine.

In the midst of his admiration, Dolph remarked a pile of bright, snowy clouds, peering above the western heights. It was succeeded by another, and another, each seemingly pushing onwards its predecessor, and towering, with dazzling brilliancy, in the deep-blue atmosphere; and now muttering peals of thunder were faintly heard rolling behind the mountains. The river, hitherto still and glassy, reflecting pictures of the sky and land, now showed a dark ripple at a distance, as the breeze came creeping up it. The fish-hawks wheeled and screamed, and sought their nests on the high dry trees; the crows flew clamorously to the crevices of the rocks, and all nature seemed conscious of the approaching thunder-gust.

The clouds now rolled in volumes over the mountain-tops; their summits still bright and snowy, but the lower parts of an inky blackness. The rain began to patter down in broad and scattered drops; the wind freshened and curled up the waves; at length it seemed as if the bellying clouds were torn open by the mountain-tops, and complete torrents of rain came rattling down. The lightning leaped from cloud to cloud, and streamed quivering against the rocks, splitting and rending the stoutest forest-trees. The thunder burst in tremendous explosions; the peals were echoed from mountain to mountain; they crashed upon Dunderberg, and rolled up the long defile of the highlands, each headland making a new echo, until old Bull Hill seemed to bellow back the storm.

For a time the scudding rack and mist, and the sheeted rain, almost hid the landscape from the sight. There was a fearful gloom, illumined still more fearfully by the streams of lightning which glittered among the rain-drops. Never had Dolph beheld such an absolute warring of the elements; it seemed as if the storm was tearing and rending its way through this mountain defile, and had brought all the artillery of heaven into action.

The vessel was hurried on by the increasing wind, until she came to where the river makes a sudden bend, the only one in the whole course of its majestic career.[2] Just as they turned the point, a violent flaw of wind came sweeping down a mountain gully, bending the forest before it, and, in a moment, lashing up the river into white froth and foam. The captain saw the

[2]This must have been the bend at West Point.

danger, and cried out to lower the sail. Before the order could be obeyed, the flaw struck the sloop and threw her on her beam ends. Everything now was fright and confusion: the flapping of the sails, the whistling and rushing of the wind, the bawling of the captain and crew, the shrieking of the passengers, all mingled with the rolling and bellowing of the thunder. In the midst of the uproar the sloop righted; at the same time the mainsail shifted, the boom came sweeping the quarterdeck, and Dolph, who was gazing unguardedly at the clouds, found himself, in a moment, floundering in the river.

For once in his life one of his idle accomplishments was of use to him. The many truant hours he had devoted to sporting in the Hudson had made him an expert swimmer; yet with all his strength and skill he found great difficulty in reaching the shore. His disappearance from the deck had not been noticed by the crew, who were all occupied by their own danger. The sloop was driven along with inconceivable rapidity. She had hard work to weather a long promontory on the eastern shore, round which the river turned, and which completely shut her from Dolph's view.

It was on a point of the western shore that he landed, and, scrambling up the rocks, threw himself, faint and exhausted, at the foot of a tree. By degrees the thunder-gust passed over. The clouds rolled away to the east, where they lay piled in feathery masses, tinted with the last rosy rays of the sun. The distant play of the lightning might be seen about the dark bases, and now and then might be heard the faint muttering of the thunder. Dolph rose, and sought about to see if any path led from the shore, but all was savage and trackless. The rocks were piled upon each other; great trunks of trees lay shattered about, as they had been blown down by the strong winds which draw through these mountains, or had fallen through age. The rocks, too, were overhung with wild vines and briers, which completely matted themselves together, and opposed a barrier to all ingress; every movement that he made shook down a shower from the dripping foliage. He attempted to scale one of these almost perpendicular heights; but, though strong and agile, he found it an Herculean undertaking. Often he was supported merely by crumbling projections of the rock, and sometimes he clung to roots and branches of trees, and hung almost suspended in the air. The wood-pigeon came cleaving his whistling flight by him, and the eagle screamed from the brow of the impending cliff. As he was thus climbing, he was on the point of seizing hold of a shrub to aid his ascent, when something rustled among the leaves, and he saw a snake quivering along like lightning, almost from under his hand. It coiled itself up immediately, in an attitude of defiance, with flattened head, distended jaws, and quickly vibrating tongue, that played like a little flame about its mouth. Dolph's heart turned faint within him, and he had well-nigh let go his hold and tumbled down the precipice. The serpent stood on the defensive but for an instant; and finding there was no attack, glided away into a cleft of the rock. Dolph's eye followed it with fearful intensity, and saw a nest of adders, knotted, and writhing, and hissing in the chasm. He hastened with all speed from so frightful a neighborhood. His imagination, full of this new horror, saw an adder in every curling vine, and heard the tail of a rattlesnake in every dry leaf that rustled.

At length he succeeded in scrambling to the summit of a precipice; but it was covered by a dense forest. Wherever he could gain a lookout between trees, he beheld heights and cliffs, one rising beyond another, until huge mountains over-topped the whole. There were no signs of cultivation; no smoke curling among the trees to indicate a human residence. Every-thing was wild and solitary. As he was standing on the edge of a precipice overlooking a deep ravine fringed with trees, his feet detached a great fragment of rock; it fell, crashing its way through the tree-tops, down into the chasm. A loud whoop, or rather yell, issued from the bottom of the glen; the moment after there was a report of a gun; and a ball came whistling over his head, cutting the twigs and leaves, and burying itself deep in the bark of a chestnut-tree.

Dolph did not wait for a second shot, but made a precipi-tate retreat; fearing every moment to hear the enemy in pur-suit. He succeeded, however, in returning unmolested to the shore, and determined to penetrate no farther into the country so beset with savage perils.

He sat himself down, dripping, disconsolately, on a stone. What was to be done? Where was he to shelter himself? The hour of repose was approaching: the birds were seeking their nests, the bat began to flit about in the twilight, and the night-hawk, soaring high in the heaven, seemed to be calling out the stars. Night gradually closed in, and wrapped everything in gloom; and though it was the latter part of summer, the breeze stealing along the river, and among these dripping forests, was chilly and penetrating, especially to a half-drowned man.

As he sat drooping and despondent in this comfortless con-dition, he perceived a light gleaming through the trees near the shore, where the winding of the river made a deep bay. It cheered him with the hope of a human habitation, where he might get something to appease the clamorous cravings of his stomach, and what was equally necessary in his shipwrecked condition, a comfortable shelter for the night. With extreme difficulty he made his way toward the light, along ledges of rocks, down which he was in danger of sliding into the river, and over great trunks of fallen trees; some of which had been blown down in the late storm, and lay so thickly together that he had to struggle through their branches. At length he came to the brow of the rock overhanging a small dell, whence the light proceeded. It was from a fire at the foot of a great tree in the midst of a grassy interval or plat among the rocks. The fire cast up a red glare among the gray crags, and impending trees; leaving chasms of deep gloom, that resembled entrances to caverns. A small brook rippled close by, betrayed by the quivering reflection of the flame. There were two figures moving about the fire, and others squatted before it. As they were between him and the light, they were in complete shadow: but one of them happening to move round to the opposite side, Dolph was startled at perceiving, by the glare falling on painted features, and glittering on silver ornaments, that he was an Indian. He now looked more narrowly, and saw guns leaning against a tree, and a dead body lying on the ground. Here was the very foe that had fired at him from the glen. He endeavored to retreat quietly, not caring to intrust himself to these half-human beings in so savage and lonely a place. It was too late: the Indian, with that eagle quickness of eye so remarkable in his race, perceived something stirring among the bushes on the rock. He seized one of the guns that leaned against the tree; one moment more, and Dolph might have had his passion for adventure cured by a bullet. He

halloed loudly, with the Indian salutation of friendship; the whole party sprang upon their feet; the salutation was returned, and the straggler was invited to join them at the fire.

On approaching, he found to his consolation, the party was composed of white men as well as Indians. One, evidently the principal personage, or commander, was seated on a trunk of a tree before the fire. He was a large, stout man, somewhat advanced in life, but hale and hearty. His face was bronzed almost to the color of an Indian's; he had strong but rather jovial features, an aquiline nose, and a mouth shaped like a mastiff's. His face was half thrown in the shade by a broad hat, with a buck's tail in it. His gray hair hung short in his neck. He wore a hunting-frock, with Indian leggins, and moccasins, and a tomahawk in the broad wampum-belt round his waist. As Dolph caught a distinct view of his person and features, something reminded him of the old man of the haunted house. The man before him, however, was different in dress and age; he was more cheery too in aspect, and it was hard to find where the vague resemblance lay; but a resemblance there certainly was. Dolph felt some degree of awe in approaching him; but was assured by a frank, hearty welcome. He was still further encouraged by perceiving that the dead body, which had caused him some alarm, was that of a deer; and his satisfaction was complete in discerning, by savory steams from a kettle, suspended by a hooked stick over the fire, that there was a part cooking for the evening's repast.

He had, in fact, fallen in with a rambling hunting-party, such as often took place in those days among the settlers along the river. The hunter is always hospitable; and nothing makes men more social and unceremonious than meeting in the

wilderness. The commander of the party poured out a dram of cheering liquor, which he gave him with a merry leer, to warm his heart; and ordered one of his followers to fetch some garments from a pinnace, moored in a cove close by, while those in which our hero was dripping might be dried before the fire.

Dolph found, as he had suspected, that the shot from the glen, which had come so near giving him his quietus when on the precipice, was from the party before him. He had nearly crushed one of them by the fragment of rock which he had detached; and the jovial old hunter, in the broad hat and bucktail, had fired at the place where he saw the bushes move, supposing it to be the sound of some wild animal. He laughed heartily at the blunder, it being what is considered an exceeding good joke among hunters. "But faith, my lad," said he, "if I had but caught a glimpse of you to take sight at, you would have followed the rock. Antony Vander Heyden is seldom known to miss his aim." These last words were at once a clue to Dolph's curiosity: and a few questions let him completely into the character of the man before him, and of his band of woodland rangers. This commander in the broad hat and hunting-frock was no less a personage than the Heer Antony Vander Heyden, of Albany, of whom Dolph had many a time heard. He was, in fact, the hero of many a story, his singular humors and whimsical habits being matters of wonder to his quiet Dutch neighbors. As he was a man of property, having had a father before him from whom he inherited large tracts of wild land, and whole barrels full of wampum, he could indulge his humors without control. Instead of staying quietly at home, eating and drinking at regular mealtimes, amusing himself by smoking his pipe on a bench before the door, and then turning into a comfortable bed at night, he delighted in all kinds of rough, wild expeditions: never so happy as when on a hunting-party in the wilderness, sleeping under trees or bark sheds, or cruising down the river, or on some woodland lake, fishing and fowling, and living the Lord knows how.

He was a great friend to Indians, and to an Indian mode of life; which he considered true natural liberty and manly enjoyment. When at home he had always several Indian hangers-on who loitered about his house, sleeping like hounds in the sunshine; or preparing hunting and fishing tackle for some new expedition; or shooting at marks with bows and arrows.

Over these vagrant beings Heer Antony had as perfect command as a huntsman over his pack; though they were great nuisances to the regular people of his neighborhood. As he was a rich man, no one ventured to thwart his humors; indeed, his hearty, joyous manner made him universally popular. He would troll a Dutch song as he tramped along the street; hail everyone a mile off, and when he entered a house, would slap the good man familiarly on the back, shake him by the hand till he roared, and kiss his wife and daughter before his face— in short there was no pride or ill-humor about Heer Antony.

Besides his Indian hangers-on, he had three or four humble friends among the white men, who looked up to him as a patron, and had the run of his kitchen, and the favor of being taken with him occasionally on his expeditions. With a medley of such retainers he was at present on a cruise along the shores of the Hudson, in a pinnace kept for his own recreation. There were two white men with him, dressed partly in Indian style, with moccasins and hunting-shirts; the rest of his crew consisted of four favorite Indians. They had been prowling about the river, without any definite object, until they found themselves in the highlands; where they had passed two or three days, hunting the deer which still lingered among these mountains.

"It is lucky for you, young man," said Antony Vander Heyden, "that you happened to be knocked overboard to-day, as to-morrow morning we start early on our return homewards; and you might then have looked in vain for a meal among the mountains—but come, lads, stir about! Stir about! Let's see what prog we have for supper; the kettle has boiled long enough; my stomach cries cupboard; and I'll warrant our guest is in no mood to dally with his trencher."

There was a bustle now in the little encampment; one took off the kettle and turned a part of the contents into a huge wooden bowl. Another prepared a flat rock for a table; while a third brought various utensils from the pinnace; Heer Antony himself brought a flask or two of precious liquor from his own private locker; knowing his boon companions too well to trust any of them with the key.

A rude but hearty repast was soon spread; consisting of venison smoking from the kettle, with cold bacon, boiled Indian corn, and mighty loaves of good brown household bread. Never had Dolph made a more delicious repast; and when he had washed it down with two or three draughts from the Heer Antony's flask, and felt the jolly liquor sending its warmth through his veins, and glowing round his very heart, he would not have changed his situation, no, not with the governor of the province.

The Heer Antony, too, grew chirping and joyous; told half a dozen fat stories, at which his white followers laughed immoderately, though the Indians, as usual, maintained an invincible gravity.

"This is your true life, my boy!" said he, slapping Dolph on the shoulder. "A man is never a man till he can defy wind and weather, range woods and wilds, sleep under a tree, and live on bass-wood leaves!"

And then would he sing a stave or two of a Dutch drinking-song, swaying a short swab Dutch bottle in his hand, while his myrmidons would join in the chorus, until the woods echoed again—as the good old song has it,

> "They all with a shout made the elements ring
>   So soon as the office was o'er,
> To feasting they went, with true merriment,
>   And tippled strong liquor gillore."

In the midst of his joviality, however, Heer Antony did not lose sight of discretion. Though he pushed the bottle without reserve to Dolph, he always took care to help his followers himself, knowing the beings he had to deal with; and was particular in granting but a moderate allowance to the Indians. The repast being ended, the Indians having drunk their liquor, and smoked their pipes, now wrapped themselves in their blankets, stretched themselves on the ground, with their feet to the fire, and soon fell asleep, like so many tired hounds. The rest of the party remained chatting before the fire, which the gloom of the forest, and the dampness of the air from the late storm, rendered extremely grateful and comforting. The conversation gradually moderated from the hilarity of supper time, and turned upon hunting-adventures, and exploits and perils in the wilderness, many of which were so strange and improbable, that I will not venture to repeat them, lest the veracity of Antony Vander Heyden and his comrades should be brought into question. There were many legendary tales told, also, about the river, and the settlements on its borders; in which valuable kind of lore the Heer Antony seemed deeply versed. As the sturdy bush-beater sat in a twisted root of a tree, that served him for an arm-chair, dealing forth these wild stories, with the fire gleaming on his strongly marked visage, Dolph was again repeatedly perplexed by something that reminded him of the phantom of the haunted house; some vague resemblance not to be fixed upon any precise feature or lineament, but pervading the general air of his countenance and figure.

The circumstance of Dolph's falling overboard led to the relation of divers disasters and singular mishaps that had befallen voyagers on this great river, particularly in the earlier periods of colonial history; most of which the Heer deliberately attributed to supernatural causes. Dolph stared at this suggestion; but the old gentleman assured him it was very currently believed by the settlers along the river, that these highlands were under the dominion of supernatural and mischievous beings, which seemed to have taken some pique against the Dutch colonists in the early time of the settlement. In consequence of this, they have ever taken particular delight in venting their spleen, and indulging their humors, upon the Dutch skippers; bothering them with flaws, head-winds, counter-currents, and all kinds of impediments: insomuch, that a Dutch navigator was always obliged to be exceedingly wary and deliberate in his proceedings; to come to anchor at dusk;

to drop his peak, or take to sail, whenever he saw a swag-bellied cloud rolling over the mountains; in short, to take so many precautions, that he was often apt to be an incredible time in toiling up the river.

Some, he said, believed these mischievous powers of the air to be the evil spirits conjured up by the Indian wizards, in the early times of the province, to revenge themselves on the strangers who had dispossessed them of their country. They even attributed to their incantations the misadventure which befell the renowned Hendrick Hudson, when he sailed so gallantly up this river in quest of a northwest passage, and, as he thought, ran his ship aground; which they affirm was nothing more nor less than a spell of these same wizards, to prevent his getting to China in this direction.

The greater part, however, Heer Antony observed, accounted for all the extraordinary circumstances attending this river, and the perplexities of the skippers who navigated it, by the old legend of the Storm-Ship which haunted Point-no-point. On finding Dolph to be utterly ignorant of this tradition, the Heer stared at him for a moment with surprise, and wondered where he had passed his life, to be uninformed on so important a point of history. To pass away the remainder of the evening, therefore, he undertook the tale, as far as his memory would serve, in the very words in which it had been written out by Mynheer Selyne, an early poet of the New Netherlandts. Giving, then, a stir to the fire, that sent up its sparks among the trees like a little volcano, he adjusted himself comfortably in his root of a tree, and throwing back his head, and closing his eyes for a few moments, to summon up his recollection, he related the following legend.

The Legend
of
the Storm-Ship

In the golden age of the province of the New Netherlands,
when under the sway of Wouter Van Twiller, otherwise called
the Doubter, the people of the Manhattoes were alarmed one
sultry afternoon, just about the time of the summer solstice,
by a tremendous storm of thunder and lightning. The rain
fell in such torrents as absolutely to spatter up and smoke
along the ground. It seemed as if the thunder rattled and rolled
over the very roofs of the houses; the lightning was seen to
play about the church of St. Nicholas, and to strive three times,
in vain, to strike its weather-cock. Garret Van Horne's new

chimney was split almost from top to bottom; and Doffue Mildeberger was struck speechless from his bald-faced mare, just as he was riding into town. In a word, it was one of those unparalleled storms which only happen once within the memory of that venerable personage known in all towns by the appellation of "the oldest inhabitant."

Great was the terror of the good old women of the Manhattoes. They gathered their children together, and took refuge in the cellars; after having hung a shoe on the iron point of every bedpost, lest it should attract the lightning. At length the storm abated; the thunder sank into a growl, and the setting sun, breaking from under the fringed borders of the clouds, made the broad bosom of the bay to gleam like a sea of molten gold.

The word was given from the fort that a ship was standing up the bay. It passed from mouth to mouth, and street to street, and soon put the little capital in a bustle. The arrival of a ship, in those early times of the settlement, was an event of vast importance to the inhabitants. It brought them news from the Old World, from the land of their birth, from which they were so completely severed: to the yearly ship, too, they looked for their supply of luxuries, of finery, of comforts, and almost of necessaries. The good vrouw could not have her new cap nor new gown until the arrival of the ship; the artist waited for it for his tools, the burgomaster for his pipe and his supply of Hollands, the schoolboy for his top and marbles, and the lordly landholder for the bricks with which he was to build his new mansion. Thus everyone, rich and poor, great and small, looked out for the arrival of the ship. It was the great yearly event of the town of New Amsterdam; and from one end of the year to the other, the ship—the ship—the ship—was the continual topic of conversation.

The news from the fort, therefore, brought all the populace down to the Battery, to behold the wished-for sight. It was not exactly the time when she had been expected to arrive, and the circumstance was a matter of some speculation. Many were the groups collected about the Battery. Here and there might be seen a burgomaster, of slow and pompous gravity, giving his opinion with great confidence to a crowd of old women and idle boys. At another place was a knot of old weather-beaten fellows, who had been seamen or fishermen in their times, and were great authorities on such occasions; these gave different opinions, and caused great disputes among their several adherents: but the man most looked up to, and followed and watched by the crowd, was Hans Van Pelt, an old Dutch sea-captain retired from service, the nautical oracle of the place. He reconnoitred the ship through an ancient telescope, covered with tarry canvas, hummed a Dutch tune to himself, and said nothing. A hum, however, from Hans Van Pelt, had always more weight with the public than a speech from another man.

In the meantime the ship became more distinct to the naked eye: she was a stout, round, Dutch-built vessel, with high bow and poop, and bearing Dutch colors. The evening sun gilded her bellying canvas, and she came riding over the long waving billows. The sentinel who had given notice of her approach, declared, that he first got sight of her when she was in the centre of the bay; and that she broke suddenly on his sight, just as if she had come out of the bosom of the black thundercloud. The by-standers looked at Hans Van Pelt, to see what

he would say to this report: Hans Van Pelt screwed his mouth closer together, and said nothing; upon which some shook their heads, and others shrugged their shoulders.

The ship was now repeatedly hailed, but made no reply, and passing by the fort, stood on up the Hudson. A gun was brought to bear on her, and, with some difficulty, loaded and fired by Hans Van Pelt, the garrison not being expert in artillery. The shot seemed absolutely to pass through the ship, and to skip along the water on the other side, but no notice was taken of it! What was strange, she had all her sails set, and sailed right against wind and tide, which were both down the river. Upon this Hans Van Pelt, who was likewise harbormaster, ordered his boat, and set off to board her; but after rowing two or three hours, he turned without success. Sometimes he would get within one or two hundred yards of her, and then, in a twinkling, she would be half a mile off. Some said it was because his oarsmen, who were rather pursy and short-winded, stopped every now and then to take breath, and

spit on their hands; but this it is probable was a mere scandal. He got near enough, however, to see the crew; who were all dressed in Dutch style, the officers in doublets and high hats and feathers; not a word was spoken by anyone on board; they stood as motionless as so many statues, and the ship seemed as if left to her own government. Thus she kept on, away up the river, lessening and lessening in the evening sunshine, until she faded from sight, like a little white cloud melting away in the summer sky.

The appearance of this ship threw the governor into one of the deepest doubts that ever beset him in the whole course of his administration. Fears were entertained for the security of the infant settlements on the river, lest this might be an enemy's ship in disguise, sent to take possession. The governor called together his council repeatedly to assist him with their conjectures. He sat in his chair of state, built of timber from the sacred forest of the Hague, smoking his long jasmin pipe, and listening to all that his counsellors had to say on a subject about which they knew nothing; but in spite of all the conjecturing of the sagest and oldest heads, the governor still continued to doubt.

Messengers were dispatched to different places on the river; but they returned without any tidings—the ship had made no port. Day after day, and week after week, elapsed, but she never returned down the Hudson. As, however, the council seemed solicitous for intelligence, they had it in abundance. The captains of the sloops seldom arrived without bringing some report of having seen the strange ship at different parts of the river; sometimes near the Pallisadoes, sometimes off Croton Point, and sometimes in the highlands; but she never was reported as having been seen above the highlands. The crews of the sloops, it is true, generally differed among them-selves in their accounts of these apparitions; but that may have arisen from the uncertain situations in which they saw her. Sometimes it was by the flashes of the thunder-storm lighting up a pitchy night, and giving glimpses of her careering across Tappaan Zee, or the wide waste of Haverstraw Bay. At one moment she would appear close upon them, as if likely to run them down, and would throw them into great bustle and alarm; but the next flash would show her far off, always sailing against the wind. Sometimes, in quiet moonlight nights, she would be seen under some high bluff of the highlands, all in deep shadow, excepting her topsails glittering in the moon-beams; by the time, however, that the voyagers reached the place, no ship was to be seen; and when they had passed on for some distance, and looked back, behold! there she was again, with her topsails in the moonshine! Her appearance was always just after, or just before, or just in the midst of unruly weather; and she was known among the skippers and voyagers of the Hudson by the name of "the Storm-Ship."

These reports perplexed the governor and his council more than ever; and it would be endless to repeat the conjectures and opinions uttered on the subject. Some quoted cases in point, of ships seen off the coast of New England, navigated by witches and goblins. Old Hans Van Pelt, who had been more than once to the Dutch colony at the Cape of Good Hope, insisted that this must be the flying Dutchman, which had so long haunted Table Bay; but being unable to make port, had now sought another harbor. Others suggested, that, if it really was a supernatural apparition, as there was every natural reason to believe, it might be Hendrick Hudson, and his crew of the *Half-Moon;* who, it was well known, had once run aground in the upper part of the river in seeking a north-west passage to China. This opinion had very little weight with the governor, but it passed current out of doors; for in-deed it had already been reported, that Hendrick Hudson and his crew haunted the Kaatskill Mountains; and it appeared very reasonable to suppose, that his ship might infest the river where the enterprise was baffled, or that it might bear the shadowy crew to their periodical revels in the mountain.

Other events occurred to occupy the thoughts and doubts of the sage Wouter and his council, and the Storm-Ship ceased to be a subject of deliberation at the board. It continued, however, a matter of popular belief and marvellous anecdote through the whole time of the Dutch government, and partic-ularly just before the capture of New Amsterdam, and the subjugation of the province by the English squadron. About that time the Storm-Ship was repeatedly seen in the Tappaan Zee, and about Weehawk, and even down as far as Hoboken; and her appearance was supposed to be ominous of the ap-proaching squall in public affairs, and the downfall of Dutch domination.

Since that time we have no authentic accounts of her; though it is said she still haunts the highlands, and cruises about Point-no-point. People who live along the river insist that they sometimes see her in summer moonlight; and that in a deep still midnight they have heard the chant of her crew, as if heaving the lead; but sights and sounds are so deceptive along the mountainous shores, and about the wide bays and long reaches of this great river, that I confess I have very strong doubts upon the subject.

It is certain, nevertheless, that strange things have been seen in these highlands in storms, which are considered as connected with the old story of the ship. The captains of the river craft talk of the bulbous-bottomed Dutch goblin, in trunk-hose and sugar-loafed hat, with a speaking-trumpet in his hand, which they say keeps about the Dunderberg.[1] They declare that they have heard him, in stormy weather, in the midst of the turmoil, giving orders in Low Dutch for the piping up of a fresh gust of wind, or the rattling off of another thunder-clap. That sometimes he has been seen surrounded by a crew of little imps in broad breeches and short doublets; tumbling head-over-heels in the rack and mist, and playing a thousand gambols in the air; or buzzing like a swarm of flies about Antony's Nose; and that, at such times, the hurry-scurry of the storm was always greatest. One time a sloop, in passing by the Dunderberg, was overtaken by a thunder-gust, that came scouring round the mountain, and seemed to burst just over the vessel. Though tight and well ballasted, she labored dreadfully, and the water came over the gunwale. All the crew were amazed when it was discovered that there was a little white sugar-loaf hat on the mast-head, known at once to be the hat of the Heer of the Dunderberg. Nobody, however, dared to climb to the mast-head, and get rid of this terrible hat. The sloop continued laboring and rocking, as if she would have rolled her mast overboard, and seemed in continual danger either of upsetting or of running on shore. In this way she

[1] *i.e.,* The "Thunder-Mountain," so-called from its echoes.

drove quite through the highlands, until she had passed Pollopol's Island, where, it is said, the jurisdiction of the Dunderberg potentate ceases. No sooner had she passed this bourn, than the little hat spun up into the air like a top, whirled up all the clouds into a vortex, and hurried them back to the summit of the Dunderberg; while the sloop righted herself, and sailed on as quietly as if in a mill-pond. Nothing saved her from utter wreck but the fortunate circumstance of having a horse-shoe nailed against the mast—a wise precaution against evil spirits, since adopted by all the Dutch captains that navigate this haunted river.

There is another story told of this foul-weather urchin, by Skipper Daniel Ouselsticker, of Fishkill, who was never known to tell a lie. He declared that, in a severe squall, he saw him seated astride of his bowsprit, riding the sloop ashore, full butt against Antony's Nose, and that he was exorcised by Dominie Van Gieson, of Esopus, who happened to be on board, and who sang the hymn of St. Nicholas; whereupon the goblin threw himself up in the air like a ball, and went off in a whirlwind, carrying away with him the nightcap of the Dominie's wife; which was discovered the next Sunday morning hanging on the weather-cock of Esopus church-steeple, at least forty miles off! Several events of this kind having taken place, the regular skippers of the river, for a long time, did not venture to pass the Dunderberg without lowering their peaks, out of homage to the Heer of the mountain; and it was observed that all such as paid this tribute of respect were suffered to pass unmolested.[2]

[2]Among the superstitions which prevailed in the colonies, during the early times of the settlements, there seems to have been a singular one

"Such," said Antony Vander Heyden, "are a few of the stories written down by Selyne, the poet, concerning the Storm-Ship, which he affirms to have brought a crew of mischievous imps into the province, from some old ghost-ridden country of Europe. I could give a host more, if necessary; for all the accidents that so often befall the river craft in the highlands are said to be tricks played off by these imps of the Dunderberg; but I see that you are nodding, so let us turn in for the night."

The moon had just raised her silver horns above the round back of Old Bull Hill, and lit up the gray rocks and shagged forests, and glittered on the waving bosom of the river. The night-dew was falling, and the late gloomy mountains began to soften and put on a gray aërial tint in the dewy light. The hunters stirred the fire, and threw on fresh fuel to qualify the

about phantom ships. The superstitious fancies of men are always apt to turn upon those objects which concern their daily occupations. The solitary ship, which, from year to year, came like a raven in the wilderness, bringing to the inhabitants of a settlement the comforts of life from the world from which they were cut off, was apt to be present to their dreams, whether sleeping or waking. The accidental sight from shore of a sail gliding along the horizon in those as yet lonely seas, was apt to be a matter of much talk and speculation. There is mention made in one of the early New England writers of a ship navigated by witches, with a great horse that stood by the mainmast. I have met with another story, somewhere, of a ship that drove on shore, in fair, sunny, tranquil weather, with sails all set, and a table spread in the cabin, as if to regale a number of guests, yet not a living being on board. These phantom ships always sailed in the eye of the wind; or ploughed their way with great velocity, making the smooth sea foam before their bows, when not a breath of air was stirring.

Moore has finely wrought up one of these legends of the sea into a little tale, which, within a small compass, contains the very essence of this species of supernatural fiction. I allude to his Spectre ship, bound to Deadman's Isle.

damp of the night air. They then prepared a bed of branches and dry leaves under a ledge of rocks for Dolph; while Antony Vander Heyden, wrapping himself in a huge coat of skins, stretched himself before the fire. It was some time, however, before Dolph could close his eyes. He lay contemplating the strange scene before him: the wild woods and rocks around; the fire throwing fitful gleams on the faces of the sleeping savages; and the Heer Antony, too, who so singularly, yet vaguely, reminded him of the nightly visitant to the haunted house. Now and then he heard the cry of some wild animal from the forest; or the hooting of the owl; or the notes of the whippoorwill, which seemed to abound among these solitudes; or the splash of a sturgeon, leaping out of the river and falling back full-length on its placid surface. He contrasted all this with his accustomed nest in the garret-room of the doctor's mansion, where the only sounds at night were the church-clock telling the hour; the drowsy voice of the watchman, drawling out all was well; the deep snoring of the doctor's clubbed nose from below-stairs; or the cautious labors of some carpenter rat gnawing in the wainscot. His thoughts then wandered to his poor old mother: what would she think of his mysterious disappearance—what anxiety and distress would she not suffer? This thought would continually intrude itself to mar his present enjoyment. It brought with it a feeling of pain and compunction, and he fell asleep with the tears yet standing in his eyes.

Were this a mere tale of fancy, here would be a fine opportunity for weaving in strange adventures among these wild mountains, and roving hunters; and, after involving my hero in a variety of perils and difficulties, rescuing him from them all by some miraculous contrivance. But as this is absolutely a true story, I must content myself with simple facts, and keep to probabilities.

At an early hour of the next day, therefore, after a hearty morning's meal, the encampment broke up, and our adventurers embarked in the pinnace of Antony Vander Heyden. There being no wind for the sails, the Indians rowed her gently along, keeping time to a kind of chant of one of the white men. The day was serene and beautiful; the river without a wave; and as the vessel cleft the glassy water, it left a long, undulating track behind. The crows, who had scented the hunters' banquet, were already gathering and hovering in the air, just where a column of thin, blue smoke, rising from among the trees showed the place of their last night's quarters. As they coasted along the bases of the mountains, the Heer Antony pointed out to Dolph a bald eagle, the sovereign of these regions, who sat perched on a dry tree that projected over the river, and, with eye turned upwards, seemed to be drinking in the splendor of the morning sun. Their approach disturbed the monarch's meditations. He first spread one wing, and then the other; balanced himself for a moment; and then, quitting his perch with dignified composure, wheeled slowly over their heads. Dolph snatched up a gun, and sent a whistling ball after him, that cut some of the feathers from his wing; the report of the gun leaped sharply from rock to rock, and awakened a thousand echoes; but the monarch of the air sailed calmly on, ascending higher and higher, and wheeling widely as he ascended, soaring up the green bosom of the woody mountain, until he disappeared over the brow of a beetling precipice. Dolph felt in a manner rebuked by this proud tranquillity, and almost reproached himself for having so wantonly insulted this majestic bird. Heer Antony told him, laughing, to remember that he was not yet out of the territories of the lord of the Dunderberg; and an old Indian shook his head, and observed that there was bad luck in killing an eagle; the hunter, on the contrary, should always leave him a portion of his spoils.

Nothing, however, occurred to molest them on their voyage. They passed pleasantly through magnificent and lonely scenes, until they came to where Pollopol's Island lay, like a floating bower at the extremity of the highlands. Here they landed, until the heat of the day should abate, or a breeze spring up that might supersede the labor of the oar. Some prepared the mid-day meal, while others reposed under the shade of the trees, in luxurious summer indolence, looking drowsily forth upon the beauty of the scene. On the one side were the highlands, vast and cragged, feathered to the top with forests, and throwing their shadows on the glassy water that dimpled at their feet. On the other side was a wide expanse of the river, like a broad lake, with long sunny reaches, and green headlands; and the distant line of Shawangunk Mountains waving along a clear horizon, or checkered by a fleecy cloud.

But I forbear to dwell on the particulars of their cruise along the river; this vagrant, amphibious life, careering across silver sheets of water; coasting wild woodland shores, banqueting on shady promontories, with the spreading tree overhead, the river curling its light foam to one's feet, and distant mountain, and rock, and tree, and snowy cloud, and deep-blue sky, all mingling in summer beauty before one; all this, though never cloying in the enjoyment, would be but tedious in narration.

When encamped by the water-side, some of the party would

go into the woods and hunt; others would fish. Sometimes they would amuse themselves by shooting at a mark, by leaping, by running, by wrestling; and Dolph gained great favor in the eyes of Antony Vander Heyden, by his skill and adroitness in all these exercises; which the Heer considered as the highest of manly accomplishments.

Thus did they coast jollily on, choosing only the pleasant hours for voyaging; sometimes in the cool morning dawn, sometimes in the sombre evening twilight, and sometimes when the moonshine spangled the crisp curling waves that whispered along the sides of their little bark. Never had Dolph felt so completely in his element; never had he met with anything so completely to his taste as this wild haphazard life. He was the very man to second Antony Vander Heyden in his rambling humors, and gained continually on his affections. The heart of the old bushwhacker yearned toward the young man, who seemed thus growing up in his own likeness; and as they approached to the end of their voyage, he could not help inquiring a little into his history. Dolph frankly told him his course of life, his severe medical studies, his little proficiency, and his very dubious prospects. The Heer was shocked to find that such amazing talents and accomplishments were to be cramped and buried under a doctor's wig. He had a sovereign contempt for the healing art, having never had any other physician than the butcher. He bore a mortal grudge to all kinds of study also, ever since he had been flogged about an unintelligible book when he was a boy. But to think that a young fellow like Dolph, of such wonderful abilities, who could shoot, fish, run, jump, ride, and wrestle, should be obliged to roll pills, and administer juleps for a living—'twas monstrous! He told Dolph never to despair, but to "throw physic to the dogs"; for a young fellow of his prodigious talents could never fail to make his way. "As you seem to have no acquaintance in Albany," said Heer Antony, "you shall go home with me, and remain under my roof until you can look about you; and in the meantime we can take an occasional bout at shooting and fishing, for it is a pity that such talents should lie idle."

Dolph, who was at the mercy of chance, was not hard to be persuaded. Indeed, on turning over matters in his mind, which he did very sagely and deliberately, he could not but think that Antony Vander Heyden was, "somehow or other," connected with the story of the Haunted House; that the misadventure in the highlands, which had thrown them so strangely together, was, "somehow or other," to work out something good; in short, there is nothing so convenient as this "somehow-or-other" way of accommodating one's self to circumstances; it is the mainstay of a heedless actor, and tardy reasoner, like Dolph Heyliger; and he who can, in this loose, easy way, link foregone evil to anticipated good, possesses a secret of happiness almost equal to the philosopher's stone.

On their arrival at Albany, the sight of Dolph's companion seemed to cause universal satisfaction. Many were the greetings at the river-side, and the salutations in the streets; the dogs bounded before him; the boys whooped as he passed; everybody seemed to known Antony Vander Heyden. Dolph followed on in silence, admiring the neatness of this worthy burgh; for in those days Albany was in all its glory, and inhabited almost exclusively by the descendants of the original Dutch settlers, not having as yet been discovered and colonized

by the restless people of New England. Everything was quiet
and orderly; everything was conducted calmly and leisurely;
no hurry, no bustle, no struggling and scrambling for existence.
The grass grew about the unpaved streets, and relieved the
eye by its refreshing verdure. Tall sycamores or pendent willows shaded the houses, with caterpillars swinging, in
long silken strings, from their branches; or moths, fluttering
about like coxcombs, in joy at their gay transformation. The
houses were built in the old Dutch style with gabled-ends towards the street. The thrifty housewife was seated on a bench
before her door, in close-crimped cap, bright-flowered gown,
and white apron, busily employed in knitting. The husband
smoked his pipe on the opposite bench; and the little pet
Negro girl, seated on the step at her mistress's feet, was in-
dustriously plying her needle. The swallows sported about the
eaves, or skimmed along the streets, and brought back some
rich booty for their clamorous young; and the little housekeeping wren flew in and out of a Liliputian house, or an old hat
nailed against the wall. The cows were coming home, lowing
through the streets, to be milked at their owner's door; and if,
perchance, there were any loiterers, some Negro urchin, with a
long goad, was gently urging them homewards.

As Dolph's companion passed on, he received a tranquil nod
from the burghers, and a friendly word from their wives; all
calling him familiarly by the name of Antony; for it was the
custom in this stronghold of the patriarchs, where they had all
grown up together from childhood, to call each other by the
Christian name. The Heer did not pause to have his usual
jokes with them, for he was impatient to reach his home. At
length they arrived at his mansion. It was of some magnitude,

in the Dutch style, with large iron figures on the gables, that gave the date of its erection, and showed that it had been built in the earliest times of the settlement.

The news of Heer Antony's arrival had preceded him, and the whole household was on the look-out. A crew of Negroes, large and small, had collected in front of the house to receive him. The old, white-headed ones, who had grown gray in his service, grinned for joy, and made many awkward bows and grimaces, and the little ones capered about his knees. But the most happy being in the household was a little, plump, blooming lass, his only child, and the darling of his heart. She came bounding out of the house; but the sight of a strange young man with her father called up, for a moment, all the bashfulness of a homebred damsel.

Dolph gazed at her with wonder and delight; never had he seen, as he thought, anything so comely in the shape of a woman. She was dressed in the good old Dutch taste, with long stays, and full, short petticoats, so admirably adapted to show and set off the female form. Her hair, turned up under a small round cap, displayed the fairness of her forehead; she had fine blue, laughing eyes, a trim, slender waist, and soft swell—but, in a word, she was a little Dutch divinity; and Dolph, who never stopped half-way in a new impulse, fell desperately in love with her.

Dolph was now ushered into the house with a hearty welcome. In the interior was a mingled display of Heer Antony's taste and habits, and of the opulence of his predecessors. The chambers were furnished with good old mahogany; the beaufets and cupboards glittered with embossed silver and painted china. Over the parlor fireplace was, as usual, the family coat-of-arms, painted and framed; above which was a long duck fowling-piece, flanked by an Indian pouch, and a powder horn. The room was decorated with many Indian articles, such as pipes of peace, tomahawks, scalping-knives, hunting-pouches, and belts of wampum; and there were various kinds of fishing-tackle, and two or three fowling-pieces in the corners. The household affairs seemed to be conducted, in some measure, after the master's humors; corrected, perhaps, by a little quiet management of the daughter's. There was a great degree of patriarchal simplicity, and good-humored indulgence. The Negroes came into the room without being called, merely to look at their master, and hear of his adventures; they would stand listening at the door until he had finished a story, and then go off on a broad grin, to repeat it in the kitchen. A couple of pet Negro children were playing about the floor with the dogs, and sharing with them their bread and butter. All the domestics looked hearty and happy; and when the table was set for the evening repast, the variety and abundance of good household luxuries bore testimony to the open-handed liberality of the Heer, and the notable housewifery of his daughter.

In the evening there dropped in several of the worthies of the place, the Van Rensselaers, and the Gansevoorts, and the Rosebooms, and others of Antony Vander Heyden's intimates, to hear an account of his expedition; for he was the Sinbad of Albany, and his exploits and adventures were favorite topics of conversation among the inhabitants. While these sat gossiping together about the door of the hall, and telling long twilight stories, Dolph was cosily seated, entertaining the daughter, on a window-bench. He had already got on intimate

terms; for those were not times of false reserve and idle ceremony; and, besides, there is something wonderfully propitious
to a lover's suit in the delightful dusk of a long summer evening; it gives courage to the most timid tongue, and hides the
blushes of the bashful. The stars alone twinkled brightly; and
now and then a fire-fly streamed his transient light before the
window, or, wandering into the room, flew gleaming about the
ceiling.

What Dolph whispered in her ear that long summer evening, it is impossible to say; his words were so low and indistinct, that they never reached the ear of the historian. It is
probable, however, that they were to the purpose; for he had
a natural talent at pleasing the sex, and was never long in
company with a petticoat without paying proper court to it. In
the meantime the visitors, one by one, departed; Antony Vander Heyden, who had fairly talked himself silent, sat nodding
alone in his chair by the door, when he was suddenly aroused
by a hearty salute with which Dolph Heyliger had unguardedly rounded off one of his periods, and which echoed through
the still chamber like the report of a pistol. The Heer started
up, rubbed his eyes, called for lights, and observed that it was
high time to go to bed; though, on parting for the night, he
squeezed Dolph heartily by the hand, looked kindly in his
face, and shook his head knowingly; for the Heer well remembered what he himself had been at the youngster's age.

The chamber in which our hero was lodged was spacious,
and panelled with oak. It was furnished with clothes-presses,
and mighty chests of drawers, well waxed, and glittering with
brass ornaments. These contained ample stock of family linen;

for the Dutch housewives had always a laudable pride in showing off their household treasures to strangers.

Dolph's mind, however, was too full to take particular note of the objects around him; yet he could not help continually comparing the free open-hearted cheeriness of this establishment with the starveling, sordid, joyless housekeeping at Doctor Knipperhausen's. Still something marred the enjoyment: the idea that he must take leave of his hearty host, and pretty hostess, and cast himself once more adrift upon the world. To linger here would be folly: he should only get deeper in love; and for a poor varlet, like himself, to aspire to the daughter of the great Heer Vander Heyden—it was madness to think of such a thing! The very kindness that the girl had shown towards him prompted him, on reflection, to hasten his departure; it would be a poor return for the frank hospitality of his host to entangle his daughter's heart in an injudicious attachment. In a word, Dolph was like many other young reasoners of exceeding good hearts and giddy heads—who think after they act, and act differently from what they think—who make excellent determinations overnight, and forget to keep them the next morning.

"This is a fine conclusion, truly, of my voyage," said he, as he almost buried himself in a sumptuous feather-bed, and drew the fresh white sheets up to his chin. "Here am I, instead of finding a bag of money, to carry home, launched in a strange place, with scarcely a stiver in my pocket; and, what is worse, have jumped ashore up to my very ears in love into the bargain. However," added he, after some pause, stretching himself, and turning himself in bed, "I'm in good quarters for the present, at least; so I'll e'en enjoy the present moment, and let the next take care of itself; I dare say all will work out, 'somehow or other,' for the best."

As he said these words, he reached out his hand to extinguish the candle, when he was suddenly struck with astonishment and dismay, for he thought he beheld the phantom of the haunted house, staring on him from a dusky part of the the chamber. A second look reassured him, as he perceived that what he had taken for the spectre was, in fact, nothing but a Flemish portrait, hanging in a shadowy corner, just behind a clothes-press. It was, however, the precise representation of his nightly visitor. The same cloak and belted jerkin, the same grizzled beard and fixed eye, the same broad slouched hat, with a feather hanging over one side. Dolph now called to mind the resemblance he had frequently remarked between his host and the old man of the haunted house; and was fully convinced they were in some way connected, and that some especial destiny had governed his voyage. He lay gazing on the portrait with almost as much awe as he had gazed on the ghostly oirginal, until the shrill house-clock warned him of the lateness of the hour. He put out the light; but remained for a long time turning over these curious circumstances and coincidences in his mind, until he fell asleep. His dreams partook of the nature of his waking thoughts. He fancied that he still lay gazing on the picture, until, by degrees, it became animated; that the figure descended from the wall, and walked out of the room; that he followed it, and found himself by the well to which the old man pointed, smiled on him, and disappeared.

In the morning, when he waked, he found his host standing

by his bedside, who gave him a hearty morning's salutation, and asked him how he had slept. Dolph answered cheerily; but took occasion to inquire about the portrait that hung against the wall. "Ah," said Heer Antony, "that's a portrait of old Killian Vander Spiegel, once a burgomaster of Amsterdam, who, on some popular troubles, abandoned Holland, and came over to the province during the government of Peter Stuyvesant. He was my ancestor by the mother's side, and an old miserly curmudgeon he was. When the English took possession of New Amsterdam, in 1664, he retired into the country. He fell into a melancholy, apprehending that his wealth would be taken from him and he come to beggary. He turned all his property into cash, and used to hide it away. He was for a year or two concealed in various places, fancying himself sought after by the English, to strip him of his wealth; and finally he was found dead in his bed one morning, without anyone being able to discover where he had concealed the greater part of his money."

When his host had left the room, Dolph remained for some time lost in thought. His whole mind was occupied by what he had heard. Vander Spiegel was his mother's family name; and he recollected to have heard her speak of this very Killian Vander Spiegel as one of her ancestors. He had heard her say, too, that her father was Killian's rightful heir, only that the old man died without leaving anything to be inherited. It now appeared that Heer Antony was likewise a descendant, and perhaps an heir also, of this poor rich man; and that thus the Heyligers and the Vander Heydens were remotely connected. "What," thought he, "if, after all, this is the interpretation of my dream, that this is the way I am to make my fortune by this voyage to Albany, and that I am to find the old man's hidden wealth in the bottom of that well? But what an odd round-about mode of communicating the matter! Why the plague could not the old goblin have told me about the well at once, without sending me all the way to Albany, to hear a story that was to send me all the way back again?"

These thoughts passed through his mind while he was dressing. He descended the stairs, full of perplexity, when the bright face of Marie Vander Heyden suddenly beamed in smiles upon him, and seemed to give him a clue to the whole mystery. "After all," thought he, "the old goblin is in the right. If I am to get his wealth, he means that I shall marry his pretty descendant; thus both branches of the family will again be united, and the property go in the proper channel."

No sooner did this idea enter his head, than it carried conviction with it. He was now all impatience to hurry back and secure the treasure, which, he did not doubt, lay at the bottom of the well, and which he feared every moment might be discovered by some other person. "Who knows," thought he, "but this night-walking old fellow of the haunted house may be in the habit of haunting every visitor, and may give a hint to some shrewder fellow than myself, who will take a shorter cut to the well than by the way of Albany?" He wished a thousand times that the babbling old ghost was laid in the Red Sea, and his rambling portrait with him. He was in a perfect fever to depart. Two or three days elapsed before any opportunity presented for returning down the river. They were ages to Dolph, notwithstanding that he was basking in the smiles of the pretty Marie, and daily getting more and more enamoured.

At length the very sloop from which he had been knocked overboard prepared to make sail. Dolph made an awkward apology to his host for his sudden departure. Antony Vander Heyden was sorely astonished. He had concerted half a dozen excursions into the wilderness; and his Indians were actually preparing for a grand expedition to one of the lakes. He took Dolph aside, and exerted his eloquence to get him to abandon all thoughts of business and to remain with him, but in vain; and he at length gave up the attempt, observing, "that it was a thousand pities so fine a young man should throw himself away." Heer Antony, however, gave him a hearty shake by the hand at parting, with a favorite fowling-piece, and an invitation to come to his house whenever he revisited Albany. The pretty little Marie said nothing; but as he gave her a farewell kiss, her dimpled cheek turned pale, and a tear stood in her eye.

Dolph sprang lightly on board of the vessel. They hoisted sail; the wind was fair; they soon lost sight of Albany, its green hills and embowered islands. They were wafted gayly past the Kaatskill Mountains, whose fairy heights were bright and cloudless. They passed prosperously through the highlands, without any molestation from the Dunderberg goblin and his crew; they swept on across Haverstraw Bay, and by Croton Point, and through the Tappaan Zee, and under the Palisadoes, until, in the afternoon of the third day, they saw the promontory of Hoboken hanging like a cloud in the air; and, shortly after, the roofs of the Manhattoes rising out of the water.

Dolph's first care was to repair to his mother's house; for he was continually goaded by the idea of the uneasiness she must experience on his account. He was puzzling his brains, as he went along, to think how he should account for his absence without betraying the secrets of the haunted house. In the midst of these cogitations he entered the street in which his mother's house was situated, when he was thunderstruck at beholding it a heap of ruins.

There had evidently been a great fire, which had destroyed several large houses, and the humble dwelling of poor Dame Heyliger had been involved in the conflagration. The walls were not so completely destroyed, but that Dolph could distinguish some traces of the scene of his childhood. The fireplace, about which he had often played, still remained, ornamented with Dutch tiles, illustrating passages in Bible history, on which he had many a time gazed with admiration. Among the rubbish lay the wreck of the good dame's elbow-chair, from which she had given him so many a wholesale precept; and hard by it was the family Bible, with brass clasps; now, alas! reduced almost to a cinder.

For a moment Dolph was overcome by this dismal sight, for he was seized with the fear that his mother had perished in the flames. He was relieved, however, from his horrible apprehension by one of the neighbors, who happened to come by and informed him that his mother was yet alive.

The good woman had, indeed, lost everything by this unlooked-for calamity; for the populace had been so intent upon saving the fine furniture of her rich neighbors, that the little tenement, and the little all of poor Dame Heyliger, had been suffered to consume without interruption; nay, had it not been for the gallant assistance of her old crony, Peter de Groodt, the worthy dame and her cat might have shared the fate of their habitation.

As it was, she had been overcome with fright and affliction, and lay ill in body and sick at heart. The public, however, had showed her its wonted kindness. The furniture of her rich neighbors being, as far as possible rescued from the flames; themselves duly and ceremoniously visited and condoled with on the injury of their property, and their ladies commiserated on the agitation of their nerves; the public, at length, began to recollect something about poor Dame Heyliger. She forthwith became again a subject of universal sympathy; everybody pitied her more than ever; and if pity could but have been coined into cash—good Lord! how rich she would have been!

It was now determined, in good earnest, that something ought to be done for her without delay. The Dominie, therefore, put up prayers for her on Sunday, in which all the congregation joined most heartily. Even Cobus Groesbeek, the alderman, and Mynheer Milledollar, the great Dutch merchant, stood up in their pews, and did not spare their voices on the occasion; and it was thought the prayers of such great men could not but have their due weight. Doctor Knipperhausen, too, visited her professionally, and gave her abundance of advice gratis, and was universally lauded for his charity. As to her old friend, Peter de Groodt, he was a poor man, whose pity, and prayers, and advice could be of but little avail, so he gave her all that was in his power—he gave her shelter.

To the humble dwelling of Peter de Groodt, then, did Dolph turn his steps. On his way thither he recalled all the tenderness and kindness of his simple-hearted parent, her indulgence of his errors, her blindness to his faults; and then he bethought himself of his own idle, harum-scarum life. "I've been a sad scapegrace," said Dolph, shaking his head sorrowfully. "I've been a complete sink-pocket, that's the truth of it. But," added he briskly, and clasping his hands, "only let her live—only let her live—and I will show myself indeed a son!"

As Dolph approached the house he met Peter de Groodt coming out of it. The old man started back aghast, doubting whether it was not a ghost that stood before him. It being bright daylight, however, Peter soon plucked up heart, satisfied that no ghost dare show his face in such clear sunshine. Dolph now learned from the worthy sexton the consternation and rumor to which his mysterious disappearance had given rise. It had been universally believed that he had been spirited away by those hobgoblin gentry that infested the haunted house; and old Abraham Vandozer, who lived by the great button-wood-trees, near the three-mile stone, affirmed, that he had heard a terrible noise in the air, as he was going home late at night, which seemed just as if a flock of wild geese were over-head, passing off towards the northward. The haunted house was, in consequence, looked upon with ten times more awe than ever; nobody would venture to pass a night in it for the world, and even the doctor had ceased to make his expeditions to it in the daytime.

It required some preparation before Dolph's return could be made known to his mother, the poor soul having bewailed him as lost; and her spirits having been sorely broken down by a number of comforters, who daily cheered her with stories of ghosts, and of people carried away by the devil. He found her confined to her bed, with the other member of the Heyliger family, the good dame's cat, purring beside her, but sadly singed, and utterly despoiled of those whiskers which were the glory of her physiognomy. The poor woman threw her arms about Dolph's neck. "My boy! My boy! Art thou still alive?" For a time she seemed to have forgotten all her losses and troubles in her joy at his return. Even the sage grimalkin showed indubitable signs of joy at the return of the youngster. She saw, perhaps, that they were a forlorn and undone family, and felt a touch of that kindliness which fellow-sufferers only know. But, in truth, cats are a slandered people; they have more affection in them than the world commonly gives them credit for.

The good dame's eyes glistened as she saw one being at least, besides herself, rejoiced at her son's return. "Tib knows thee! Poor dumb beast!" said she, smoothing down the mottled coat of her favorite; then recollecting herself, with a melancholy shake of the head, "Ah, my poor Dolph!" exclaimed she. "Thy mother can help thee no longer! She can no longer help herself! What will become of thee, my poor boy!"

"Mother," said Dolph, "don't talk in that strain; I've been too long a charge upon you; it's now my part to take care of you in your old days. Come! Be of good cheer! You, and I, and Tib will all see better days. I'm here, you see, young, and sound, and hearty; then don't let us despair; I dare say things will all, somehow or other, turn out for the best."

While this scene was going on with the Heyliger family, the news was carried to Doctor Knipperhausen of the safe return of his disciple. The little doctor scarce knew whether to rejoice or be sorry at the tidings. He was happy at having the foul reports which had prevailed concerning his country mansion thus disproved; but he grieved at having his disciple, of whom he had supposed himself fairly disencumbered, thus drifting back, a heavy charge upon his hands. While balancing between these two feelings, he was determined by the counsels of Frau Ilsy, who advised him to take advantage of the truant absence of the youngster, and shut the door upon him forever.

At the hour of bedtime, therefore, when it was supposed the recreant disciple would seek his old quarters, everything was prepared for his reception. Dolph, having talked his mother into a state of tranquillity, sought the mansion of his quondam master, and raised the knocker with a faltering hand. Scarcely, however, had it given a dubious rap, when the doctor's head, in a red nightcap, popped out of one window, and the housekeeper's, in a white nightcap, out of another. He was now greeted with a tremendous volley of hard names and hard language, mingled with invaluable pieces of advice, such as are seldom ventured to be given excepting to a friend in distress, or a culprit at the bar. In a few moments not a window in the street but had its particular nightcap, listening to the shrill treble of Frau Ilsy, and the guttural croaking of Dr. Knipperhausen; and the word went from window to window, "Ah! Here's Dolph Heyliger come back, and at his old pranks again." In short, poor Dolph found he was likely to get nothing from the doctor but good advice; a commodity so abundant as even to be thrown out of the window; so he was fain to beat a retreat, and take up his quarters for the night under the lowly roof of honest Peter de Groodt.

The next morning, bright and early, Dolph was out at the haunted house. Everything looked just as he had left it. The fields were grass-grown and matted, and appeared as if nobody had traversed them since his departure. With palpitating heart he hastened to the well. He looked down into it, and saw that it was of great depth, with water at the bottom. He had provided himself with a strong line, such as the fishermen use on the banks of Newfoundland. At the end was a heavy plummet and a large fish-hook. With this he began to sound the bottom of the well, and to angle about in the water. The water was of some depth; there was also much rubbish, stones from the top having fallen in. Several times his hook got entangled, and he came near breaking his line. Now and then, too, he hauled up mere trash, such as the skull of a horse, an iron hoop, and a shattered iron-bound bucket. He had now been several hours employed without finding anything to repay his trouble, or to encourage him to proceed. He began to think himself a great fool, to be thus decoyed into a wild-goose chase by mere dreams, and was on the point of throwing line and all into the well, and giving up all further angling.

"One more cast of the line," said he, "and that shall be the last." As he sounded, he felt the plummet slip, as it were, through the interstices of loose stones; and as he drew back the line, he felt that the hook had taken hold of something heavy. He had to manage his line with great caution, lest it should be broken by the strain upon it. By degrees the rubbish which lay upon the article he had hooked gave way; he drew it to the surface of the water, and what was his rapture at seeing something like silver glittering at the end of his line! Almost breathless with anxiety, he drew it up to the mouth of the well, surprised at its great weight, and fearing every instant that his hook would slip from its hold, and his prize tumble again to the bottom. At length he landed it safe beside the well. It was a great silver porringer, of an ancient form, richly embossed, and with armorial bearings engraved on its side, similar to those over his mother's mantelpiece. The lid was fastened down by several twists of wire; Dolph loosened them with a trembling hand, and, on lifting the lid, behold! the vessel was filled with broad golden pieces, of a coinage which he had never seen before! It was evident he had hit on the place where Killian Vander Spiegel had concealed his treasure.

Fearful of being seen by some straggler, he cautiously retired, and buried his pot of money in a secret place. He now spread terrible stories about the haunted house, and deterred everyone from approaching it, while he made frequent visits to it in stormy days, when no one was stirring in the neighboring fields; though, to tell the truth, he did not care to venture there in the dark. For once in his life he was diligent and industrious, and followed up his new trade of angling with such perseverance and success, that in a little while he had hooked up wealth enough to make him, in those moderate days, a rich burgher for life.

It would be tedious to detail minutely the rest of this story. To tell how he gradually managed to bring his property into use without exciting surprise and inquiry—how he satisfied all scruples with regard to retaining the property, and at the same time gratified his own feelings by marrying the pretty Marie Vander Heyden—and how he and Heer Antony had many a merry and roving expedition together.

I must not omit to say, however, that Dolph took his mother home to live with him, and cherished her in her old days. The good dame, too, had the satisfaction of no longer hearing her son made the theme of censure; on the contrary, he grew daily in public esteem; everybody spoke well of him and his wines; and the lordliest burgomaster was never known to decline his invitation to dinner. Dolph often related, at his own table, the wicked pranks which had once been the abhorrence of the town; but they were now considered excellent jokes, and the gravest dignitary was fain to hold his sides when listening to them. No one was more struck with Dolph's increasing merit than his old master the doctor; and so forgiving was Dolph, that he absolutely employed the doctor as his family physician, only taking care that his prescriptions should be always thrown out of the window. His mother had often her junto of old cronies to take a snug cup of tea with her in her comfortable little parlor; and Peter de Groodt, as he sat by the fireside, with one of her grandchildren on his knee, would many a time congratulate her upon her son turning out so great a man; upon which the good old soul would wag her head with exultation, and exclaim, "Ah, neighbor, neighbor! Did I not say that Dolph would one day or other hold up his head with the best of them?"

Thus did Dolph Heyliger go on, cheerily and prosperously, growing merrier as he grew older and wiser, and completely falsifying the old proverb about money got over the devil's back; for he made good use of his wealth, and became a distinguished citizen, and a valuable member of the community. He was a great promoter of public institutions, such as beefsteak societies and catch-clubs. He presided at all public dinners, and was the first that introduced turtle from the West Indies. He improved the breed of race-horses and game-cocks, and was so great a patron of modest merit, that anyone who could sing a good song, or tell a good story, was sure to find a place at his table.

He was a member, too, of the corporation, made several laws for the protection of game and oysters, and bequeathed to the board a large silver punch-bowl, made out of the identical porringer before mentioned, and which is in the possession of the corporation to this very day.

Finally, he died, in a florid old age, of an apoplexy at a corporation feast, and was buried with great honors in the yard of the little Dutch church in Garden Street, where his tombstone may still be seen with a modest epitaph in Dutch, by his friend Mynheer Justus Benson, an ancient and excellent poet of the province.

The foregoing tale rests on better authority than most tales of the kind, as I have it at second-hand from the lips of Dolph Heyliger himself. He never related it till towards the latter part of his life, and then in great confidence (for he was very discreet), to a few of his particular cronies at his own table, over a supernumerary bowl of punch; and, strange as the hobgoblin parts of the story may seem, there never was a single doubt expressed on the subject by any of his guests. It may not be amiss, before concluding, to observe that, in addition to his other accomplishments, Dolph Heyliger was noted for being the ablest drawer of the long-bow in the whole province.

Kidd the Pirate

In old times, just after the territory of the New Netherlands had been wrested from the hands of their High Mightinesses, the Lords States-General of Holland, by King Charles the Second, and while it was as yet in an unquiet state, the province was a great resort of random adventurers, loose livers, and all that class of haphazard fellows who live by their wits, and dislike the old-fashioned restraint of law and gospel. Among these, the foremost were the buccaneers. These were rovers of the deep, who perhaps in time of war had been educated in those schools of piracy, the privateers; but having once tasted the sweets of plunder, had ever retained a hankering after it. There is but a slight step from the privateersman to the pirate; both fight for the love of plunder; only that the latter is the bravest, as he dares both the enemy and the gallows.

But in whatever school they had been taught, the buccaneers that kept about the English colonies were daring fellows, and made sad work in times of peace among the Spanish settlements and Spanish merchantmen. The easy access to the harbor of the Manhattoes, the number of hiding-places about its waters, and the laxity of its scarcely organized government, made it a great rendezvous of the pirates; where they might dispose of their booty, and concert new depredations. As they brought home with them wealthy lading of all kinds, the luxuries of the tropics, and the sumptuous spoils of the Spanish provinces, and disposed of them with the proverbial carelessness of freebooters, they were welcome visitors to the thrifty traders of the Manhattoes. Crews of these desperadoes, therefore, the runagates of every country and every clime, might be seen swaggering in open day about the streets of the little burgh, elbowing its quiet mynheers; trafficking away their rich outlandish plunder at half or quarter price to the wary merchant; and then squandering their prize money in taverns, drinking, gambling, singing, swearing, shouting, and astounding the neighborhood with midnight brawl and ruffian revelry.

At length these excesses rose to such a height as to become a scandal to the provinces, and to call loudly for the interposition of government. Measures were accordingly taken to put a stop to the widely extended evil, and to ferret this vermin brood out of the colonies.

Among the agents employed to execute this purpose was the notorious Captain Kidd. He had long been an equivocal character; one of those nondescript animals of the ocean that are neither fish, flesh, nor fowl. He was somewhat of a trader, something more of a smuggler, with a considerable dash of the picaroon. He had traded for many years among the pirates, in a little rakish mosquito-built vessel, that could run into all kinds of waters. He knew all their haunts and lurking-places; was always hooking about on mysterious voyages, and was as busy as a Mother Carey's chicken in a storm.

This nondescript personage was pitched upon by government as the very man to hunt the pirates by sea, upon the good old maxim of "setting a rogue to catch a rogue"; or as otters are sometimes used to catch their cousins german, the fish.

Kidd accordingly sailed for New York, in 1695, in a gallant vessel called the *Adventure Galley,* well armed and duly commissioned. On arriving at his old haunts, however, he shipped his crew on new terms; enlisted a number of his old comrades, lads of the knife and the pistol; and then set sail for the East. Instead of cruising against pirates, he turned pirate himself; steered to the Madeiras, to Bonavista, and Madagascar, and cruised about the entrance of the Red Sea. Here, among other maritime robberies, he captured a rich Quedah merchantman, manned by Moors, though commanded by an Englishman. Kidd would fain have passed this off for a worthy exploit, as being a kind of crusade against the infidels; but government had long since lost all relish for such Christian triumphs.

After roaming the seas, trafficking his prizes, and changing from ship to ship, Kidd had the hardihood to return to Boston, laden with booty, with a crew of swaggering companions at his heels.

Times, however, were changed. The buccaneers could no longer show a whisker in the colonies with impunity. The new Governor, Lord Bellamont, had signalized himself by his zeal in extirpating these offenders; and was doubly exasperated against Kidd, having been instrumental in appointing him to the trust which he had betrayed. No sooner, therefore, did he show himself in Boston, than the alarm was given of his reappearance, and measures were taken to arrest this cutpurse of the ocean. The daring character which Kidd had acquired, however, and the desperate fellows who followed like bulldogs at his heels, caused a little delay in his arrest. He took advantage of this, it is said, to bury the greater part of his treasures, and then carried a high head about the streets of Boston. He even attempted to defend himself when arrested, but was secured and thrown into prison, with his followers. Such was the formidable character of this pirate and his crew, that it was thought advisable to despatch a frigate to bring them to England. Great exertions were made to screen him from justice, but in vain; he and his comrades were tried, condemned, and hanged at Execution Dock in London. Kidd died hard, for the rope with which he was first tied up broke with his weight, and he tumbled to the ground. He was tied up a second time, and more effectually; hence came, doubtless, the story of Kidd's having a charmed life, and that he had to be twice hanged.

Such is the main outline of Kidd's history; but it has given birth to an innumerable progeny of traditions. The report of his having buried great treasures of gold and jewels before his arrest, set the brains of all the good people along the coast in a ferment. There were rumors on rumors of great sums of money found here and there, sometimes in one part of the country, sometimes in another; of coins with Moorish inscriptions, doubtless the spoils of his eastern prizes, but which the common people looked upon with superstitious awe, regarding the Moorish letters as diabolical or magical characters.

Some reported the treasure to have been buried in solitary, unsettled places, about Plymouth and Cape Cod; but by degrees various other parts, not only on the eastern coast, but along the shores of the Sound, and even of Manhattan and Long Island, were gilded by these rumors. In fact, the rigorous measures of Lord Bellamont spread sudden consternation among the buccaneers in every part of the provinces: they secreted their money and jewels in lonely out-of-the-way places, about the wild shores of the rivers and sea-coast, and dispersed themselves over the face of the country. The hand of justice prevented many of them from ever returning to regain their buried treasures, which remained, and remain probably to this day, as objects of enterprise for the money-digger.

This is the cause of those frequent reports of trees and rocks bearing mysterious marks, supposed to indicate the spots where treasures lay hidden; and many have been the ransackings after the pirate's booty. In all the stories which once abounded of these enterprises the devil played a conspicuous part. Either he was conciliated by ceremonies and invocations, or some solemn compact was made with him. Still he was ever prone to play the money-diggers some slippery trick. Some would dig so far as to come to an iron chest, when some baffling circumstance was sure to take place. Either the earth would fall in and fill up the pit, or some direful noise or apparition would frighten the party from the place: sometimes the devil himself would appear, and bear off the prize when within their very grasp; and if they revisited the place the next day, not a trace would be found of their labors of the preceding night.

All these rumors, however, were extremely vague, and for a long time tantalized, without gratifying, my curiosity. There is nothing in this world so hard to get at as truth, and there is nothing in this world but truth that I care for. I sought among all my favorite sources of authentic information, the oldest inhabitants, and particularly the old Dutch wives of the province; but though I flatter myself that I am better versed than most men in the curious history of my native province, yet for a long time my inquiries were unattended with any substantial result.

At length it happened that, one calm day in the later part of summer, I was relaxing myself from the toils of severe study, by a day's amusement in fishing in those waters which had been the favorite resort of my boyhood. I was in company with several worthy burghers of my native city, among whom were more than one illustrious member of the corporation, whose names, did I dare to mention them, would do honor to my humble page. Our sport was indifferent. The fish did not bite freely, and we frequently changed our fishing-ground without bettering our luck. We were at length anchored close under a ledge of rocky coast, on the eastern side of the island of Manhatta. It was a still, warm day. The stream whirled and dimpled by us, without a wave or even a ripple; and everything was so calm and quiet, that it was almost startling when the kingfisher would pitch himself from the branch of some high tree, and suspending himself for a moment in the air, to take his aim, would souse into the smooth water after his prey. While we were lolling in our boat, half drowsy with the warm stillness of the day, and the dullness of our sport, one of our party, a worthy alderman, was overtaken by a slumber, and, as he dozed, suffered the sinker of his drop-line to lie upon the bottom of the river. On waking, he found he had caught something of importance from the weight. On drawing it to the surface, we were much surprised to find it a long pistol of very curious and outlandish fashion, which, from its rusted condition, and its stock being worm-eaten and covered with barnacles, appeared to have lain a long time under water. The unexpected appearance of this document of warfare occasioned much speculation among my pacific companions. One supposed it to have fallen there during the Revolutionary War; another, from the peculiarity of its fashion, attributed it to the voyagers in the earliest days of the settlement; perchance to the renowned Adrian Block, who explored the Sound, and discovered Block Island, since so noted for its cheese. But a third, after regarding it for some time, pronounced it to be of veritable Spanish workmanship.

"I'll warrant," said he, "if this pistol could talk, it would tell strange stories of hard fights among the Spanish Dons. I've no doubt but it is a relic of the buccaneers of old times—who knows but it belonged to Kidd himself?"

"Ah! That Kidd was a resolute fellow," cried an old iron-faced Cape-Cod whaler. "There's a fine old song about him, all to the tune of—

Kidd the Pirate

"My name is Captain Kidd,
As I sailed, as I sailed—

and then it tells about how he gained the devil's good graces by
burying the Bible—

"I had the Bible in my hand,
As I sailed, as I sailed,
And I buried it in the sand,
As I sailed—"

"Odsfish, if I thought this pistol had belonged to Kidd, I
should set great store by it, for curiosity's sake."

The Devil
and
Tom Walker

A few miles from Boston in Massachusetts, there is a deep inlet, winding several miles into the interior of the country from Charles Bay, and terminating in a thickly-wooded swamp or morass. On one side of this inlet is a beautiful dark grove; on the opposite side the land rises abruptly from the water's edge into a high ridge, on which grow a few scattered oaks of great age and immense size. Under one of these gigantic trees, according to old stories, there was a great amount of treasure buried by Kidd the pirate. The inlet allowed a facility to bring the money in a boat secretly and at night to the very foot of the hill; the elevation of the place permitted a good lookout to be kept that no one was at hand; while the remarkable trees formed good landmarks by which the place might easily be found again. The old stories add, moreover, that the devil presided at the hiding of the money, and took it under his guardianship; but this, it is well known, he always does with buried treasure, particularly when it has been ill-gotten. Be that as it may, Kidd never returned to recover his wealth; being shortly after seized at Boston, sent out to England and there hanged for a pirate.

About the year 1727, just at the time that earthquakes were prevalent in New England, and shook many tall sinners down upon their knees, there lived near this place a meagre, miserly fellow, of the name of Tom Walker. He had a wife as miserly as himself: they were so miserly that they even conspired to cheat each other. Whatever the woman could lay hands on, she hid away; a hen could not cackle but she was on the alert to secure the new-laid egg. Her husband was continually prying about to detect her secret hoards, and many and fierce were the conflicts that took place about what ought to have been common property. They lived in a forlorn-looking house that stood alone, and had an air of starvation. A few straggling savin-trees, emblems of sterility, grew near it; no smoke ever curled from its chimney; no traveller stopped at its door. A miserable horse, whose ribs were as articulate as the bars of a gridiron, stalked about a field, where a thin carpet of moss, scarcely covering the ragged beds of pudding-stone, tantalized and balked his hunger; and sometimes he would lean his head over the fence, look piteously at the passer-by, and seem to petition deliverance from this land of famine.

The house and its inmates had altogether a bad name. Tom's wife was a tall termagant, fierce of temper, loud of tongue, and strong of arm. Her voice was often heard in wordy warfare with her husband; and his face sometimes showed signs that their conflicts were not confined to words. No one ventured, however, to interfere between them. The lonely wayfarer shrunk within himself at the horrid clamor and clapper-clawing; eyed the den of discord askance; and hurried on his way, rejoicing, if a bachelor, in his celibacy.

One day that Tom Walker had been to a distant part of the neighborhood, he took what he considered a short cut homeward, through the swamp. Like most short cuts, it was an ill-chosen route. The swamp was thickly grown with great gloomy pines and hemlocks, some of them ninety feet high, which made it dark at noonday, and a retreat for all the owls of the neighborhood. It was full of pits and quagmires, partly covered with weeds and mosses, where the green surface often betrayed the traveller into a gulf of black, smothering mud: there were also dark and stagnant pools, the abodes of the tadpole, the bull-frog, and the water-snake; where the trunks of pines and hemlocks lay half-drowned, half-rotting, looking like alligators sleeping in the mire.

Tom had long been picking his way cautiously through this treacherous forest; stepping from tuft to tuft of rushes and roots, which afforded precarious footholds among deep sloughs; or pacing carefully, like a cat, along the prostrate trunks of trees; startled now and then by the sudden screaming of the bittern, or the quacking of a wild duck rising on the wing from some solitary pool. At length he arrived at a firm piece of ground, which ran out like a peninsula into the deep bosom of the swamp. It had been one of the strongholds of the Indians during their wars with the first colonists. Here they had thrown up a kind of fort, which they had looked upon as almost impregnable, and had used as a place of refuge for their squaws and children. Nothing remained of the old Indian fort but a few embankments, gradually sinking to the level of the surrounding earth, and already overgrown in part by oaks and other forest trees, the foliage of which formed a contrast to the dark pines and hemlocks of the swamp.

It was late in the dusk of evening when Tom Walker reached the old fort, and he paused there awhile to rest himself. Anyone but he would have felt unwilling to linger in this lonely, melancholy place, for the common people had a bad opinion of it, from the stories handed down from the time of the Indian wars; when it was asserted that the savages held incantations here, and made sacrifices to the evil spirit.

Tom Walker, however, was not a man to be troubled with any fears of the kind. He reposed himself for some time on the trunk of a fallen hemlock, listening to the boding cry of the tree-toad, and delving with his walking-staff into a mound of black mould at his feet. As he turned up the soil unconsciously, his staff struck against something hard. He raked it out of the vegetable mould, and lo! a cloven skull, with an Indian tomahawk buried deep in it, lay before him. The rust on the weapon showed the time that had elapsed since this death-blow had been given. It was a dreary memento of the fierce struggle that had taken place in this last foothold of the Indian warriors.

"Humph!" said Tom Walker, as he gave it a kick to shake the dirt from it.

"Let that skull alone!" said a gruff voice. Tom lifted up his eyes, and beheld a great black man seated directly opposite him, on the stump of a tree. He was exceedingly surprised, having neither heard nor seen anyone approach; and he was still more perplexed on observing, as well as the gathering gloom would permit, that the stranger was neither Negro nor Indian. It is true he was dressed in a rude half-Indian garb, and had a red belt or sash swathed round his body; but his face was neither black nor copper-color, but swarthy and dingy, and begrimed with soot, as if he had been accustomed to toil among fires and forges. He had a shock of coarse black hair, that stood out from his head in all directions, and bore an axe on his shoulder.

He scowled for a moment at Tom with a pair of great red eyes.

"What are you doing on my grounds?" said the black man, with a hoarse growling voice.

"Your grounds!" said Tom, with a sneer. "No more your grounds than mine; they belong to Deacon Peabody."

"Deacon Peabody be d——d," said the stranger, "as I flatter myself he will be, if he does not look more to his own sins and less to those of his neighbors. Look yonder, and see how Deacon Peabody is faring."

Tom looked in the direction that the stranger pointed, and beheld one of the great trees, fair and flourishing without, but rotten at the core, and saw that it had been nearly hewn through, so that the first high wind was likely to blow it down. On the bark of the tree was scored the name of Deacon Peabody, an eminent man, who had waxed wealthy by driving shrewd bargains with the Indians. He now looked around, and

found most of the tall trees marked with the name of some great man of the colony, and all more or less scored by the axe. The one on which he had been seated, and which had evidently just been hewn down, bore the name of Crowninshield; and he recollected a mighty rich man of that name, who made a vulgar display of wealth, which it was whispered he had acquired by buccaneering.

"He's just ready for burning!" said the black man, with a growl of triumph. "You see I am likely to have a good stock of firewood for winter."

"But what right have you," said Tom, "to cut down Deacon Peabody's timber?"

"The right of a prior claim," said the other. "This woodland belonged to me long before one of your white-faced race put foot upon the soil."

"And pray, who are you, if I may be so bold?" said Tom.

"Oh, I go by various names. I am the wild huntsman in some countries; the black miner in others. In this neighborhood I am known by the name of the black woodsman. I am he to whom the red men consecrated this spot, and in honor of whom they now and then roasted a white man, by way of sweet-smelling sacrifice. Since the red men have been exterminated by you white savages, I amuse myself by presiding at the persecutions of Quakers and Anabaptists; I am the great patron and prompter of slave-dealers, and the grand-master of the Salem witches."

"The upshot of all which is, that, if I mistake not," said Tom, sturdily, "you are he commonly called Old Scratch."

"The same, at your service!" replied the black man, with a half-civil nod.

Such was the opening of this interview, according to the old story; though it has almost too familiar an air to be credited. One would think that to meet with such a singular personage, in this wild, lonely place, would have shaken any man's nerves; but Tom was a hard-minded fellow, not easily daunted, and he had lived so long with a termagant wife, that he did not even fear the devil.

It is said that after this commencement they had a long and earnest conversation together, as Tom returned homeward. The black man told him of great sums of money buried by Kidd the pirate, under the oak-trees on the high ridge, not far from the morass. All these were under his command, and protected by his power, so that none could find them but such as propitiated his favor. These he offered to place within Tom Walker's reach having conceived an especial kindness for him; but they were to be had only on certain conditions. What these conditions were may be easily surmised, though Tom never disclosed them publicly. They must have been very hard, for he required time to think of them, and he was not a man to stick at trifles when money was in view. When they had reached the edge of the swamp, the stranger paused. "What proof have I that all you have been telling me is true?" said Tom. "There's my signature," said the black man, pressing his finger on Tom's forehead. So saying he turned off among the thickets of the swamp, and seemed, as Tom said, to go down, down, down, into the earth, until nothing but his head and shoulders could be seen, and so on, until he totally disappeared.

When Tom reached home, he found the black print of a finger burnt, as it were, into his forehead, which nothing could obliterate.

The first news his wife had to tell him was the sudden death of Absalom Crowninshield, the rich buccaneer. It was announced in the papers with the usual flourish, that "A great man had fallen in Israel."

Tom recollected the tree which his black friend had just hewn down, and which was ready for burning. "Let the freebooter roast," said Tom. "Who cares!" He now felt convinced that all he had heard and seen was no illusion.

He was not prone to let his wife into his confidence; but as this was an uneasy secret, he willingly shared it with her. All her avarice was awakened at the mention of hidden gold, and she urged her husband to comply with the black man's terms, and secure what would make them wealthy for life. However Tom might have felt disposed to sell himself to the Devil, he was determined not to do so to oblige his wife; so he flatly refused, out of the mere spirit of contradiction. Many and bitter were the quarrels they had on the subject; but the more she talked, the more resolute was Tom not to be damned to please her.

At length she determined to drive the bargain on her own account, and if she succeeded, to keep all the gain to herself. Being of the same fearless temper as her husband, she set off for the old Indian fort towards the close of a summer's day. She was many hours absent. When she came back, she was reserved and sullen in her replies. She spoke something of a black man, whom she had met about twilight hewing at the root of a tall tree. He was sulky, however, and would not come to terms: she was to go again with a propitiatory offering, but what it was she forebore to say.

The next evening she set off again for the swamp, with her apron heavily laden. Tom waited and waited for her, but in vain; midnight came, but she did not make her appearance, morning, noon, night returned, but still she did not come. Tom now grew uneasy for her safety, especially as he found she had carried off in her apron the silver tea-pot and spoons, and every portable article of value. Another night elapsed, another morning came; but no wife. In a word, she was never heard of more.

What was her real fate nobody knows, in consequence of so many pretending to know. It is one of those facts which have become confounded by a variety of historians. Some asserted that she lost her way among the tangled mazes of the swamp, and sank into some pit or slough; others, more uncharitable, hinted that she had eloped with the household booty, and made off to some other province; while others surmised that the tempter had decoyed her into a dismal quagmire, on the top of which her hat was found lying. In confirmation of this, it was said a black man, with an axe on his shoulder, was seen late that very evening coming out of the swamp, carrying a bundle tied in a check apron, with an air of surly triumph.

The most current and probable story, however, observes, that Tom Walker grew so anxious about the fate of his wife and his property, that he set out at length to seek them both at the Indian fort. During a long summer's afternoon he searched about the gloomy place, but no wife was to be seen. He called her name repeatedly, but she was nowhere to be heard. The bittern alone responded to his voice, as he flew screaming by; or the bull-frog croaked dolefully from a neighboring pool. At length, it is said, just in the brown hour of twilight, when the owls began to hoot, and the bats to flit about, his attention was attracted by the clamor of carrion crows hovering about a cypress-tree. He looked up, and beheld a bundle tied in a check apron, and hanging in the branches of the tree, with a great vulture perched hard by, as if keeping watch upon it. He leaped with joy; for he recognized his wife's apron, and supposed it to contain the household valuables.

"Let us get hold of the property," said he, consolingly to himself, "and we will endeavor to do without the woman."

As he scrambled up the tree, the vulture spread its wide wings, and sailed off, screaming, into the deep shadows of the forest. Tom seized the checked apron, but, woful sight! found nothing but a heart and liver tied up in it!

Such, according to this most authentic old story, was all that was to be found of Tom's wife. She had probably attempted to deal with the black man as she had been accustomed to deal with her husband; but though a female scold is generally considered a match for the devil, yet in this instance she appears to have had the worst of it. She must have died game, however; for it is said Tom noticed many prints of cloven feet deeply stamped about the tree, and found handfuls of hair, that looked as if they had been plucked from the coarse black shock of the woodman. Tom knew his wife's prowess by experience. He shrugged his shoulders, as he looked at the signs of a fierce clapper-clawing. "Egad," said he to himself, "Old Scratch must have had a tough time of it!"

Tom consoled himself for the loss of his property, with the loss of his wife, for he was a man of fortitude. He even felt something like gratitude towards the black woodman, who, he considered, had done him a kindness. He sought, therefore, to cultivate a further acquaintance with him, but for some time without success; the old black-legs played shy, for whatever people may think, he is not always to be had for calling for: he knows how to play his cards when pretty sure of his game.

At length, it is said, when delay had whetted Tom's eagerness to the quick, and prepared him to agree to anything rather than not gain the promised treasure, he met the black man one evening in his usual woodman's dress, with his axe on his shoulder, sauntering along the swamp, and humming a tune. He affected to receive Tom's advances with great indifference, made brief replies, and went on humming his tune.

By degrees, however, Tom brought him to business, and they began to haggle about the terms on which the former was to have the pirate's treasure. There was one condition which need not be mentioned, being generally understood in all cases where the devil grants favors; but there were others about which, though of less importance, he was inflexibly obstinate. He insisted that the money found through his means should be employed in his service. He proposed, therefore, that Tom should employ it in the black traffic, that is to say, that he should fit out a slave-ship. This, however, Tom resolutely refused: he was bad enough in all conscience; but the devil himself could not tempt him to turn slave-trader.

Finding Tom so squeamish on this point, he did not insist upon it, but proposed, instead, that he should turn usurer; the devil being extremely anxious for the increase of usurers, looking upon them as his peculiar people.

To this no objections were made, for it was just to Tom's taste.

"You shall open a broker's shop in Boston next month," said the black man.

"I'll do it to-morrow, if you wish," said Tom Walker.

"You shall lend money at two per cent a month."

"Egad, I'll charge four!" replied Tom Walker.

"You shall extort bonds, foreclose mortgages, drive the merchants to bankruptcy——"

"I'll drive them to the d——l," cried Tom Walker.

"You are the usurer for my money!" said black-legs with delight. "When will you want the rhino?"

"This very night."

"Done!" said the devil.

"Done!" said Tom Walker. So they shook hands and struck a bargain.

A few days' time saw Tom Walker seated behind his desk in a counting-house in Boston.

His reputation for a ready-moneyed man, who would lend money out for a good consideration, soon spread abroad. Everybody remembers the time of Governor Belcher, when money was particularly scarce. It was a time of paper credit. The country had been deluged with government bills, the famous Land Bank had been established; there had been a rage for speculating; the people had run mad with schemes for new settlements; for building cities in the wilderness; land-jobbers went about with maps of grants, and townships, and Eldorados, lying nobody knew where, but which everybody was ready to purchase. In a word, the great speculating fever which breaks out every now and then in the country, had raged to an alarming degree, and everybody was dreaming of making sudden fortunes from nothing. As usual the fever had subsided; the dream had gone off, and the imaginary fortunes with it; the patients were left in doleful plight, and the whole country resounded with the consequent cry of "hard times."

At this propitious time of public distress did Tom Walker

set up as usurer in Boston. His door was soon thronged by customers. The needy and adventurous; the gambling speculator; the dreaming land-jobber; the thriftless tradesman; the merchant with cracked credit; in short, everyone driven to raise money by desperate means and desperate sacrifices, hurried to Tom Walker.

Thus Tom was the universal friend of the needy, and acted like a "friend in need" that is to say, he always exacted good pay and good security. In proportion to the distress of the applicant was the hardness of his terms. He accumulated bonds and mortgages; gradually squeezed his customers closer and closer: and sent them at length, dry as a sponge, from his door.

In this way he made money hand over hand; became a rich and mighty man, and exalted his cocked hat upon 'Change. He built himself, as usual, a vast house, out of ostentation; but left the greater part of it unfinished and unfurnished, out of parsimony. He even set up a carriage in the fulness of his vainglory, though he nearly starved the horses which drew it; and as the ungreased wheels groaned and screeched on the axletrees, you would have thought you heard the souls of the poor debtors he was squeezing.

As Tom waxed old, however, he grew thoughtful. Having secured the good things of this world, he began to feel anxious about those of the next. He thought with regret on the bargain he had made with his black friend, and set his wits to work to cheat him out of the conditions. He became, therefore, all of a sudden, a violent church-goer. He prayed loudly and strenuously, as if heaven were to be taken by force of lungs. Indeed, one might always tell when he had sinned most during the week, by the clamor of his Sunday devotion. The quiet Christians who had been modestly and steadfastly travelling Zionward, were struck with self-reproach at seeing themselves so suddenly outstripped in their career by this new-made convert. Tom was as rigid in religious as in money matters; he was a stern supervisor and censurer of his neighbors, and seemed to think every sin entered up to their account became a credit on his own side of the page. He even talked of the expediency of reviving the persecution of Quakers and Anabaptists. In a word, Tom's zeal became as notorious as his riches.

Still, in spite of all this strenuous attention to forms, Tom had a lurking dread that the devil, after all, would have his due. That he might not be taken unawares, therefore, it is said he always carried a small Bible in his coat-pocket. He had also a great folio Bible on his counting-house desk, and would frequently be found reading it when people called on business; on such occasions he would lay his green spectacles in the book, to mark the place, while he turned round to drive some usurious bargain.

Some say that Tom grew a little crack-brained in his old days, and that, fancying his end approaching, he had his horse new shod, saddled and bridled, and buried with his feet uppermost; because he supposed that at the last day the world would be turned upside down; in which case he should find his horse standing ready for mounting, and he was determined at the worst to give his old friend a run for it. This, however, is probably a mere old wives' fable. If he really did take such a precaution, it was totally superfluous; at least so says the authentic old legend; which closes his story in the following manner.

One hot summer afternoon in the dog-days, just as a terrible black thunder-gust was coming up, Tom sat in his counting-house, in his white linen cap and India silk morning-gown. He was on the point of foreclosing a mortgage, by which he would complete the ruin of an unlucky land-speculator for whom he had professed the greatest friendship. The poor land-jobber begged him to grant a few months' indulgence. Tom had grown testy and irritated, and refused another day.

"My family will be ruined, and brought upon the parish," said the land-jobber. "Charity begins at home," replied Tom; "I must take care of myself in these hard times."

"You have made so much money out of me," said the speculator.

Tom lost his patience and his piety. "The devil take me," said he, "if I have made a farthing!"

Just then there were three loud knocks at the street-door. He stepped out to see who was there. A black man was holding a black horse, which neighed and stamped with impatience.

"Tom, you're come for," said the black fellow, gruffly. Tom shrank back, but too late. He had left his little Bible at the bottom of his coat-pocket, and his big Bible on the desk buried under the mortgage he was about to forclose: never was sinner taken more unawares. The black man whisked him like a child into the saddle, gave the horse the lash, and away he galloped, with Tom on his back, in the midst of the thunderstorm. The clerks stuck their pens behind their ears, and stared after him from the windows. Away went Tom Walker, dashing down the streets; his white cap bobbing up and down; his morning-gown fluttering in the wind, and his steed striking fire out of the pavement at every bound. When the clerks turned to look for the black man, he had disappeared.

Tom Walker never returned to forclose the mortgage. A countryman, who lived on the border of the swamp, reported that in the height of the thunder-gust he had heard a great clattering of hoofs and a howling along the road, and running to the window caught sight of a figure, such as I have described, on a horse that galloped like mad across the fields, over the hills, and down into the black hemlock swamp towards the old Indian fort; and that shortly after a thunder-bolt falling in that direction seemed to set the whole forest in a blaze.

The good people of Boston shook their heads and shrugged their shoulders, but had been so much accustomed to witches and goblins, and tricks of the devil, in all kinds of shapes, from the first settlement of the colony, that they were not so much horror-struck as might have been expected. Trustees were appointed to take charge of Tom's effects. There was nothing, however, to administer upon. On searching his coffers, all his bonds and mortgages were found reduced to cinders. In place of gold and silver, his iron chest was filled with chips and shavings; two skeletons lay in his stable instead of his half-starved horses, and the very next day his great house took fire and was burnt to the ground.

Such was the end of Tom Walker and his ill-gotten wealth. Let all griping money-brokers lay this story to heart. The truth of it is not to be doubted. The very hole under the oak-trees, whence he dug Kidd's money, is to be seen to this day; and the neighboring swamp and old Indian fort are often haunted in stormy nights by a figure on horseback, in morning-gown and white cap, which is doubtless the troubled spirit of the usurer. In fact, the story has resolved itself into a proverb, and is the origin of that popular saying, so prevalent throughout New England, of "The Devil and Tom Walker."

Philip of Pokanoket

AN INDIAN MEMOIR
BY WASHINGTON IRVING

As monumental bronze unchanged his look:
A soul that pity touch'd but never shook:
Train'd from his tree-rock'd cradle to his bier,
The fierce extremes of good and ill to brook
Impassive—fearing but the shame of fear—
A stoic of the woods—a man without a tear.

CAMPBELL

It is to be regretted that those early writers, who treated of the discovery and settlement of America, have not given us more particular and candid accounts of the remarkable characters that flourished in savage life. The scanty anecdotes which have reached us are full of peculiarity and interest; they furnish us with nearer glimpses of human nature, and show what man is in a comparatively primitive state, and what he owes to civilization. There is something of the charm of discovery in lighting upon these wild and unexplored tracts of human nature; in witnessing, as it were, the native growth of moral sentiment, and perceiving those generous and romantic qualities which have been artificially cultivated by society, vegetating in spontaneous hardihood and rude magnificence.

In civilized life, where the happiness, and indeed almost the existence, of man depends so much upon the opinion of his fellow-men, he is constantly acting a studied part. The bold and peculiar traits of native character are refined away, or softened down by the levelling influence of what is termed good-breeding; and he practises so many petty deceptions, and affects so many generous sentiments, for the purposes of popularity, that it is difficult to distinguish his real from his artificial character. The Indian, on the contrary, free from the restraints and refinements of polished life, and, in a great degree, a solitary and independent being, obeys the impulses of his inclination or the dictates of his judgment; and thus the attributes of his nature, being freely indulged, grow singly great and striking. Society is like a lawn, where every roughness is smoothed, every bramble eradicated, and where the eye is delighted by the smiling verdure of a velvet surface. He, however, who would study nature in its wildness and variety, must plunge into the forest, must explore the glen, must stem the torrent, and dare the precipice.

These reflections arose on casually looking through a volume of early colonial history, wherein are recorded, with great bitterness, the outrages of the Indians, and their wars with the settlers of New England. It is painful to perceive even from these partial narratives, how the footsteps of civilization may be traced in the blood of the aborigines; how easily the colonists were moved to hostility by the lust of conquest; how merciless and exterminating was their warfare. The imagination shrinks at the idea, how many intellectual beings were hunted from the earth, how many brave and noble hearts, of nature's sterling coinage, were broken down and trampled in the dust!

Such was the fate of PHILIP OF POKANOKET, an Indian warrior, whose name was once a terror throughout Massachusetts and Connecticut. He was the most distinguished of a number of contemporary Sachems who reigned over the Pequods, the Narragansets, the Wampanoags, and the other eastern tribes, at the time of the first settlement of New England; a band of native untaught heroes, who made the most generous struggle of which human nature is capable, fighting to the last gasp in the cause of their country, without a hope of victory or a thought of renown. Worthy of an age of poetry, and fit subjects for local story and romantic fiction, they have left scarcely any authentic traces on the page of history, but stalk, like gigantic shadows, in the dim twilight of tradition.[1]

When the pilgrims, as the Plymouth settlers are called by their descendants, first took refuge on the shores of the New World, from the religious persecutions of the Old, their situation was to the last degree gloomy and disheartening. Few in number, and that number rapidly perishing away through sickness and hardships; surrounded by a howling wilderness and savage tribes; exposed to the rigors of an almost arctic winter, and the vicissitudes of an ever-shifting climate; their minds were filled with doleful forebodings, and nothing preserved them from sinking into despondency but the strong excite-

---

[1]While correcting the proof sheets of this article, the author is informed that a celebrated English poet has nearly finished an heroic poem on the story of Philip of Pokanoket.

ment of religious enthusiasm. In this forlorn situation they were visited by Massasoit, chief Sagamore of the Wampanoags, a powerful chief, who reigned over a great extent of country. Instead of taking advantage of the scanty number of the strangers, and expelling them from his territories, into which they had intruded, he seemed at once to conceive for them a generous friendship, and extended towards them the rites of primitive hospitality. He came early in the spring to their settlement of New Plymouth, attended by a mere handful of followers, entered into a solemn league of peace and amity; sold them a portion of the soil, and promised to secure for them the good-will of his savage allies. Whatever may be said of Indian perfidy, it is certain that the integrity and good faith of Massasoit have never been impeached. He continued a firm and magnanimous friend of the white men; suffering them to extend their possessions, and to strengthen themselves in the land; and betraying no jealousy of their increasing power and prosperity. Shortly before his death he came once more to New Plymouth, with his son Alexander, for the purpose of renewing the covenant of peace, and of securing it to his posterity.

At this conference he endeavored to protect the religion of his forefathers from the encroaching zeal of the missionaries; and stipulated that no further attempt should be made to draw off his people from their ancient faith; but, finding the English obstinately opposed to any such condition, he mildly relinquished the demand. Almost the last act of his life was to bring his two sons, Alexander and Philip (as they had been named by the English), to the residence of a principal settler, recommending mutual kindness and confidence; and entreating that the same love and amity which had existed between the white men and himself might be continued afterwards with his children. The good old Sachem died in peace, and was happily gathered to his fathers before sorrow came upon his tribe; his children remained behind to experience the ingratitude of white men.

His eldest son, Alexander, succeeded him. He was of a quick and impetuous temper, and proudly tenacious of his hereditary rights and dignity. The intrusive policy and dictatorial conduct of the strangers excited his indignation; and he beheld with uneasiness their exterminating wars with the neighboring tribes. He was doomed soon to incur their hostility, being accused of plotting with the Narragansets to rise against the English and drive them from the land. It is impossible to say whether this accusation was warranted by facts or was grounded on mere suspicion. It is evident, however, by the violent and overbearing measures of the settlers, that they had by this time begun to feel conscious of the rapid increase of their power, and to grow harsh and inconsiderate in their treatment of the natives. They despatched an armed force to seize upon Alexander, and to bring him before their courts. He was traced to his woodland haunts, and surprised at a hunting house, where he was reposing with a band of his followers, unarmed, after the toils of the chase. The suddenness of his arrest, and the outrage offered to his sovereign dignity, so preyed upon the irascible feelings of this proud savage, as to throw him into a raging fever. He was permitted to return home, on condition of sending his son as a pledge for his reappearance; but the blow he had received was fatal, and before he had reached his home he fell a victim to the agonies of a wounded spirit.

The successor of Alexander was Metacomet, or King Philip, as he was called by the settlers, on account of his lofty spirit and ambitious temper. These, together with his well-known energy and enterprise, had rendered him an object of great jealousy and apprehension, and he was accused of having always cherished a secret and implacable hostility towards the whites. Such may very probably, and very naturally, have been the case. He considered them as originally but mere intruders into the country, who had presumed upon indulgence, and were extending an influence baneful to savage life. He saw the whole race of his countrymen melting before them from the face of the earth; their territories slipping from their hands, and their tribes becoming feeble, scattered and dependent. It may be said that the soil was originally purchased by the settlers; but who does not know the nature of Indian purchases, in the early period of colonization? The Europeans always made thrifty bargains through their superior adroitness in traffic; and they gained vast accessions of territory by easily provoked hostilities. An uncultivated savage is never a nice inquirer into the refinements of the law, by which an injury may be gradually and legally inflicted. Leading facts are all by which he judges; and it was enough for Philip to know that before the intrusion of the Europeans his countrymen were lords of the soil, and that now they were becoming vagabonds in the land of their fathers.

But whatever may have been his feelings of general hostility, and his particular indignation at the treatment of his brother, he suppressed them for the present, renewed the contract with the settlers, and resided peaceably for many years at Pokanoket, or, as it was called by the English, Mount Hope,[2] the ancient seat of dominion of his tribe. Suspicions, however, which were at first but vague and indefinite, began to acquire form and substance; and he was at length charged with attempting to instigate the various Eastern tribes to rise at once, and, by a simultaneous effort, to throw off the yoke of their oppressors. It is difficult at this distant period to assign the proper credit due to these early accusations against the Indians. There was a proneness to suspicion, and an aptness to acts of violence on the part of the whites, that gave weight and importance to every idle tale. Informers abounded where talebearing met with countenance and reward; and the sword was readily unsheathed when its success was certain, and it carved out empire.

The only positive evidence on record against Philip is the accusation of one Sausaman, a renegado Indian, whose natural cunning had been quickened by a partial education which he had received among the settlers. He changed his faith and allegiance two or three times, with a facility that evinced the looseness of his principles. He had acted for some time as Philip's confidential secretary and counsellor, and had enjoyed his bounty and protection. Finding, however, that the clouds of adversity were gathering round his patron, he abandoned his service and went over to the whites; and, in order to gain their favor, charged his former benefactor with plotting against their safety. A rigorous investigation took place. Philip and several of his subjects submitted to be examined, but

[2]Now Bristol, Rhode Island.

nothing was proved against them. The settlers, however, had now gone too far to retract; they had previously determined that Philip was a dangerous neighbor; they had publicly evinced their distrust; and had done enough to insure his hostility; according, therefore, to the usual mode of reasoning in these cases, his destruction had become necessary to their security. Sausaman, the treacherous informer, was shortly afterwards found dead, in a pond, having fallen a victim to the vengeance of his tribe. Three Indians, one of whom was a friend and counsellor of Philip, were apprehended and tried, and on the testimony of one very questionable witness, were condemned and executed as murderers.

This treatment of his subjects, and ignominious punishment of his friend, outraged the pride and exasperated the passions of Philip. The bolt which had fallen thus at his very feet awakened him to the gathering storm, and he determined to trust himself no longer in the power of the white men. The fate of his insulted and broken-hearted brother still rankled in his mind; and he had a further warning in the tragical story of Miantonimo, a great Sachem of the Narragansets, who, after manfully facing his accusers before a tribunal of the colonists, exculpating himself from a charge of conspiracy, and receiving assurances of amity, had been perfidiously despatched at their instigation. Philip, therefore, gathered his fighting men about him; persuaded all strangers that he could to join his cause; sent the women and children to the Narragansets for safety; and wherever he appeared, was continually surrounded by armed warriors.

When the two parties were thus in a state of distrust and irritation, the least spark was sufficient to set them in a flame.

The Indians, having weapons in their hands, grew mischievous, and committed various petty depredations. In one of their maraudings a warrior was fired on and killed by a settler. This was the signal for open hostilities; the Indians pressed to revenge the death of their comrade, and the alarm of war resounded through the Plymouth colony.

In the early chronicles of these dark and melancholy times we meet with many indications of the diseased state of the public mind. The gloom of religious abstraction, and the wildness of their situation, among trackless forests and savage tribes, had disposed the colonists to superstitious fancies, and had filled their imaginations with the frightful chimeras of witchcraft and spectrology. They were much given also to a belief in omens. The troubles with Philip and his Indians were preceded, we are told, by a variety of those awful warnings which forerun great and public calamities. The perfect form of an Indian bow appeared in the air at New Plymouth, which was looked upon by the inhabitants as a "prodigious apparition." At Hadley, Northampton, and other towns in their neighborhood, "was heard the report of a great piece of ordnance, with a shaking of the earth and a considerable echo."[3] Others were alarmed on a still, sunshiny morning, by the discharge of guns and muskets; bullets seemed to whistle past them, and the noise of drums resounded in the air, seeming to pass away to the westward; others fancied that they heard the galloping of horses over their heads; and certain monstrous births, which took place about the time, filled the superstitious in some towns with doleful forebodings. Many of these portentous sights and sounds may be ascribed to natural phe-

[3]The Rev. Increase Mather's History.

nomena: to the northern lights which occur vividly in those latitudes; the meteors which explode in the air; the casual rushing of a blast through the top branches of the forest; the crash of fallen trees or disrupted rocks; and to those other uncouth sounds and echoes which will sometimes strike the ear so strangely amidst the profound stillness of woodland solitudes. These may have startled some melancholy imaginations, may have been exaggerated by the love of the marvellous, and listened to with that avidity with which we devour whatever is fearful and mysterious. The universal currency of these superstitious fancies, and the grave record made of them by one of the learned men of the day, are strongly characteristic of the times.

The nature of the contest that ensued was such as too often distinguishes the warfare between civilized men and savages. On the part of the whites it was conducted with superior skill and success, but with a wastefulness of the blood, and a disregard of the natural rights of their antagonists: on the part of the Indians it was waged with the desperation of men fearless of death, and who had nothing to expect from peace but humiliation, dependence, and decay.

The events of the war are transmitted to us by a worthy clergyman of the time; who dwells with horror and indignation on every hostile act of the Indians, however justifiable, whilst he mentions with applause the most sanguinary atrocities of the whites. Philip is reviled as a murderer and a traitor; without considering that he was a true born prince, gallantly fighting at the head of his subjects to avenge the wrongs of his family; to retrieve the tottering power of his line; and to deliver his native land from the oppression of usurping strangers.

The project of a wide and simultaneous revolt, if such had really been formed, was worthy of a capacious mind, and, had it not been prematurely discovered, might have been overwhelming in its consequences. The war that actually broke out was but a war of detail, a mere succession of casual exploits and unconnected enterprises. Still it sets forth the military genius and daring prowess of Philip; and wherever, in the prejudiced and passionate narrations that have been given of it, we can arrive at simple facts, we find him displaying a vigorous mind, a fertility of expedients, a contempt of suffering and hardship, and an unconquerable resolution, that command our sympathy and applause.

Driven from his paternal domains at Mount Hope, he threw himself into the depths of those vast and trackless forests, that skirted the settlements and were almost impervious to anything but a wild beast, or an Indian. Here he gathered together his forces, like the storm accumulating its stores of mischief in the bosom of the thunder cloud, and would suddenly emerge at a time and place least expected, carrying havoc and dismay into the villages. There were now and then indications of these impending ravages, that filled the minds of the colonists with awe and apprehension. The report of a distant gun would perhaps be heard from the solitary woodland, where there was known to be no white man; the cattle which had been wandering in the woods would sometimes return home wounded; or an Indian or two would be seen lurking about the skirts of the forests, and suddenly disappearing; as the lightning will sometimes be seen playing silently about the edge of the cloud that is brewing up the tempest.

Though sometimes pursued and even surrounded by the settlers, yet Philip as often escaped almost miraculously from their toils, and, plunging into the wilderness, would be lost to all search or inquiry, until he again emerged at some far distant quarter, laying the country desolate. Among his strongholds, were the great swamps or morasses, which extend in some parts of New England; composed of loose bogs of deep black mud; perplexed with thickets, brambles, rank weeds, the shattered and mouldering trunks of fallen trees, overshadowed by lugubrious hemlocks. The uncertain footing and the tangled mazes of these shaggy wilds, rendered them almost impracticable to the white man, though the Indian could tread their labyrinths with the agility of a deer. Into one of these, the great swamp of Pocasset Neck, was Philip once driven with a band of his followers. The English did not dare to pursue him, fearing to venture into these dark and frightful recesses, where they might perish in fens and miry pits, or be shot down by lurking foes. They therefore invested the entrance to the Neck, and began to build a fort, with the thought of starving out the foe; but Philip and his warriors wafted themselves on a raft over an arm of the sea, in the dead of the night, leaving the women and children behind; and escaped away to the westward, kindling the flames of war among the tribes of Massachusetts and the Nipmuck country, and threatening the colony of Connecticut.

In this way Philip became a theme of universal apprehension. The mystery in which he was enveloped exaggerated his real terrors. He was an evil that walked in darkness; whose coming none could foresee, and against which none knew when to be on the alert. The whole country abounded with rumors and alarms. Philip seemed almost possessed of ubiquity; for, in whatever part of the widely-extended frontier an irruption from the forest took place, Philip was said to be its leader. Many superstitious notions also were circulated concerning him. He was said to deal in necromancy, and to be attended by an old Indian witch or prophetess, whom he consulted, and who assisted him by her charms and incantations. This indeed was frequently the case with Indian chiefs; either through their own credulity, or to act upon that of their followers: and the influence of the prophet and the dreamer over Indian superstition has been fully evidenced in recent instances of savage warfare.

At the time that Philip effected his escape from Pocasset, his fortunes were in a desperate condition. His forces had been thinned by repeated fights, and he had lost almost the whole of his resources. In this time of adversity he found a faithful friend in Canonchet, chief Sachem of all the Narragansets. He was the son and heir of Miantonimo, the great Sachem, who, as already mentioned, after an honorable acquittal of the charge of conspiracy, had been privately put to death at the perfidious instigations of the settlers. "He was the heir," says the old chronicler, "of all his father's pride and insolence, as well as of his malice towards the English." He certainly was the heir of his insults and injuries, and the legitimate avenger of his murder. Though he had forborne to take an active part in this hopeless war, yet he received Philip and his broken forces with open arms; and gave them the most generous countenance and support. This at once drew upon him the hostility of the English; and it was determined to strike a signal blow that should involve both the Sachems in one common ruin. A great force was, therefore, gathered together from Massachusetts, Plymouth, and Connecticut, and was sent into the Narraganset country in the depth of winter, when the swamps, being frozen and leafless, could be traversed with comparative facility, and would no longer afford dark and impenetrable fastnesses to the Indians.

Apprehensive of attack, Canonchet had conveyed the greater part of his stores, together with the old, the infirm, the women and children of his tribe, to a strong fortress; where he and Philip had likewise drawn up the flower of their forces. This fortress, deemed by the Indians impregnable, was situated upon a rising mound or kind of island, of five or six acres, in the midst of a swamp; it was constructed with a degree of judgment and skill vastly superior to what is usually displayed in Indian fortification, and indicative of the martial genius of these two chieftains.

Guided by a renegado Indian, the English penetrated, through December snows, to this stronghold, and came upon the garrison by surprise. The fight was fierce and tumultuous. The assailants were repulsed in their first attack, and several of their bravest officers were shot down in the act of storming the fortress sword in hand. The assault was renewed with greater success. A lodgment was effected. The Indians were driven from one post to another. They disputed their ground inch by inch, fighting with the fury of despair. Most of their veterans were cut to pieces, and after a long and bloody battle, Philip and Canonchet, with a handful of surviving warriors, retreated from the fort, and took refuge in the thickets of the surrounding forest.

The victors set fire to the wigwams and the fort; the whole was soon in a blaze; many of the old men, the women and the children perished in the flames. This last outrage overcame even the stoicism of the savage. The neighboring woods resounded with the yells of rage and despair, uttered by the fugitive warriors, as they beheld the destruction of their dwellings, and heard the agonizing cries of their wives, and offspring. "The burning of the wigwams," says a contemporary writer, "the shrieks and cries of the women and children, and the yelling of the warriors, exhibited a most horrible and affecting scene, so that it greatly moved some of the soldiers." The same writer cautiously adds, "They were in *much doubt* then, and afterwards seriously inquired, whether burning their enemies alive could be consistent with humanity, and the benevolent principles of the Gospel."[4]

The fate of the brave and generous Canonchet is worthy of particular mention: the last scene of his life is one of the noblest instances on record of Indian magnanimity.

Broken down in his power and resources by this signal defeat, yet faithful to his ally, and to the hapless cause which he had espoused, he rejected all overtures of peace, offered on condition of betraying Philip and his followers, and declared that, "he would fight it out to the last man, rather than become a servant to the English." His home being destroyed; his country harassed and laid waste by the incursions of the conquerors; he was obliged to wander away to the banks of the Connecticut; where he formed a rallying point to the whole body of western Indians, and laid waste several of the English settlements.

Early in the spring he departed on a hazardous expedition, with only thirty chosen men, to penetrate to Seaconck, in the

[4]Ms. of the Rev. W. Ruggles.

vicinity of Mount Hope, and to procure seed corn to plant for the sustenance of his troops. This little band of adventurers had passed safely through the Pequod country, and were in the centre of the Narraganset, resting at some wigwams near Pawtucket River, when an alarm was given of an approaching enemy. Having but seven men by him at the time, Canonchet despatched two of them to the top of a neighboring hill, to bring intelligence of the foe.

Panic-struck by the appearance of a troop of English and Indians rapidly advancing, they fled in breathless terror past their chieftain, without stopping to inform him of the danger. Canonchet sent another scout, who did the same. He then sent two more, one of whom, hurrying back in confusion and affright, told him that the whole British army was at hand. Canonchet saw there was no choice but immediate flight. He attempted to escape round the hill, but was perceived and hotly pursued by the hostile Indians and a few of the fleetest of the English. Finding the swiftest pursuer close upon his heels, he threw off, first his blanket, then his silver-laced coat and belt of peag, by which his enemies knew him to be Canonchet, and redoubled the eagerness of pursuit.

At length, in dashing through the river, his foot slipped upon a stone, and he fell so deep as to wet his gun. This accident so struck him with despair, that, as he afterwards confessed, "his heart and his bowels turned within him, and he became like a rotten stick, void of strength."

To such a degree was he unnerved, that, being seized by a Pequod Indian within a short distance of the river, he made no resistance, though a man of great vigor of body and boldness of heart. But on being made prisoner the whole pride of his spirit arose within him; and from that moment, we find, in the anecdotes given by his enemies, nothing but repeated flashes of elevated and prince-like heroism. Being questioned by one of the English who first came up with him, and who had not attained his twenty-second year, the proud-hearted warrior, looking with lofty contempt upon his youthful countenance, replied, "You are a child—you cannot understand matters of war—let your brother or your chief come—him will I answer."

Though repeated offers were made to him of his life, on condition of submitting with his nation to the English, yet he rejected them with disdain, and refused to send any proposals of the kind to the great body of his subjects; saying, that he knew none of them would comply. Being reproached with his breach of faith towards the whites; his boast that he would not deliver up a Wampanoag nor the paring of a Wampanoag's nail; and his threat that he would burn the English alive in their houses; he disdained to justify himself, haughtily answering that others were as forward for the war as himself, and "he desired to hear no more thereof."

So noble and unshaken a spirit, so true a fidelity to his cause and his friend, might have touched the feelings of the generous and the brave; but Canonchet was an Indian; a being towards whom war had no courtesy, humanity no law, religion no compassion—he was condemned to die. The last words of him that are recorded, are worthy the greatness of his soul. When sentence of death was passed upon him, he observed, "that he liked it well, for he should die before his heart was soft, or he had spoken anything unworthy of himself." His enemies gave him the death of a soldier, for he was shot at Stoningham, by three young Sachems of his own rank.

The defeat at the Narraganset fortress, and the death of Canonchet, were fatal blows to the fortunes of King Philip. He made an ineffectual attempt to raise a head of war by stirring up the Mohawks to take arms; but though possessed of the native talents of a statesman, his arts were counteracted by the superior arts of his enlightened enemies, and the terror of their warlike skill began to subdue the resolution of the neighboring tribes. The unfortunate chieftain saw himself daily stripped of power, and his ranks rapidly thinning around him. Some were suborned by the whites; others fell victims to hunger and fatigue, and to the frequent attacks by which they were harassed. His stores were all captured; his chosen friends were swept away from before his eyes; his uncle was shot down by his side; his sister was carried into captivity; and in one of his narrow escapes he was compelled to leave his beloved wife and only son to the mercy of the enemy. "His ruin," says the historian, "being thus gradually carried on, his misery was not prevented, but augmented thereby; being himself made acquainted with the sense and experimental feeling of the captivity of his children, loss of friends, slaughter of his subjects, bereavement of all family relations, and being stripped of all outward comforts, before his own life should be taken away."

To fill up the measure of his misfortunes, his own followers began to plot against his life, that by sacrificing him they might purchase dishonorable safety. Through treachery a number of his faithful adherents, the subjects of Wetamoe, an Indian princess of Pocasset, near kinswoman and confederate of Philip, were betrayed into the hands of the enemy. Wetamoe was among them at the time, and attempted to make her escape by crossing a neighboring river: either exhausted by swimming, or starved by cold and hunger, she was found dead and naked near the water side. But persecution ceased not at the grave. Even death, the refuge of the wretched, where the wicked commonly cease from troubling, was no protection to this outcast female, whose great crime was affectionate fidelity to her kinsman and her friend. Her corpse was the object of unmanly and dastardly vengeance; the head was severed from the body and set upon a pole, and was thus exposed at Taunton, to the view of her captive subjects. They immediately recognized the features of their unfortunate queen, and were so affected at this barbarous spectacle, that we are told they broke forth into the "most horrible and diabolical lamentations."

However Philip had borne up against the complicated miseries and misfortunes that surrounded him, the treachery of his followers seemed to wring his heart and reduce him to despondency. It is said that "he never rejoiced afterwards, nor had success in any of his designs." The spring of hope was broken—the ardor of enterprise was extinguished—he looked around, and all was danger and darkness; there was no eye to pity, nor any arm that could bring deliverance. With a scanty band of followers, who still remained true to his desperate fortunes, the unhappy Philip wandered back to the vicinity of Mount Hope, the ancient dwelling of his fathers. Here he lurked about, like a spectre, among the scenes of former power and prosperity, now bereft of home, of family, and friend. There needs no better picture of his destitute and piteous situation, than that furnished by the homely pen of the chronicler, who is unwarily enlisting the feelings of the reader in favor of the hapless warrior whom he reviles. "Philip," he says, "like a savage wild beast, having been hunted by the English forces through the woods, above a hundred miles backward and forward, at last was driven to his own den upon Mount Hope, where he retired, with a few of his best friends, into a swamp, which proved but a prison to keep him fast till the messengers of death came by divine permission to execute vengeance upon him."

Even in this last refuge of desperation and despair, a sullen grandeur gathers round his memory. We picture him to ourselves seated among his care-worn followers, brooding in silence over his blasted fortunes, and acquiring a savage sublimity from the wildness and dreariness of his lurking-place. Defeated, but not dismayed—crushed to the earth, but not humiliated—he seemed to grow more haughty beneath disaster, and to experience a fierce satisfaction in draining the last dregs of bitterness. Little minds are tamed and subdued by misfortune; but great minds rise above it. The very idea of submission awakened the fury of Philip, and he smote to death one of his followers, who proposed an expedient of peace. The brother of the victim made his escape, and in revenge betrayed the retreat of his chieftain. A body of white men and Indians were immediately despatched to the swamp where Philip lay crouched, glaring with fury and despair. Before he was aware of their approach, they had begun to surround him. In a little while he saw five of his trustiest followers laid dead at his feet; all resistance was vain; he rushed forth from his covert, and made a headlong attempt to escape, but was shot through the heart by a renegado Indian of his own nation.

Such is the scanty story of the brave, but unfortunate, King Philip; persecuted while living, slandered and dishonored when dead. If, however, we consider even the prejudiced anecdotes furnished us by his enemies, we may perceive in them traces of amiable and lofty character sufficient to awaken sympathy for his fate, and respect for his memory. We find that, amidst all the harassing cares and ferocious passions of constant warfare, he was alive to the softer feelings of connubial love and paternal tenderness, and to the generous sentiment of friendship. The captivity of his "beloved wife and only son" are mentioned with exultation as causing him poignant misery: the death of any near friend is triumphantly recorded as a new blow on his sensibilities; but the treachery and desertion of many of his followers, in whose affections he had confided, is said to have desolated his heart, and to have bereaved him of all further comfort. He was a patriot attached to his native soil—a prince true to his subjects, and indignant of their wrongs—a soldier, daring in battle, firm in adversity, patient of fatigue, of hunger, of every variety of bodily suffering, and ready to perish in the cause he had espoused. Proud of heart, and with an untamable love of natural liberty, he preferred to enjoy it among the beasts of the forests or in the dismal and famished recesses of swamps and morasses, rather than bow his haughty spirit to submission, and live dependent and despised in the ease and luxury of the settlements. With heroic qualities and bold achievements that would have graced a civilized warrior, and have rendered him the theme of the poet and the historian, he lived a wanderer and a fugitive in his native land, and went down, like a lonely bark foundering amid darkness and tempest—without a pitying eye to weep his fall, or a friendly hand to record his struggle.

The Early Experiences
of
Ralph Ringwood

NOTED DOWN FROM HIS CONVERSATIONS:
BY GEOFFREY CRAYON, GENT[1]
BY WASHINGTON IRVING

"I am a Kentuckian by residence and choice, but a Virginian by birth. The cause of my first leaving the 'Ancient Dominion,' and emigrating to Kentucky, was a jackass! You stare, but have a little patience, and I'll soon show you how it came to

[1]Ralph Ringwood, though a fictitious name, is a real personage—the late Govenor Duval of Florida. I have given some ancedotes of his early and eccentric career, in, as nearly as I can recollect, the very words in which he related them. They certainly afford strong temptations to the embellishments of fiction; but I thought them so strikingly characteristic of the individual, and of the scenes and society into which his peculiar humors carried him, that I preferred giving them in their original simplicity.

pass. My father, who was of one of the old Virginian families, resided in Richmond. He was a widower, and his domestic affairs were managed by a housekeeper of the old school, such as used to administer the concerns of opulent Virginian households. She was a dignitary that almost rivalled my father in importance, and seemed to think everything belonged to her; in fact, she was so considerate in her economy, and so careful of expense, as sometimes to vex my father, who would swear she was disgracing him by her meanness. She always appeared with that ancient insignia of housekeeping trust and authority, a great bunch of keys jingling at her girdle. She superintended the arrangements of the table at every meal, and saw that the dishes were all placed according to her primitive notions of symmetry. In the evening she took her stand and served out tea with a mingled respectfulness and pride of station truly exemplary. Her great ambition was to have everything in order, and that the establishment under her sway should be cited as a model of good housekeeping. If anything went wrong, poor old Barbara would take it to heart, and sit in her room and cry, until a few chapters in the Bible would quiet her spirits, and make all calm again. The Bible, in fact, was her constant resort in time of trouble. She opened it indiscriminately, and whether she chanced among the Lamentations of Jeremiah, the Canticles of Solomon, or the rough enumeration of the tribes in Deuteronomy, a chapter was a chapter, and operated like balm to her soul. Such was our good old housekeeper Barbara; who was destined, unwittingly, to have a most important effect upon my destiny.

"It came to pass, during the days of my juvenility, while I was yet what is termed 'an unlucky boy,' that a gentleman of our neighborhood, a great advocate for experiments and improvements of all kinds, took it into his head that it would be an immense public advantage to introduce a breed of mules, and accordingly imported three jacks to stock the neighborhood. This in a part of the country where the people cared for nothing but blood horses! Why, sir, they would have considered their mares disgraced, and their whole stud dishonored by such a misalliance. The whole matter was a town-talk, and a town-scandal. The worthy amalgamator of quadrupeds found himself in a dismal scrape; so he backed out in time, abjured the whole doctrine of amalgamation, and turned his jacks loose to shift for themselves upon the town common. There they used to run about and lead an idle, good-for-nothing, holiday life, the happiest animals in the country.

"It so happened that my way to school lay across the common. The first time that I saw one of these animals, it set up a braying and frightened me confoundedly. However, I soon got over my fright, and seeing that it had something of a horse look, my Virginian love for anything of the equestrian species predominated, and I determined to back it. I accordingly applied at a grocer's shop, procured a cord that had been round a loaf of sugar, and made a kind of halter; then, summoning some of my school-fellows, we drove master Jack about the common until we hemmed him in in an angle of a 'wormfence.' After some difficulty, we fixed the halter round his muzzle, and I mounted. Up flew his heels, away I went over his head, and off he scampered. However, I was on my legs in a twinkling, gave chase, caught him, and remounted. By dint of repeated tumbles I soon learned to stick to his back, so that he could no more cast me than he could his own skin. From that

time, master Jack and his companions had a scampering life of it, for we all rode them between school-hours, and on holiday afternoons; and you may be sure school-boys' nags are never permitted to suffer the grass to grow under their feet. They soon became so knowing, that they took to their heels at sight of a school-boy; and we were generally much longer in chasing than we were in riding them.

"Sunday approached, on which I projected an equestrian excursion on one of these long-eared steeds. As I knew the jacks would be in great demand on Sunday morning, I secured one over night, and conducted him home, to be ready for an early outset. But where was I to quarter him for the night? I could not put him in the stable; our old black groom George was as absolute in that domain as Barbara was within doors, and would have thought his stable, his horses, and himself disgraced by the introduction of a jackass. I recollected the smoke-house—an outbuilding appended to all Virginian establishments, for the smoking of hams and other kinds of meat. So I got the key, put master Jack in, locked the door, returned the key to its place, and went to bed, intending to release my prisoner at an early hour, before any of the family were awake. I was so tired, however, by the exertions I had made in catching the donkey, that I fell into a sound sleep, and the morning broke without my waking.

"Not so with dame Barbara, the housekeeper. As usual, to use her own phrase, 'she was up before the crow put his shoes on,' and bustled about to get things in order for breakfast. Her first resort was to the smoke-house. Scarce had she opened the door, when master Jack, tired of his confinement, and glad to be released from darkness, gave a loud bray, and rushed forth.

Down dropped old Barbara; the animal trampled over her, and made off for the common. Poor Barbara! She had never before seen a donkey; and having read in the Bible that the Devil went about like a roaring lion, seeking whom he might devour, she took it for granted that this was Beelzebub himself. The kitchen was soon in a hubbub; the servants hurried to the spot. There lay old Barbara in fits; as fast as she got out of one, the thought of the Devil came over her, and she fell into another, for the good soul was devoutly superstitious.

"As ill luck would have it, among those attracted by the noise, was a little, cursed, fidgety, crabbed uncle of mine; one of those uneasy spirits that cannot rest quietly in their beds in the morning, but must be up early, to bother the household. He was only a kind of half-uncle, after all, for he had married my father's sister; yet he assumed great authority on the strength of this left-handed relationship, and was a universal intermeddler and family pest. This prying little busybody soon ferreted out the truth of the story, and discovered, by hook and by crook, that I was at the bottom of the affair, and had locked up the donkey in the smoke-house. He stopped to inquire no further, for he was one of those testy curmudgeons with whom unlucky boys are always in the wrong. Leaving old Barbara to wrestle in imagination with the Devil, he made for my bedchamber, where I still lay wrapped in rosy slumbers, little dreaming of the mischief I had done, and the storm about to break over me.

"In an instant I was awakened by a shower of thwacks, and started up in wild amazement. I demanded the meaning of this attack, but received no other reply than that I had murdered the housekeeper; while my uncle continued whacking

away during my confusion. I seized a poker, and put myself on the defensive. I was a stout boy for my years, while my uncle was a little wiffet of a man; one that in Kentucky we would not call even an 'individual'; nothing more than a 're-mote circumstance.' I soon, therefore, brought him to a parley, and learned the whole extent of the charge brought against me. I confessed to the donkey and the smoke-house, but pleaded not guilty of the murder of the housekeeper. I soon found out that old Barbara was still alive. She continued under the doctor's hands, however, for several days; and whenever she had an ill turn, my uncle would seek to give me another flogging. I appealed to my father, but got no redress. I was considered an 'unlucky boy,' prone to all kinds of mischief; so that prepossessions were against me, in all cases of appeal.

"I felt stung to the soul at all this. I had been beaten, de-graded, and treated with slighting when I complained. I lost my usual good spirits and good-humor; and, being out of tem-per with everybody, fancied everybody out of temper with me. A certain wild, roving spirit of freedom, which I believe is as inherent in me as it is in the partridge, was brought into sudden activity by the checks and restraints I suffered. 'I'll go from home,' thought I, 'and shift for myself.' Perhaps this notion was quickened by the rage for emigrating to Kentucky which was at that time prevalent in Virginia. I had heard such stories of the romantic beauties of the country, of the abun-dance of game of all kinds, and of the glorious independent life of the hunters who ranged its noble forests, and lived by the rifle, that I was as much agog to get there as boys who live in seaports are to launch themselves among the wonders and adventures of the ocean.

"After a time, old Barbara got better in mind and body, and matters were explained to her; and she became gradually convinced that it was not the Devil she had encountered. When she heard how harshly I had been treated on her account, the good old soul was extremely grieved, and spoke warmly to my father in my behalf. He had himself remarked the change in my behavior, and thought punishment might have been carried too far. He sought, therefore, to have some conversation with me, and to soothe my feelings; but it was too late. I frankly told him the course of mortification that I had experienced, and the fixed determination I had made to go from home.

" 'And where do you mean to go?'

" 'To Kentucky.'

" 'To Kentucky! Why, you know nobody there.'

" 'No matter; I can soon make acquaintances.'

" 'And what will you do when you get there?'

" 'Hunt!'

"My father gave a long, low whistle, and looked in my face with a serio-comic expression. I was not far in my teens, and to talk of setting off alone for Kentucky, to turn hunter, seemed doubtless the idle prattle of a boy. He was little aware of the dogged resolution of my character; and his smile of incredulity but fixed me more obstinately in my purpose. I assured him I was serious in what I said, and would certainly set off for Kentucky in the spring.

"Month after month passed away. My father now and then adverted slightly to what had passed between us; doubtless for the purpose of sounding me. I always expressed the same grave and fixed determination. By degrees he spoke to me more directly on the subject, endeavoring earnestly but kindly to dissuade me. My only reply was, 'I had made up my mind.'

"Accordingly, as soon as the spring had fairly opened, I sought him one day in his study, and informed him I was about to set out for Kentucky, and had come to take my leave. He made no objection, for he had exhausted persuasion and remonstrance, and doubtless thought it best to give way to my humor, trusting that a little rough experience would soon bring me home again. I asked money for my journey. He went to a chest, took out a long green silk purse, well filled, and laid it on the table. I now asked for a horse and servant.

" 'A horse!' said my father sneeringly, 'why, you would not go a mile without racing him, and breaking your neck; and as to a servant, you cannot take care of yourself, much less of him.'

" 'How am I to travel, then?'

"Why, I suppose you are man enough to travel on foot.'

"He spoke jestingly, little thinking I would take him at his word; but I was thoroughly piqued in respect to my enterprise; so I pocketed the purse, went to my room, tied up three or four shirts in a pocket-handkerchief, put a dirk in my bosom, girt a couple of pistols round my waist, and felt like a knight-errant armed *cap-a-pie*, and ready to rove the world in quest of adventures.

"My sister (I had but one) hung round me and wept, and entreated me to stay. I felt my heart swell in my throat; but I gulped it back to its place, and straightened myself up: I would not suffer myself to cry. I at length disengaged myself from her, and got to the door.

" 'When will you come back?' cried she.

" 'Never, by heavens!' cried I. 'Until I come back a member of Congress from Kentucky. I am determined to show that I am not the tail-end of the family.'

"Such was my first outset from home. You may suppose what a greenhorn I was, and how little I knew of the world I was launching into.

"I do not recollect any incident of importance, until I reached the borders of Pennsylvania. I had stopped at an inn to get some refreshment; as I was eating in a back-room, I overheard two men in the bar-room conjecture who and what I could be. One determined, at length, that I was a runaway apprentice, and ought to be stopped, to which the other assented. When I had finished my meal, and paid for it, I went out at the back-door, lest I should be stopped by my supervisors. Scorning, however, to steal off like a culprit, I walked round to the front of the house. One of the men advanced to the front door. He wore his hat on one side, and had a consequential air that nettled me.

" 'Where are you going, youngster?' demanded he.

" 'That's none of your business!' replied I, rather pertly.

" 'Yes, but it is though! You have run away from home, and must give an account of yourself.'

"He advanced to seize me, when I drew forth a pistol. 'If you advance another step, I'll shoot you!'

"He sprang back as if he had trodden upon a rattle-snake, and his hat fell off in the movement.

" 'Let him alone!' cried his companion. 'He's a foolish mad-headed boy, and don't know what he's about. He'll shoot you, you may rely on it.'

"He did not need any caution in the matter; he was afraid

even to pick up his hat; so I pushed forward on my way without molestation. This incident, however, had its effect upon me. I became fearful of sleeping in any house at night, lest I should be stopped. I took my meals in the houses, in the course of the day, but would turn aside at night into some wood or ravine, make a fire and sleep before it. This I considered was true hunter's style, and I wished to inure myself to it.

"At length I arrived at Brownsville, leg-weary and wayworn, and in a shabby plight, as you may suppose, having been 'camping out' for some nights past. I applied at some of the inferior inns but could gain no admission. I was regarded for a moment with a dubious eye, and then informed they did not receive foot-passengers. At last I went boldly to the principal inn. The landlord appeared as unwilling as the rest to receive a vagrant boy beneath his roof; but his wife interfered in the midst of his excuses, and, half elbowing him aside—

" 'Where are you going, my lad?' said she.

" 'To Kentucky.'

" 'What are you going there for?'

" 'To hunt.'

"She looked earnestly at me for a moment or two. 'Have you a mother living?' said she at length.

" 'No, madam; she has been dead for some time.'

" 'I thought so!' cried she, warmly. 'I knew if you had a mother living, you would not be here.' From that moment the good woman treated me with a mother's kindness.

"I remained several days beneath her roof, recovering from the fatigue of my journey.

"While here, I purchased a rifle, and practised daily at a

mark, to prepare myself for a hunter's life. When sufficiently recruited in strength I took leave of my kind host and hostess, and resumed my journey.

"At Wheeling I embarked in a flat-bottomed family boat, technically called a broad-horn, a prime river conveyance in those days. In this ark for two weeks I floated down the Ohio. The river was as yet in all its wild beauty. Its loftiest trees had not been thinned out. The forest overhung the water's edge, and was occasionally skirted by immense canebrakes. Wild animals of all kinds abounded. We heard them rushing through the thickets and plashing in the water. Deer and bears would frequently swim across the river; others would come down to the bank, and gaze at the boat as it passed. I was incessantly on the alert with my rifle; but, somehow or other, the game was never within shot. Sometimes I got a chance to land and try my skill on shore. I shot squirrels, and small birds, and even wild turkeys; but though I caught glimpses of deer bounding away through the woods, I never could get a fair shot at them.

"In this way we glided in our broad-horn past Cincinnati, the 'Queen of the West,' as she is now called, then a mere group of log-cabins; and the site of the bustling city of Louisville, then designated by a solitary house. As I said before, the Ohio was as yet a wild river; all was forest, forest, forest! Near the confluence of Green River with the Ohio I landed, bade adieu to the broad-horn, and struck for the interior of Kentucky. I had no precise plan; my only idea was to make for one of the wildest parts of the country. I had relatives in Lexington and other settled places, to whom I thought it probable my father would write concerning me; so, as I full of manhood and independence, and resolutely bent on making my way in the world without assistance or control, I resolved to keep clear of them all.

"In the course of my first day's trudge I shot a wild turkey, and slung it on my back for provisions. The forest was open and clear from underwood. I saw deer in abundance, but always running, running. It seemed to me as if these animals never stood still.

"At length I came to where a gang of half-starved wolves were feasting on the carcass of a deer which they had run down, and snarling and snapping, and fighting like so many dogs. They were all so ravenous and intent upon their prey that they did not notice me, and I had time to make my observations. One, larger and fiercer than the rest, seemed to claim the larger share, and to keep the others in awe. If anyone came too near him while eating, he would fly off, seize and shake him, and then return to his repast. 'This,' thought I, 'must be the captain; if I can kill him, I shall defeat the whole army.' I accordingly took aim, fired, and down dropped the old fellow. He might be only shamming dead; so I loaded and put a second ball through him. He never budged; all the rest ran off, and my victory was complete.

"It would not be easy to describe my triumphant feelings on this great achievement. I marched on with renovated spirit, regarding myself as absolute lord of the forest. As night drew near, I prepared for camping. My first care was to collect dry wood, and make a roaring fire to cook and sleep by, and to frighten off wolves, and bears, and panthers. I then began to pluck my turkey for supper. I had camped out several times in the early part of my expedition; but that was in comparatively more settled and civilized regions, where there were no wild animals of consequence in the forest. This was my first camping out in the real wilderness, and I was soon made sensible of the loneliness and wildness of my situation.

"In a little while a concert of wolves commenced; there might have been a dozen or two, but it seemed to me as if there were thousands. I never heard such howling and whining. Having prepared my turkey, I divided it into two parts, thrust two sticks into one of the halves, and planted them on end before the fire—the hunter's mode of roasting. The smell of roast meat quickened the appetites of the wolves, and their concert became truly infernal. They seemed to be all around me, but I could only now and then get a glimpse of one of them, as he came within the glare of the light.

"I did not much care for the wolves, who I knew to be a cowardly race, but I had heard terrible stories of panthers, and began to fear their stealthy prowlings in the surrounding darkness. I was thirsty, and heard a brook bubbling and tinkling along at no great distance, but absolutely dared not go there, lest some panther might lie in wait and spring upon me. By and by a deer whistled. I had never heard one before, and thought it must be a panther. I now felt uneasy lest he might climb the trees, crawl along the branches overhead, and plump down upon me; so I kept my eyes fixed on the branches, until my head ached. I more than once thought I saw fiery eyes glaring down from among the leaves. At length I thought of my supper, and turned to see if my half turkey was cooked. In crowding so near the fire, I had pressed the meat into the flames, and it was consumed. I had nothing to do but roast the other half, and take better care of it. On that half I made my supper, without salt or bread. I was still so possessed with the dread of panthers, that I could not close my eyes all night, but lay watching the trees until daybreak, when all my fears were dispelled with the darkness; and as I saw the morning sun sparkling down through the branches of the trees, I smiled to think how I suffered myself to be dismayed by sounds and shadows; but I was a young woodsman, and a stranger in Kentucky.

"Having breakfasted on the remainder of my turkey and slaked my thirst at the bubbling stream, without further dread of panthers, I resumed my wayfaring with buoyant feelings. I again saw deer, but, as usual, running, running! I tried in vain to get a shot at them, and began to fear I never should. I was gazing with vexation after a herd in full scamper, when I was startled by a human voice. Turning round, I saw a man at a short distance from me in a hunting-dress.

" 'What are you after, my lad?' cried he.

" 'Those deer,' replied I pettishly; 'but it seems as if they never stand still.'

"Upon that he burst out laughing. 'Where are you from?' said he.

" 'From Richmond.'

" 'What! In old Virginny?'

" 'The same.'

" 'And how on earth did you get here?'

" 'I landed at Green River from a broad-horn.'

" 'And where are your companions?'

" 'I have none.'

" 'What! All alone?'

" 'Yes.'

" 'Where are you going?'

" 'Anywhere.'

" 'And what have you come here for?'

" 'To hunt.'

" 'Well,' said he, laughingly, 'you'll make a real hunter; there's no mistaking that! Have you killed anything?'

" 'Nothing but a turkey; I can't get within shot of a deer; they are always running.'

" 'Oh, I'll tell you the secret of that. You're always pushing forward, and startling the deer at a distance, and gazing at those that are scampering; but you must step as slow and silent and cautious as a cat, and keep your eyes close around you, and lurk from tree to tree, if you wish to get a chance at deer. But come, go home with me. My name is Bill Smithers; I live not far off, stay with me a little while, and I'll teach you how to hunt.'

"I gladly accepted the invitation of honest Bill Smithers. We soon reached his habitation, a mere log-hut, with a square hole for a window, and a chimney made of sticks and clay. Here he lived, with a wife and child. He had 'girdled' the trees for an acre or two around, preparatory to clearing a space for corn and potatoes. In the meantime he maintained his family entirely by his rifle, and I soon found him to be a first-rate huntsman. Under his tutelage I received my first effective lessons in 'woodcraft.'

"The more I knew of a hunter's life, the more I relished it. The country, too, which had been the promised land of my boyhood, did not, like most promised lands, disappoint me. No wilderness could be more beautiful than this part of Kentucky in those times. The forests were open and spacious, with noble trees, some of which looked as if they had stood for centuries. There were beautiful prairies, too, diversified with groves and clumps of trees, which looked like vast parks, and in which you could see the deer running, at a great distance. In the proper season, these prairies would be covered in many places with wild strawberries, where your horse's hoofs would be dyed to the fetlock. I thought there could not be another place in the world equal to Kentucky—and I think so still.

"After I had passed ten or twelve days with Bill Smithers, I thought it time to shift my quarters, for his house was scarce large enough for his own family, and I had no idea of being an encumbrance to anyone. I accordingly made up my bundle, shouldered my rifle, took a friendly leave of Smithers and his wife, and set out in quest of a Nimrod of the wilderness, one John Miller, who lived alone, nearly forty miles off, and who I hoped would be well pleased to have a hunting companion.

"I soon found out that one of the most important items in woodcraft, in a new country, was the skill to find one's way in the wilderness. There were no regular roads in the forests, but they were cut up and perplexed by paths leading in all directions. Some of these were made by the cattle of the settlers, and were called 'stock-tracks,' but others had been made by the immense droves of buffaloes which roamed about the country from the flood until recent times. These were called buffalo-tracks, and traversed Kentucky from end to end, like highways. Traces of them may still be seen in uncultivated parts, or deeply worn in the rocks where they crossed the mountains. I was a young woodsman, and sorely puzzled to distinguish one kind of track from the other, or to make out my course through this tangled labyrinth. While thus perplexed, I heard a distant roaring and rushing sound; a gloom stole over the forest. On looking up, when I could catch a stray glimpse of the sky, I beheld the clouds rolled up like balls, the lower part as black as ink. There was now and then an explosion, like a burst of cannonry afar off, and the crash of a falling tree. I had heard of hurricanes in the woods, and surmised that one was at hand. It soon came crashing its way, the forest writhing, and twisting, and groaning before it. The hurricane did not extend far on either side, but in a manner ploughed a furrow through the woodland, snapping off or uprooting trees that had stood for centuries, and filling the air with whirling branches. I was directly in its course, and took my stand behind an immense poplar, six feet in diameter. It bore for a time the full fury of the blast, but at length began to yield. Seeing it falling, I scrambled nimbly around the trunk like a squirrel. Down it went, bearing down another tree with it. I crept under the trunk as a shelter, and was protected from other trees which fell around me, but was sore all over, from the twigs and branches driven against me by the blast.

"This was the only incident of consequence that occurred on my way to John Miller's, where I arrived on the following day, and was received by the veteran with the rough kindness of a backwoodsman. He was a gray-haired man, hardy and weather-beaten, with a blue wart, like a great bead, over one eye, whence he was nicknamed by the hunters, 'Blue-bead Miller.' He had been in these parts from the earliest settlements, and had signalized himself in the hard conflicts with the Indians, which gained Kentucky the appellation of the 'Bloody Ground.' In one of these fights he had had an arm broken; in another he had narrowly escaped, when hotly pur-

sued, by jumping from a precipice thirty feet high into a river.

"Miller willingly received me into his house as an inmate, and seemed pleased with the idea of making a hunter of me. His dwelling was a small log-house, with a loft or garret of boards, so that there was ample room for both of us. Under his instruction, I soon made a tolerable proficiency in hunting. My first exploit of any consequence was killing a bear. I was hunting in company with two brothers, when we came upon the track of Bruin, in a wood where there was an undergrowth of canes and grape-vines. He was scrambling up a tree, when I shot him through the breast; he fell to the ground, and lay motionless. The brothers sent in their dog, who seized the bear by the throat. Bruin raised one arm, and gave the dog a hug that crushed his ribs. One yell, and all was over. I don't know which was first dead, the dog or the bear. The two brothers sat down and cried like children over their unfortunate dog. Yet they were mere rough huntsmen, almost as wild and untamable as Indians; but they were fine fellows.

"By degrees I became known, and somewhat of a favorite among the hunters of the neighborhood; that is to say, men who lived within a circle of thirty or forty miles, and came occasionally to see John Miller, who was a patriarch among them. They lived widely apart, in log-huts and wigwams, almost with the simplicity of Indians, and wellnigh as destitute of the comforts and inventions of civilized life. They seldom saw each other; weeks, and even months would elapse, without their visiting. When they did meet, it was very much after the manner of Indians; loitering about all day, without having much to say, but becoming communicative as evening advanced, and sitting up half the night before the fire, telling hunting-stories, and terrible tales of the fights of the Bloody Ground.

"Sometimes several would join in a distant hunting expedition, or rather campaign. Expeditions of this kind lasted from November until April, during which we laid up our stock of summer provisions. We shifted our hunting-camps from place to place, according as we found the game. They were generally pitched near a run of water, and close by a canebrake, to screen us from the wind. One side of our lodge was open towards the fire. Our horses were hoppled and turned loose in the canebrakes, with bells round their necks. One of the party stayed at home to watch the camp, prepare the meals, and keep off the wolves; the others hunted. When a hunter killed a deer at a distance from the camp, he would open it and take out the entrails; then, climbing a sapling, he would bend it down, tie the deer to the top, and let it spring up again, so as to suspend the carcass out of reach of the wolves. At night he would return to the camp, and give an account of his luck. The next morning early he would get a horse out of the canebrake and bring home his game. That day he would stay at home to cut up the carcass, while the others hunted.

"Our days were thus spent in silent and lonely occupations. It was only at night that we would gather together before the fire, and be sociable. I was a novice, and used to listen with open eyes and ears to the strange and wild stories told by the old hunters, and believed everything I heard. Some of their stories bordered upon the supernatural. They believed that their rifles might be spell-bound, so as not to be able to kill a buffalo, even at arm's length. This superstition they had derived from the Indians, who often think the white hunters

had laid a spell upon their rifles. Miller partook of this superstition, and used to tell of his rifle's having a spell upon it;
but it often seemed to me to be a shuffling way of accounting
for a bad shot. If a hunter grossly missed his aim, he would
ask, 'Who shot last with his rifle?'—and hint that he must have
charmed it. The sure mode to disenchant the gun was to
shoot a silver bullet out of it.

"By the opening of spring we would generally have quanti-
ties of bear's meat and venison salted, dried, and smoked, and
numerous packs of skins. We would then make the best of our
way home from our distant hunting-grounds, transporting our
spoils, sometimes in canoes along the rivers, sometimes on
horseback over land, and our return would often be celebrated
by feasting and dancing, in true backwoods style. I have given
you some idea of our hunting; let me now give you a sketch
of our frolicking.

"It was on our return from a winter's hunting in the neighborhood of Green River, when we received notice that there
was to be a grand frolic at Bob Mosely's, to greet the hunters.
This Bob Mosely was a prime fellow throughout the country.
He was an indifferent hunter, it is true, and rather lazy, to
boot; but then he could play the fiddle, and that was enough
to make him of consequence. There was no other man within
a hundred miles that could play the fiddle, so there was no
having a regular frolic without Bob Mosely. The hunters,
therefore, were always ready to give him a share of their game
in exchange for his music, and Bob was always ready to get
up a carousal whenever there was a party returning from a
hunting expedition. The present frolic was to take place at
Bob Mosely's own house, which was on the Pigeon-Roost

Fork of the Muddy, which is a branch of Rough Creek, which is a branch of Green River.

"Everybody was agog for the revel at Bob Mosely's; and as all the fashion of the neighborhood was to be there, I thought I must brush up for the occasion. My leathern hunting-dress, which was the only one I had, was somewhat the worse for wear, it is true, and considerably japanned with blood and grease; but I was up to hunting expedients. Getting into a periogue, I paddled off to a part of the Green River where there was sand and clay, that might serve for soap; then, taking off my dress, I scrubbed and scoured it, until I thought it looked very well. I then put it on the end of a stick, and hung it out of the periogue to dry, while I stretched myself very comfortably on the green bank of the river. Unluckily a flaw struck the periogue, and tipped over the stick; down went my dress to the bottom of the river, and I never saw it more. Here was I, left almost in a state of nature. I managed to make a kind of Robinson Crusoe garb of undressed skins, with the hair on, which enabled me to get home with decency; but my dream of gayety and fashion was at an end; for how could I think of figuring in high life at the Pigeon-Roost, equipped like a mere Orson?

"Old Miller, who really began to take some pride in me, was confounded when he understood that I did not intend to go to Bob Mosely's; but when I told him my misfortune, and that I had no dress, 'By the powers,' cried he, 'but you *shall* go, and you shall be the best dressed and the best mounted lad there!'

"He immediately set to work to cut out and make up a hunting-shirt, of dressed deer-skin, gayly fringed at the shoulders, and leggins of the same, fringed from hip to heel. He then made me a rakish raccoon-cap, with a flaunting tail to it, mounted me on his best horse; and I may say, without vanity, that I was one of the smartest fellows that figured on that occasion at the Pigeon-Roost Fork of the Muddy.

"It was no small occasion, either, let me tell you. Bob Mosely's house was a tolerably large bark shanty, with a clapboard roof; and there were assembled all the young hunters and pretty girls of the country for many a mile round. The young men were in their best hunting-dresses, but not one could compare with mine; and my raccoon-cap, with its flowing tail, was the admiration of everybody. The girls were mostly in doe-skin dresses; for there was no spinning and weaving as yet in the woods, nor any need of it. I never saw girls that seemed to me better dressed, and I was somewhat of a judge, having seen fashions at Richmond. We had a hearty dinner, and a merry one; for there was Jemmy Kiel, famous for raccoon-hunting, and Bob Tarleton, and Wesley Pigman, and Joe Taylor, and several other prime fellows for a frolic, that made all ring again, and laughed that you might have heard them a mile.

"After dinner we began dancing, and were hard at it when, about three o'clock in the afternoon, there was a new arrival—the two daughters of old Simon Schultz; two young ladies that affected fashion and late hours. Their arrival had nearly put an end to all our merriment. I must go a little round about in my story to explain to you how that happened.

"As old Schultz, the father, was one day looking in the canebrakes for his cattle, he came upon the track of horses. He knew they were none of his, and that none of his neighbors had horses about that place. They must be stray horses, or must belong to some traveller who had lost his way, as the track led nowhere. He accordingly followed it up, until he came to an unlucky peddler, with two or three pack-horses, who had been bewildered among the cattle-tracks, and had wandered for two or three days among woods and canebrakes, until he was almost famished.

"Old Schultz brought him to his house, fed him on venison, bear's meat, and hominy, and at the end of a week put him in prime condition. The peddler could not sufficiently express his thankfulness, and when about to depart, inquired what he had to pay. Old Schultz stepped back with surprise. 'Stranger,' said he, 'you have been welcome under my roof. I've given you nothing but wild meat and hominy, because I had no better, but have been glad of your company. You are welcome to stay as long as you please; but, by zounds! if anyone offers to pay Simon Schultz for food, he affronts him!' So saying, he walked out in a huff.

"The peddler admired the hospitality of his host, but could not reconcile it to his conscience to go away without making some recompense. There were honest Simon's two daughters, two strapping, red-haired girls. He opened his packs and displayed riches before them of which they had no conception; for in those days there were no country stores in those parts, with their artificial finery and trinketry; and this was the first peddler that had wandered into that part of the wilderness. The girls were for a time completely dazzled, and knew not what to choose; but what caught their eyes most were two looking-glasses, about the size of a dollar, set in gilt tin. They had never seen the like before, having used no other mirror than a pail of water. The peddler presented them these jewels without the least hesitation; nay, he gallantly hung them round their necks by red ribbons, almost as fine as the glasses themselves. This done, he took his departure, leaving them as much astonished as two princesses in a fairy tale, that have received a magic gift from an enchanter.

"It was with these looking-glasses hung round their necks as lockets, by red ribbons, that old Schultz's daughters made their appearance at three o'clock in the afternoon, at the frolic at Bob Moseley's, on the Pigeon-Roost Fork of the Muddy.

"By the powers, but it was an event! Such a thing had never before been seen in Kentucky. Bob Tarleton, a strapping fellow, with a head like a chestnut-burr, and a look like a boar in an apple-orchard, stepped up, caught hold of the looking-glass of one of the girls, and gazing at it for a moment, cried out, 'Joe Taylor, come here! Come here! I'll be darn'd if Patty Schultz ain't got a locket that you can see your face in, as clear as in a spring of water!'

"In a twinkling all the young hunters gathered round old Schultz's daughters. I, who knew what looking-glasses were, did not budge. Some of the girls who sat near me were excessively mortified at finding themselves thus deserted. I heard Peggy Pugh say to Sally Pigman, 'Goodness knows it's well Schultz's daughters is got them things round their necks, for it's the first time the young men crowded round them!'

"I saw immediately the danger of the case. We were a small community, and could not afford to be split up by feuds. So I stepped up to the girls, and whispered to them: 'Polly,' said I, 'those lockets are powerful fine, and become you amazingly, but you don't consider that the country is not advanced enough in these parts for such things. You and I understand these matters, but these people don't. Fine things like these may do very well in the old settlements, but they won't answer at the Pigeon-Roost Fork of the Muddy. You had better lay them aside for the present, or we shall have no peace.'

"Polly and her sister luckily saw their error; they took off the lockets, laid them aside, and harmony was restored; otherwise, I verily believe there would have been an end of our community. Indeed, notwithstanding the great sacrifice they made on this occasion, I do not think old Schultz's daughters were ever much liked afterwards among the young women.

"This was the first time that looking-glasses were ever seen in the Green River part of Kentucky.

"I had now lived some time with old Miller, and had become a tolerably expert hunter. Game, however, began to grow scarce. The buffalo had gathered together, as if by universal understanding, and had crossed the Mississippi, never to return. Strangers kept pouring into the country, clearing away the forests, and building in all directions. The hunters began to grow restive. Jemmy Kiel, the same of whom I have already spoken for his skill in raccoon catching, came to me one day. 'I can't stand this any longer,' said he, 'we're getting too thick here. Simon Schultz crowds me so that I have no comfort of my life.'

"'Why, how you talk!' said I; 'Simon Schultz lives twelve miles off.'

"'No matter; his cattle run with mine, and I've no idea of living where another man's cattle can run with mine. That's too close neighborhood; I want elbow room. This country, too, is growing too poor to live in; there's no game; so two or three of us have made up our minds to follow the buffalo to the Missouri, and we should like to have you of the party.' Other hunters of my acquaintance talked in the same manner. This set me thinking; but the more I thought, the more I was perplexed. I had no one to advise with; old Miller and his associates knew of but one mode of life, and I had no experience in any other, but I had a wider scope of thought. When out hunting alone, I used to forget the sport, and sit for hours together on the trunk of a tree, with rifle in hand, buried in thought, and debating with myself: 'Shall I go with Jemmy Kiel and his company, or shall I remain here? If I remain here, there will soon be nothing left to hunt. But am I to be a hunter all my life? Have not I something more in me than to be carrying a rifle on my shoulder, day after day, and dodging about after bears, and deer, and other brute beasts?' My vanity told me I had; and I called to mind my boyish boast to my sister, that I would never return home until I returned a member of Congress from Kentucky; but was this the way to fit myself for such a station?

"Various plans passed through my mind, but they were abandoned almost as soon as formed. At length I determined on becoming a lawyer. True it is, I knew almost nothing. I had left school before I had learnt beyond the 'Rule of Three.' 'Never mind,' said I to myself, resolutely, 'I am a terrible fellow for hanging on to anything when I've once made up my mind; and if a man has but ordinary capacity, and will set to work with heart and soul, and stick to it, he can do almost anything.' With this maxim, which has been pretty much my main stay throughout life, I fortified myself in my determination to attempt the law. But how was I to set about it? I must quit this forest life, and go to one or other of the towns, where I might be able to study and to attend the courts. This, too, required funds. I examined into the state of my finances. The purse given me by my father had remained untouched, in the bottom of an old chest up in the loft, for money was scarcely needed in these parts. I had bargained away the skins acquired in hunting, for a horse and various other matters, on which, in case of need, I could raise funds. I therefore thought I could make shift to maintain myself until I was fitted for the bar.

"I informed my worthy host and patron, old Miller, of my plan. He shook his head at my turning my back upon the woods when I was in a fair way of making a first-rate hunter; but he made no effort to dissuade me. I accordingly set off in September, on horseback, intending to visit Lexington, Frankfort, and other of the principal towns, in search of a favorable place to prosecute my studies. My choice was made sooner than I expected. I had put up one night at Bardstown, and found, on inquiry, that I could get comfortable board and accommodation in a private family for a dollar and a half a week. I liked the place, and resolved to look no farther. So the next morning I prepared to turn my face homeward, and take my final leave of forest life.

"I had taken my breakfast, and was waiting for my horse, when, in pacing up and down the piazza, I saw a young girl seated near a window, evidently a visitor. She was very pretty, with auburn hair and blue eyes, and was dressed in white. I had seen nothing of the kind since I had left Richmond, and at that time I was too much of a boy to be much struck by female charms. She was so delicate and dainty-looking, so different from the hale, buxom, brown girls of the woods; and then her white dress—it was perfectly dazzling! Never was poor youth more taken by surprise and suddenly bewitched. My heart yearned to know her; but how was I to accost her? I had grown wild in the woods, and had none of the habitudes of polite life. Had she been like Peggy Pugh, or Sally Pigman, or any other of my leathern-dressed belles of the Pigeon-Roost, I should have approached her without dread; nay, had she been as fair as Schultz's daughters, with their looking-glass lockets, I should not have hesitated; but that white dress and those auburn ringlets, and blue eyes, and delicate looks, quite daunted while they fascinated me. I don't know what put it into my head, but I thought, all at once, that I would kiss her! It would take a long acquaintance to arrive at such a boon, but I might seize upon it by sheer robbery. Nobody knew me here. I would just step in, snatch a kiss, mount my horse, and ride off. She would not be the worse for it; and that kiss—oh! I should die if I did not get it!

"I gave no time for the thought to cool, but entered the house, and stepped lightly into the room. She was seated with her back to the door, looking out at the window, and did not hear my approach. I tapped her chair, and as she turned and looked up, I snatched as sweet a kiss as ever was stolen, and vanished in a twinkling. The next moment I was on horseback, galloping homeward, my very ears tingling at what I had done.

"On my return home, I sold my horse and turned everything to cash, and found, with the remains of the paternal purse, that I had nearly four hundred dollars—a little capital which I resolved to manage with the strictest economy.

"It was hard parting with old Miller, who had been like a father to me; it cost me, too, something of a struggle to give up the free, independent, wild-wood life I had hitherto led; but I had marked out my course, and have never been one to flinch or turn back.

"I footed it sturdily to Bardstown, took possession of the quarters for which I had bargained, shut myself up, and set to work with might and main to study. But what a task I had before me! I had everything to learn; not merely law, but all the elementary branches of knowledge. I read and read for sixteen hours out of the four-and-twenty, but the more I read the more I became aware of my own ignorance, and shed bitter tears over my deficiency. It seemed as if the wilderness of knowledge expanded and grew more perplexed as I advanced. Every height gained only revealed a wider region to be traversed, and nearly filled me with despair. I grew moody, silent, and unsocial, but studied on doggedly and incessantly. The only person with whom I held any conversation, was the worthy man in whose house I was quartered. He was honest and well-meaning, but perfectly ignorant, and I believe would have liked me much better if I had not been so much addicted to reading. He considered all books filled with lies and impositions, and seldom could look into one without finding something to rouse his spleen. Nothing put him into a greater passion than the assertion that the world turned on its own axis every four-and-twenty hours. He swore it was an outrage upon common sense. 'Why, if it did,' said he, 'there would not be a drop of water in the well by morning, and all the milk and cream in the dairy would be turned topsy-turvy!' And then to talk of the earth going round the sun! 'How do they know it? I've seen the sun rise every morning and set every evening for more than thirty years. They must not talk to *me* about the earth's going round the sun!'

"At another time he was in a perfect fret at being told the distance between the sun and moon. 'How can anyone tell the distance?' cried he. 'Who surveyed it? who carried the chain? By Jupiter! They only talk this way before me to annoy me. But then there's some people of sense who give in to this cursed humbug! There's Judge Broadnax, now, one of the best lawyers we have; isn't it surprising he should believe in such stuff? Why, sir, the other day I heard him talk of the distance from a star he called Mars to the sun! He must have got it out of one or other of those confounded books he's so fond of reading; a book some impudent fellow has written, who knew nobody could swear the distance was more or less.'

"For my own part, feeling my own deficiency in scientific lore, I never ventured to unsettle his conviction that the sun made his daily circuit round the earth; and for aught I said to the contrary, he lived and died in that belief.

"I had been about a year at Bardstown, living thus studiously and reclusely, when, as I was one day walking the street, I met two young girls, in one of whom I immediately recalled the little beauty whom I had kissed so impudently. She blushed up to the eyes, and so did I; but we both passed on without further sign of recognition. This second glimpse of her, however, caused an odd fluttering about my heart. I could not get her out of my thoughts for days. She quite interfered with my studies. I tried to think of her as a mere child, but it would not do; she had improved in beauty, and was tending toward womanhood: and then I myself was little better than a stripling. However, I did not attempt to seek after her, or even to find out who she was, but returned doggedly to my books. By degrees she faded from my thoughts, or if she did cross them occasionally, it was only to increase my despondency, for I feared that, with all my exertions, I should never be able to fit myself for the bar, or enable myself to support a wife.

"One cold stormy evening I was seated, in dumpish mood, in the bar-room of the inn, looking into the fire and turning over uncomfortable thoughts, when I was accosted by someone who had entered the room without my perceiving it. I looked up, and saw before me a tall, and, as I thought, pompous-looking man, arrayed in small-clothes and knee-buckles, with powdered head, and shoes nicely blacked and polished; a style of dress unparalleled in those days in that rough country. I took a pique against him from the very portliness of his appearance and stateliness of his manner, and bristled up as he accosted me. He demanded if my name was not Ringwood.

"I was startled, for I supposed myself perfectly *incognito*; but I answered in the affirmative.

" 'Your family, I believe, lives in Richmond.'

"My gorge began to rise. 'Yes, sir,' replied I, sulkily, 'my family does live in Richmond.'

" 'And what, may I ask, has brought you into this part of the country?'

" 'Zounds, sir!' cried I, starting on my feet. 'What business is it of yours? How dare you to question me in this manner?'

"The entrance of some persons prevented a reply; but I walked up and down the bar-room, fuming with conscious independence and insulted dignity, while the pompous-looking personage, who had thus trespassed upon my spleen, retired without proffering another word.

"The next day, while seated in my room, someone tapped at the door, and, on being bid to enter, the stranger in the powdered head, small-clothes, and shining shoes and buckles, walked in with ceremonious courtesy.

"My boyish pride was again in arms, but he subdued me. He was formal, but kind and friendly. He knew my family and understood my situation, and the dogged struggle I was making. A little conversation, when my jealous pride was once put to rest, drew everything from me. He was a lawyer of experience and of extensive practice, and offered at once to take me with him and direct my studies. The offer was too advantageous and gratifying not to be immediately accepted. From that time I began to look up. I was put into a proper track, and was enabled to study to a proper purpose. I made acquaintance, too, with some of the young men of the place who were in the same pursuit, and was encouraged at finding that I could 'hold my own' in argument with them. We instituted a debating-club, in which I soon became prominent and popular. Men of talents, engaged in other pursuits, joined it, and this diversified our subjects and put me on various tracks of inquiry. Ladies, too, attended some of our discussions, and this gave them a polite tone and had an influence on the manners of the debaters. My legal patron also may have had a favorable effect in correcting any roughness contracted in my hunter's life. He was calculated to bend me in an opposite direction, for he was of the old school; quoted 'Chesterfield' on all occasions, and talked of Sir Charles Grandison, who was his *beau ideal*. It was Sir Charles Grandison, however, Kentuckyized.

"I had always been fond of female society. My experience, however, had hitherto been among the rough daughters of the backwoodsmen, and I felt an awe of young ladies in 'store clothes,' delicately brought up. Two or three of the married ladies of Bardstown, who had heard me at the debating-club, determined that I was a genius, and undertook to bring me out. I believe I really improved under their hands, became quiet where I had been shy or sulky, and easy where I had been impudent.

"I called to take tea one evening with one of these ladies, when, to my surprise, and somewhat to my confusion, I found with her the identical blue-eyed little beauty whom I had so audaciously kissed. I was formally introduced to her, but neither of us betrayed any sign of previous acquaintance, except by blushing to the eyes. While tea was getting ready, the lady of the house went out of the room to give some directions, and left us alone.

"Heavens and earth, what a situation! I would have given all the pittance I was worth, to have been in the deepest dell of the forest. I felt the necessity of saying something in excuse of my former rudeness, but I could not conjure up an idea, nor utter a word. Every moment matters were growing worse. I felt at one time tempted to do as I had done when I robbed her of the kiss—bolt from the room, and take to flight; but I was chained to the spot, for I really longed to gain her good-will.

"At length I plucked up courage, on seeing that she was equally confused with myself, and walking desperately up to her, I exclaimed:

" 'I have been trying to muster up something to say to you, but I cannot. I feel that I am in a horrible scrape. Do have pity on me, and help me out of it!'

"A smile dimpled about her mouth, and played among the blushes of her cheek. She looked up with a shy but arch glance of the eye, that expressed a volume of comic recollection; we both broke into a laugh, and from that moment all went on well.

"A few evenings afterward I met her at a dance, and prosecuted the acquaintance. I soon became deeply attached to her, paid my court regularly, and before I was nineteen years of age had engaged myself to marry her. I spoke to her mother, a widow lady, to ask her consent. She seemed to demur; upon which, with my customary haste, I told her there would be no use in opposing the match, for if her daughter chose to have me, I would take her, in defiance of her family and the whole world.

"She laughed, and told me I need not give myself any uneasiness; there would be no unreasonable opposition. She knew my family, and all about me. The only obstacle was, that I had no means of supporting a wife, and she had nothing to give with her daughter.

"No matter; at that moment everything was bright before me. I was in one of my sanguine moods. I feared nothing, doubted nothing. So it was agreed that I should prosecute my studies, obtain a license, and as soon as I should be fairly launched in business, we would be married.

"I now prosecuted my studies with redoubled ardor, and was up to my ears in law, when I received a letter from my father, who had heard of me and my whereabouts. He applauded the course I had taken, but advised me to lay a foundation of general knowledge, and offered to defray my expenses if I would go to college. I felt the want of a general education, and was staggered with this offer. It militated somewhat against the self-dependent course I had so proudly, or rather conceitedly, marked out for myself, but it would enable me to enter more advantageously upon my legal career. I talked over the matter with the lovely girl to whom I was engaged. She sided in opinion with my father, and talked so disinterestedly, yet tenderly, that if possible, I loved her more than ever. I reluctantly, therefore, agreed to go to college for a couple of years, though it must necessarily postpone our union.

"Scarcely had I formed this resolution, when her mother was taken ill, and died, leaving her without a protector. This again altered all my plans. I felt as if I could protect her. I gave up all idea of collegiate studies; persuaded myself that by dint of industry and application I might overcome the deficiencies of education, and resolved to take out a license as soon as possible.

"That very autumn I was admitted to the bar, and within a month afterward was married. We were a young couple—she not much above sixteen, I not quite twenty—and both almost without a dollar in the world. The establishment which we set up was suited to our circumstances: a log-house, with two small rooms; a bed, a table, a half-dozen chairs, a half-dozen knives and forks, a half-dozen spoons; everything by half-dozens; a little Delft ware; everything in a small way: we were so poor, but then so happy!

"We had not been married many days when court was held at a country town, about twenty-five miles distant. It was necessary for me to go there, and put myself in the way of business; but how was I to go? I had expended all my means on our establishment; and then, it was hard parting with my wife so soon after marriage. However, go I must. Money must be made, or we should soon have the wolf at the door. I accordingly borrowed a horse, and borrowed a little cash, and rode off from my door, leaving my wife standing at it, and waving her hand after me. Her last look, so sweet and beaming, went to my heart. I felt as if I could go through fire and water for her.

"I arrived at the country town on a cool October evening. The inn was crowded, for the court was to commence on the following day. I knew no one, and wondered how I, a stranger and a mere youngster, was to make my way in such a crowd, and to get business. The public room was thronged with the idlers of the country, who gather together on such occasions. There was some drinking going forward, with much noise, and a little altercation. Just as I entered the room, I saw a rough bully of a fellow, who was partly intoxicated, strike an old man. He came swaggering by me, and elbowed me as he passed. I immediately knocked him down, and kicked him into the street. I needed no better introduction. In a moment I had a dozen rough shakes of the hand and invitations to drink, and found myself quite a personage in this rough assembly.

"The next morning the court opened. I took my seat among the lawyers, but felt as a mere spectator, not having a suit in progress or prospect, nor having any idea where business was to come from. In the course of the morning, a man was put at the bar charged with passing counterfeit money, and was asked if he was ready for trial. He answered in the negative. He had been confined in a place where there were no lawyers, and had not had an opportunity of consulting any. He was told to choose counsel from the lawyers present, and to be ready for trial on the following day. He looked round the court, and selected me. I was thunderstruck. I could not tell why he should make such a choice. I, a beardless youngster, unpractised at the bar, perfectly unknown. I felt diffident, yet delighted, and could have hugged the rascal.

"Before leaving the court, he gave me one hundred dollars in a bag, as a retaining fee. I could scarcely believe my senses: it seemed like a dream. The heaviness of the fee spoke but lightly in favor of his innocence, but that was no affair of mine. I was to be advocate, not judge, nor jury. I followed him to jail, and learned from him all the particulars of his case: thence I went to the clerk's office, and took minutes of the indictment. I then examined the law on the subject, and prepared my brief in my room. All this occupied me until midnight, when I went to bed, and tried to sleep. It was all in vain. Never in my life was I more wide awake. A host of thoughts and fancies kept rushing through my mind; the shower of gold that had so unexpectedly fallen into my lap; the idea of my poor little wife at home, that I was to astonish with my good fortune! But then the awful responsibility I had undertaken—to speak for the first time in a strange court; the expectations the culprit had evidently formed of my talents; all these, and a crowd of similar notions, kept whirling through my mind. I tossed about all night, fearing the morning would find me exhausted and incompetent; in a word, the day dawned on me, a miserable fellow!

"I got up feverish and nervous. I walked out before breakfast, striving to collect my thoughts, and tranquillize my feelings. It was a bright morning; the air was pure and frosty. I bathed my forehead and my hands in a beautiful running stream; but I could not allay the fever heat that raged within. I returned to breakfast, but could not eat. A single cup of coffee formed my repast. It was time to go to court, and I went there with a throbbing heart. I believe if it had not been for the thoughts of my little wife in her lonely log-house, I should have given back to the man his hundred dollars, and relinquished the cause. I took my seat, looking, I am convinced, more like the culprit than the rogue I was to defend.

"When the time came for me to speak, my heart died within me. I rose embarrassed and dismayed, and stammered in opening my cause. I went on from bad to worse, and felt as if I was going down hill. Just then the public prosecutor, a man of talents, but somewhat rough in his practice, made a sarcastic remark on something I had said. It was like an electric spark, and ran tingling through every vein in my body. In an instant my diffidence was gone. My whole spirit was in arms. I answered with promptness and bitterness, for I felt the cruelty of such an attack upon a novice in my situation. The public prosecutor made a kind of apology; this, from a man of his redoubted powers, was a vast concession. I renewed my argument with a fearless glow; carried the case through triumphantly, and the man was acquitted.

"This was the making of me. Everybody was curious to know who this new lawyer was, that had thus suddenly risen among them, and bearded the attorney-general at the very outset. The story of my *début* at the inn, on the preceding evening, when I had knocked down a bully, and kicked him out of doors, for striking an old man, was circulated, with favorable exaggerations. Even my very beardless chin and juvenile countenance were in my favor, for people gave me far more credit than I really deserved. The chance business which occurs in our country courts came thronging upon me. I was repeatedly employed in other causes; and by Saturday night, when the court closed, and I had paid my bill at the inn, I found myself with a hundred and fifty dollars in silver, three hundred dollars in notes, and a horse that I afterwards sold for two hundred dollars more.

"Never did miser gloat on his money with more delight. I locked the door of my room, piled the money in a heap upon the table, walked round it, sat with my elbows on the table and my chin upon my hands, and gazed upon it. Was I thinking of the money? No! I was thinking of my little wife at home. Another sleepless night ensued; but what a night of golden fancies and splendid air-castles! As soon as morning dawned, I was up, mounted the borrowed horse with which I had come to court, and led the other, which I had received as a fee. All the way I was delighting myself with the thoughts of the surprise I had in store for my little wife; for both of us had expected nothing but that I should spend all the money I had borrowed, and should return in debt.

"Our meeting was joyous, as you may suppose; but I played the part of the Indian hunter, who, when he returns from the chase, never for a time speaks of his success. She had prepared a snug little rustic meal for me, and while it was getting ready, I seated myself at an old-fashioned desk in one corner, and began to count over my money and put it away. She came to me before I had finished, and asked who I had collected the money for.

" 'For myself, to be sure,' replied I, with affected coolness; 'I made it at court.'

"She looked me for a moment in the face, incredulously. I tried to keep my countenance, and to play Indian, but it would not do. My muscles began to twitch; my feelings all at once gave way. I caught her in my arms; laughed, cried, and danced about the room, like a crazy man. From that time forward, we never wanted for money.

"I had not been long in successful practice, when I was surprised one day by a visit from my woodland patron, old Miller. The tidings of my prosperity had reached him in the wilderness, and he had walked one hundred and fifty miles on foot to see me. By that time I had improved my domestic establishment, and had all things comfortable about me. He looked around him with a wondering eye, at what he considered luxuries and superfluities; but supposed they were all right, in my altered circumstances. He said he did not know, upon the whole, but that I acted for the best. It is true, if game had continued plenty, it would have been a folly for me to quit a hunter's life; but hunting was pretty nigh done up in Kentucky. The buffalo had gone to Missouri; the elk were nearly gone also; deer, too, were growing scarce; they might last out his time, as he was growing old, but they were not worth setting up life upon. He had once lived on the borders of Virginia. Game grew scarce there; he followed it up across Kentucky, and now it was again giving him the slip; but he was too old to follow it farther.

"He remained with us three days. My wife did everything in her power to make him comfortable; but at the end of that time he said he must be off again to the woods. He was tired of the village, and of having so many people about him. He accordingly returned to the wilderness, and to hunting life. But I fear he did not make a good end of it; for I understand that a few years before his death he married Sukey Thomas, who lived at the White Oak Run."

The Phantom Island

Break, Phantasie, from thy cave of cloud,
*   And wave thy purple wings,*
Now all thy figures are allowed,
*   And various shapes of things.*
Create of airy forms a stream;
*   It must have blood and naught of phlegm;*
And though it be a waking dream,
*   Yet let it like an odor rise*
To all the senses here,
*   And fall like sleep upon their eyes,*
Or music on their ear.

BEN JONSON

"There are more things in heaven and earth than are dreamed of in our philosophy," and among these may be placed that marvel and mystery of the seas, the Island of St. Brandan. Those who have read the history of the Canaries, the fortunate islands of the ancients, may remember the wonders told of this enigmatical island. Occasionally it would be visible from their shores, stretching away in the clear bright west, to all appearance substantial like themselves, and still more beautiful. Expeditions would launch forth from the Canaries to explore this land of promise. For a time its sun-gilt peaks and long, shadowy promontories would remain distinctly visible, but in proportion as the voyagers approached, peak and promontory would gradually fade away until nothing would remain but blue sky above and deep blue water below. Hence this mysterious isle was stigmatized by ancient cosmographers with the name of Aprositus or the Inaccessible. The failure of numerous expeditions sent in quest of it, both in ancient and modern days, have at length caused its very existence to be called in question, and it has been rashly pronounced a mere optical illusion, like the Fata Morgana of the Straits of Messina, or has been classed with those unsubstantial regions known to mariners as Cape Fly Away and the coast of Cloud Land.

Let us not permit, however, the doubts of worldly-wise sceptics to rob us of all the glorious realms owned by happy credulity in days of yore. Be assured, O reader of easy faith! —thou for whom it is my delight to labor—be assured that such an island actually exists, and has from time to time been revealed to the gaze and trodden by the feet of favored mortals. Historians and philosophers may have their doubts, but its existence has been fully attested by that inspired race, the poets; who, being gifted with a kind of second sight, are enabled to discern those mysteries of nature hidden from the eyes of ordinary men. To this gifted race it has ever been a kind of wonderland. Here once bloomed, and perhaps still blooms, the famous garden of the Hesperides, with its golden fruit. Here, too, the sorceress Armida had her enchanted garden, in which she held the Christian paladin, Rinaldo, in delicious but inglorious thraldom, as set forth in the immortal lay of Tasso. It was in this island that Sycorax the witch held sway, when the

good Prospero and his infant daughter Miranda were wafted
to its shores. Who does not know the tale as told in the magic
page of Shakespeare? The isle was then,

> ——"full of noises,
> Sounds, and sweet airs, that give delight, and hurt not."

The island, in fact, at different times, has been under the sway
of different powers, genii of earth, and air, and ocean, who
have made it their shadowy abode. Hither have retired many
classic but broken-down deities, shorn of almost all their attributes, but who once ruled the poetic world. Here Neptune and
Amphitrite hold a diminished court, sovereigns in exile. Their
ocean-chariot, almost a wreck, lies bottom upward in some sea-
beaten cavern; their pursy Tritons and haggard Nereids bask
listlessly like seals about the rocks. Sometimes those deities as-
sume, it is said, a shadow of their ancient pomp, and glide in
state about a summer sea; and then, as some tall Indiaman
lies becalmed with idly flapping sail, her drowsy crew may hear
the mellow note of the Triton's shell swelling upon the ear as
the invisible pageant sweeps by.

On the shores of this wondrous isle the kraken heaves its unwieldy bulk and wallows many a rood. Here the sea-serpent,
that mighty but much-contested reptile, lies coiled up during
the intervals of its revelations to the eyes of true believers. Here
even the Flying Dutchman finds a port, and casts his anchor,
and furls his shadowy sail, and takes a brief repose from his
eternal cruisings.

In the deep bays and harbors of the island lies many a spell-
bound ship, long since given up as lost by the ruined merchant.
Here, too, its crew, long, long bewailed in vain, lie sleeping

from age to age in mossy grottos, or wander about in pleasing oblivion of all things. Here in caverns are garnered up the priceless treasures lost in the ocean. Here sparkles in vain the diamond and flames the carbuncle. Here are piled up rich bales of Oriental silks, boxes of pearls, and piles of golden ingots.

Such are some of the marvels related of this island, which may serve to throw light upon the following legend, of unquestionable truth, which I recommend to the implicit belief of the reader.

The Adalantado
of
the Seven Cities

A LEGEND OF ST. BRANDAN
BY WASHINGTON IRVING

In the early part of the fifteenth century, when Prince Henry of Portugal, of worthy memory, was pushing the career of discovery along the western coast of Africa, and the world was resounding with reports of golden regions on the mainland, and new-found islands in the ocean, there arrived at Lisbon an old bewildered pilot of the seas, who had been driven by tempests, he knew not whither, and raved about an island far in the deep, upon which he had landed, and which he had found peopled with Christians, and adorned with noble cities.

The inhabitants, he said, having never before been visited

by a ship, gathered round, and regarded him with surprise. They told him they were descendants of a band of Christians, who fled from Spain when that country was conquered by the Moslems. They were curious about the state of their fatherland, and grieved to hear that the Moslems still held possession of the kingdom of Granada. They would have taken the old navigator to church, to convince him of their orthodoxy; but, either through lack of devotion, or lack of faith in their words, he declined their invitation, and preferred to return on board of his ship. He was properly punished. A furious storm arose, drove him from his anchorage, hurried him out to sea, and he saw no more of the unknown island.

This strange story caused great marvel in Lisbon and elsewhere. Those versed in history remembered to have read, in an ancient chronicle, that, at the time of the conquest of Spain, in the eighth century, when the blessed cross was cast down and the crescent erected in its place, and when Christian churches were turned into Moslem mosques, seven bishops, at the head of seven bands of pious exiles, had fled from the peninsula, and embarked in quest of some ocean island, or distant land, where they might found seven Christian cities, and enjoy their faith unmolested.

The faith of these saints errant had hitherto remained a mystery, and their story had faded from memory; the report of the old tempest-tossed pilot, however, revived this long-forgotten theme; and it was determined by the pious and enthusiastic that the island thus accidentally discovered was the identical place of refuge whither the wandering bishops had been guided by a protecting Providence, and where they had folded their flocks.

This most excitable of worlds has always some darling object of chimerical enterprise; the "Island of the Seven Cities" now awakened as much interest and longing among zealous Christians as has the renowned city of Timbuctoo among adventurous travellers, or the Northeast passage among hardy navigators; and it was a frequent prayer of the devout, that these scattered and lost portions of the Christian family might be discovered and reunited to the great body of Christendom.

No one, however, entered into the matter with half the zeal of Don Fernando de Ulmo, a young cavalier of high standing in the Portuguese court, and of most sanguine and romantic temperament. He had recently come to his estate, and had run the round of all kinds of pleasures and excitements when this theme of popular talk and wonder presented itself. The Island of the Seven Cities became now the constant subject of his thoughts by day, and his dreams by night; it even rivalled his passion for a beautiful girl, one of the greatest belles in Lisbon, to whom he was betrothed. At length his imagination became so inflamed on the subject, that he determined to fit out an expedition, at his own expense, and set sail in quest of this sainted island. It could not be a cruise of any great extent; for, according to the calculations of the tempest-tossed pilot, it must be somewhere in the latitude of the Canaries; which at that time, when the new world was as yet undiscovered, formed the frontier of ocean enterprise. Don Fernando applied to the crown for countenance and protection. As he was a favorite at court, the usual patronage was readily extended to him; that is to say, he received a commission from the king, Don Ioam II, constituting him Adalantado, or military governor, of any country he might discover, with the single proviso, that he should bear all the expenses of the discovery, and pay a tenth of the profits to the crown.

Don Fernando now set to work in the true spirit of a projector. He sold acre after acre of solid land, and invested the proceeds in ships, guns, ammunition, and sea-stores. Even his old family mansion in Lisbon was mortgaged without scruple, for he looked forward to a palace in one of the Seven Cities, of which he was to be Adalantado. This was the age of nautical romance, when the thoughts of all speculative dreamers were turned to the ocean. The scheme of Don Fernando, therefore, drew adventurers of every kind. The merchant promised himself new marts of opulent traffic; the soldier hoped to sack and plunder some one or other of those Seven Cities; even the fat monk shook off the sleep and sloth of the cloister, to join in a crusade which promised such increase to the possessions of the Church.

One person alone regarded the whole project with sovereign contempt and growing hostility. This was Don Ramiro Alvarez, the father of the beautiful Serafina, to whom Don Fernando was betrothed. He was one of those perverse, matter-of-fact old men, who are prone to oppose everything speculative and romantic. He had no faith in the Island of the Seven Cities; regarded the projected cruise as a crack-brained freak; looked with angry eye and internal heart-burning on the conduct of his intended son-in-law, chaffering away solid lands for lands in the moon; and scoffingly dubbed him Adalantado of Cloud Land. In fact, he had never really relished the intended match, to which his consent had been slowly extorted by the tears and entreaties of his daughter. It is true he could have no reasonable objections to the youth, for Don Fernando was the very flower of Portuguese chivalry. No one could excel him at the tilting match, or the riding at the ring; none was more bold and dexterous in the bull-fight; none composed more gallant madrigals in praise of his lady's charms, or sang them with sweeter tones to the accompaniment of her guitar; nor could anyone handle the castanets and dance the bolero with more captivating grace. All these admirable qualities and endowments, however, though they had been sufficient to win the heart of Serafina, were nothing in the eyes of her unreasonable father. Oh Cupid, god of Love! Why will fathers always be so unreasonable?

The engagement to Serafina had threatened at first to throw an obstacle in the way of the expedition of Don Fernando, and for a time perplexed him in the extreme. He was passionately attached to the young lady; but he was also passionately bent on this romantic enterprise. How should he reconcile the two passionate inclinations? A simple and obvious arrangement at length presented itself—marry Serafina, enjoy a portion of the honeymoon at once, and defer the rest until his return from the discovery of the Seven Cities!

He hastened to make known this most excellent arrangement to Don Ramiro, when the long-smothered wrath of the old cavalier burst forth. He reproached him with being the dupe of wandering vagabonds and wild schemers, and with squandering all his real possessions, in pursuit of empty bubbles. Don Fernando was too sanguine a projector, and too young a man, to listen tamely to such language. He acted with what is technically called "becoming spirit." A high quarrel ensued; Don Ramiro pronounced him a madman, and forbade all farther intercourse with his daughter until he should give proof of returning sanity by abandoning this madcap enterprise; while Don Fernando flung out of the house, more bent than ever on the expedition, from the idea of triumphing over the incredulity of the graybeard, when he should return successful. Don Ramiro's heart misgave him. Who knows, thought he, but this crack-brained visionary may persuade my daughter to elope with him, and share his throne in this unknown paradise of fools? If I could only keep her safe until his ships are fairly out at sea!

He repaired to her apartment, represented to her the sanguine, unsteady character of her lover and the chimerical value of his schemes, and urged the propriety of suspending all intercourse with him until he should recover from his present hallucination. She bowed her head as if in filial acquiescence, whereupon he folded her to his bosom with parental fondness and kissed away a tear that was stealing over her cheek, but as he left the chamber quietly turned the key in the lock; for though he was a fond father and had a high opinion of the submissive temper of his child, he had a still higher opinion of the conservative virtues of lock and key, and determined to trust to them until the caravels should sail. Whether the damsel had been in anywise shaken in her faith as to the schemes of her lover by her father's eloquence, tradition does not say; but certain it is, that, the moment she heard the key turn in the lock, she became a firm believer in the Island of the Seven Cities.

The door was locked; but her will was unconfined. A window of the chamber opened into one of those stone balconies, secured by iron bars, which project like huge cages from Portuguese and Spanish houses. Within this balcony the beautiful

Serafina had her birds and flowers, and here she was accustomed to sit on moonlight nights as in a bower, and touch her guitar and sing like a wakeful nightingale. From this balcony an intercourse was now maintained between the lovers, against which the lock and key of Don Ramiro were of no avail. All day would Fernando be occupied hurrying the equipments of his ships, but evening found him in sweet discourse beneath his lady's window.

At length the preparations were completed. Two gallant caravels lay at anchor in the Tagus ready to sail at sunrise. Late at night by the pale light of a waning moon the lover had his last interview. The beautiful Serafina was sad at heart and full of dark forebodings; her lover full of hope and confidence. "A few short months," said he, "and I shall return in triumph. Thy father will then blush at his incredulity, and hasten to welcome to his house the Adalantado of the Seven Cities."

The gentle lady shook her head. It was not on this point she felt distrust. She was a thorough believer in the Island of the Seven Cities, and so sure of the success of the enterprise that she might have been tempted to join it had not the balcony been high and the grating strong. Other considerations induced that dubious shaking of the head. She had heard of the inconstancy of the seas, and the inconstancy of those who roam them. Might not Fernando meet with other loves in foreign ports? Might not some peerless beauty in one or other of those Seven Cities efface the image of Serafina from his mind? Now let the truth be spoken, the beautiful Serafina had reason for her disquiet. If Don Fernando had any fault in the world, it was that of being rather inflammable and apt to take fire from every sparkling eye. He had been somewhat of a rover among the sex on shore, what might he be on sea?

She ventured to express her doubt, but he spurned at the very idea. "What! Be false to Serafina! He bow at the shrine of another beauty? Never! Never!" Repeatedly did he bend his knee, and smite his breast, and call upon the silver moon to witness his sincerity and truth.

He retorted the doubt. "Might not Serafina herself forget her plighted faith? Might not some wealthier rival present himself while he was tossing on the sea; and, backed by her father's wishes, win the treasure of her hand!"

The beautiful Serafina raised her white arms between the iron bars of the balcony, and, like her lover, invoked the moon to testify her vows. Alas! How little did Fernando know her heart. The more her father should oppose, the more would she be fixed in faith. Though years should intervene, Fernando on his return would find her true. Even should the salt sea swallow him up (and her eyes shed salt tears at the very thought), never would she be the wife of another! Never, *never*, NEVER! She drew from her finger a ring gemmed with a ruby heart, and dropped it from the balcony, a parting pledge of constancy.

Thus the lovers parted with many a tender word and plighted vow. But will they keep those vows? Perish the doubt! Have they not called the constant moon to witness?

With the morning dawn the caravels dropped down the Tagus, and put to sea. They steered for the Canaries, in those days the regions of nautical discovery and romance, and the outposts of the known world, for as yet Columbus had not steered his daring barks across the ocean. Scarce had they reached those latitudes when they were separated by a violent tempest. For many days was the caravel of Don Fernando driven about at the mercy of the elements; all seamanship was baffled, destruction seemed inevitable and the crew were in despair. All at once the storm subsided; the ocean sank into a calm; the clouds which had veiled the face of heaven were suddenly withdrawn, and the tempest-tossed mariners beheld a fair and mountainous island, emerging as if by enchantment from the murky gloom. They rubbed their eyes and gazed for a time almost incredulously, yet there lay the island spread out in lovely landscapes, with the late stormy sea laving its shores with peaceful billows.

The pilot of the caravel consulted his maps and charts; no island like the one before him was laid down as existing in those parts; it is true he had lost his reckoning in the late storm, but, according to his calculations, he could not be far from the Canaries; and this was not one of that group of islands. The caravel now lay perfectly becalmed off the mouth of a river, on the banks of which, about a league from the sea, was descried a noble city, with lofty walls and towers, and a protecting castle.

After a time, a stately barge with sixteen oars was seen emerging from the river, and approaching the caravel. It was quaintly carved and gilt; the oarsmen were clad in antique garb, their oars painted of a bright crimson, and they came slowly and solemnly, keeping time as they rowed to the cadence of an old Spanish ditty. Under a silken canopy in the stern, sat a cavalier richly clad, and over his head was a banner bearing the sacred emblem of the cross.

When the barge reached the caravel, the cavalier stepped on board. He was tall and gaunt; with a long Spanish visage, moustaches that curled up to his eyes, and a forked beard. He wore gauntlets reaching to his elbows, a Toledo blade strutting out behind, with a basket hilt, in which he carried his handkerchief. His air was lofty and precise, and bespoke indisputably the hidalgo. Thrusting out a long spindle leg, he took off a huge sombrero, and swaying it until the feather swept the ground, accosted Don Fernando in the old Castilian language, and with the old Castilian courtesy, welcoming him to the Island of the Seven Cities.

Don Fernando was overwhelmed with astonishment. Could this be true? Had he really been tempest-driven to the very land of which he was in quest?

It was even so. That very day the inhabitants were holding high festival in commemoration of the escape of their ancestors from the Moors. The arrival of the caravel at such a juncture was considered a good omen, the accomplishment of an ancient prophecy through which the island was to be restored to the great community of Christendom. The cavalier before him was grand-chamberlain, sent by the alcayde to invite him to the festivities of the capital.

Don Fernando could scarce believe that this was not all a dream. He made known his name and the object of his voyage. The grand chamberlain declared that all was in perfect accordance with the ancient prophecy, and that the moment his credentials were presented, he would be acknowledged as the Adalantado of the Seven Cities. In the meantime the day was waning; the barge was ready to convey him to the land, and would as assuredly bring him back.

Don Fernando's pilot, a veteran of the seas, drew him aside and expostulated against his venturing, on the mere word of a

stranger, to land in a strange barge on an unknown shore. "Who knows, Señor, what land this is, or what people inhabit it?"

Don Fernando was not to be dissuaded. Had he not believed in this island when all the world doubted? Had he not sought it in defiance of storm and tempest, and was he now to shrink from its shores when they lay before him in calm weather? In a word, was not faith the very corner-stone of his enterprise?

Having arrayed himself, therefore, in gala dress befitting the occasion, he took his seat in the barge. The grand chamberlain seated himself opposite. The rowers plied their oars, and renewed the mournful old ditty, and the gorgeous but unwieldy barge moved slowly through the water.

The night closed in before they entered the river, and swept along past rock and promontory, each guarded by its tower. At every post they were challenged by the sentinel.

"Who goes there?"

"The Adalantado of the Seven Cities."

"Welcome, Señor Adalantado. Pass on."

Entering the harbor they rowed close by an armed galley of ancient form. Soldiers with crossbows patrolled the deck.

"Who goes there?"

"The Adalantado of the Seven Cities."

"Welcome, Señor Adalantado. Pass on."

They landed at a broad flight of stone steps, leading up between two massive towers, and knocked at the water-gate. A sentinel, in ancient steel casque, looked from the barbican.

"Who is there?"

"The Adalantado of the Seven Cities."

"Welcome, Señor Adalantado."

The gate swung open, grating upon rusty hinges. They entered between two rows of warriors in Gothic armor, with crossbows, maces, battle-axes, and faces old fashioned as their armor. There were processions through the streets, in commemoration of the landing of the seven Bishops and their followers, and bonfires at which effigies of losel Moors expiated their invasion of Christendom by a kind of *auto-da-fé*. The groups round the fires, uncouth in their attire, looked like the fantastic figures that roam the streets in Carnival time. Even the dames who gazed down from Gothic balconies hung with antique tapestry, resembled effigies dressed up in Christmas mummeries. Everything, in short, bore the stamp of former ages, as if the world had suddenly rolled back for several centuries. Nor was this to be wondered at. Had not the Island of the Seven Cities been cut off from the rest of the world for several hundred years; and were not these the modes and customs of Gothic Spain before it was conquered by the Moors?

Arrived at the palace of the alcayde, the grand chamberlain knocked at the portal. The porter looked through a wicket, and demanded who was there.

"The Adalantado of the Seven Cities."

The portal was thrown wide open. The grand chamberlain led the way up a vast, heavily moulded, marble staircase, and into a hall of ceremony, where was the alcayde with several of the principal dignitaries of the city, who had a marvellous resemblance, in form and feature, to the quaint figures in old illuminated manuscripts.

The grand chamberlain stepped forward and announced the name and title of the stranger guest, and the extraordinary nature of his mission. The announcement appeared to create no extraordinary emotion or surprise, but to be received as the anticipated fulfilment of a prophecy.

The reception of Don Fernando, however, was profoundly gracious, though in the same style of stately courtesy which everywhere prevailed. He would have produced his credentials, but this was courteously declined. The evening was devoted to high festivity; the following day, when he should enter the port with his caravel, would be devoted to business, when the credentials would be received in due form, and he inducted into office as Adalantado of the Seven Cities.

Don Fernando was now conducted through one of those interminable suites of apartments, the pride of Spanish palaces, all furnished in a style of obsolete magnificence. In a vast saloon, blazing with tapers, was assembled all the aristocracy and fashion of the city—stately dames and cavaliers, the very counterpart of the figures in the tapestry which decorated the walls. Fernando gazed in silent marvel. It was a reflex of the proud aristocracy of Spain in the time of Roderick the Goth.

The festivities of the evening were all in the style of solemn and antiquated ceremonial. There was a dance, but it was as if the old tapestry were put in motion, and all the figures moving in stately measure about the floor. There was one exception, and one that told powerfully upon the susceptible Adalantado. The alcayde's daughter—such a ripe, melting beauty! Her dress, it is true, like the dresses of her neighbors, might have been worn before the flood, but she had the black Andalusian eye, a glance of which, through its long dark lashes, is irresistible. Her voice, too, her manner, her undulating movements, all smacked of Andalusia, and showed how female charms may be transmitted from age to age, and clime to clime, without ever going out of fashion. Those who know the witchery of the sex, in that most amorous part of amorous old Spain, may judge of the fascination to which Don Fernando was exposed, as he joined in the dance with one of its most captivating descendants.

He sat beside her at the banquet! Such an old-world feast! Such obsolete dainties! At the head of the table the peacock, that bird of state and ceremony, was served up in full plumage on a golden dish. As Don Fernando cast his eyes down the glittering board, what a vista presented itself of odd heads and head-dresses; of formal bearded dignitaries and stately dames, with castellated locks and towering plumes! Is it to be wondered at that he should turn with delight from these antiquated figures to the alcayde's daughter, all smiles and dimples, and melting looks and melting accents? Beside, for I wish to give him every excuse in my power, he was in a particularly excitable mood from the novelty of the scene before him, from this realization of all his hopes and fancies, and from frequent draughts of the wine-cup, presented to him at every moment by officious pages during the banquet.

In a word—there is no concealing the matter—before the evening was over, Don Fernando was making love outright to the alcayde's daughter. They had wandered together to a moonlit balcony of the palace, and he was charming her ear with one of those love-ditties with which, in a like balcony, he had serenaded the beautiful Serafina.

The damsel hung her head coyly. "Ah! Señor, these are flattering words; but you cavaliers, who roam the seas, are unsteady as its waves. Tomorrow you will be throned in state,

Adalantado of the Seven Cities; and will think no more of the alcayde's daughter."

Don Fernando in the intoxication of the moment called the moon to witness his sincerity. As he raised his hand in adjuration, the chaste moon cast a ray upon the ring that sparkled on his finger. It caught the damsel's eye. "Signor Adalantado," said she archly, "I have no great faith in the moon, but give me that ring upon your finger in pledge of the truth of what you profess."

The gallant Adalantado was taken by surprise; there was no parrying this sudden appeal; before he had time to reflect, the ring of the beautiful Serafina glittered on the finger of the alcayde's daughter.

At this eventful moment the chamberlain approached with lofty demeanor, and announced that the barge was waiting to bear him back to the caravel. I forbear to relate the ceremonious partings with the alcayde and his dignitaries, and the tender farewell of the alcayde's daughter. He took his seat in the barge opposite the grand chamberlain. The rowers plied their crimson oars in the same slow and stately manner, to the cadence of the same mournful old ditty. His brain was in a whirl with all that he had seen, and his heart now and then gave him a twinge as he thought of his temporary infidelity to the beautiful Serafina. The barge sallied out into the sea, but no caravel was to be seen; doubtless she had been carried to a distance by the current of the river. The oarsmen rowed on; their monotonous chant had a lulling effect. A drowsy influence crept over Don Fernando. Objects swam before his eyes.

The oarsmen assumed odd shapes as in a dream. The grand chamberlain grew larger and larger, and taller and taller. He took off his huge sombrero, and held it over the head of Don Fernando, like an extinguisher over a candle. The latter cowered beneath it; he felt himself sinking in the socket.

"Good night! Señor Adalantado of the Seven Cities!" said the grand chamberlain.

The sombrero slowly descended—Don Fernando was extinguished!

How long he remained extinct no mortal man can tell. When he returned to consciousness, he found himself in a strange cabin, surrounded by strangers. He rubbed his eyes, and looked round him wildly. Where was he? On board a Portuguese ship, bound to Lisbon. How came he there? He had been taken senseless from a wreck drifting about the ocean.

Don Fernando was more and more confounded and perplexed. He recalled, one by one, everything that had happened to him in the Island of the Seven Cities, until he had been extinguished by the sombrero of the grand chamberlain. But what had happened to him since? What had become of his caravel? Was it the wreck of her on which he had been found floating?

The people about him could give no information on the subject. He entreated them to take him to the Island of the Seven Cities, which could not be far off, told them all that had befallen him there; that he had but to land to be received as Adalantado; when he would reward them magnificently for their services.

They regarded his words as the ravings of delirium, and in their honest solicitude for the restoration of his reason, administered such rough remedies that he was fain to drop the subject, and observe a cautious taciturnity.

At length they arrived in the Tagus, and anchored before the famous city of Lisbon. Don Fernando sprang joyfully on shore, and hastened to his ancestral mansion. A strange porter opened the door, who knew nothing of him or his family; no people of the name had inhabited the house for many a year.

He sought the mansion of Don Ramiro. He approached the balcony beneath which he had bidden farewell to Serafina. Did his eyes deceive him? No! There was Serafina herself among the flowers in the balcony. He raised his arms toward her with an exclamation of rapture. She cast upon him a look of indignation, and, hastily retiring, closed the casement with a slam that testified her displeasure.

Could she have heard of his flirtation with the alcayde's daughter? But that was mere transient gallantry. A moment's interview would dispel every doubt of his constancy.

He rang at the door; as it was opened by the porter he rushed upstairs, sought the well-known chamber, and threw himself at the feet of Serafina. She started back with affright, and took refuge in the arms of a youthful cavalier.

"What mean you, Señor," cried the latter, "by this intrusion?"

"What right have you to ask the question?" demanded Don Fernando fiercely.

"The right of an affianced suitor!"

Don Fernando started and turned pale. "Oh, Serafina! Serafina!" cried he, in a tone of agony. "Is this thy plighted constancy?"

"Serafina? What mean you by Serafina, Señor? If this be the lady you intend, her name is Maria."

"May I not believe my senses? May I not believe my heart?"

cried Don Fernando. "Is not this Serafina Alvarez, the original of yon portrait, which, less fickle than herself, still smiles on me from the wall?"

"Holy Virgin!" cried the young lady, casting her eyes upon the portrait. "He is talking of my great-grandmother!"

An explanation ensued, if that could be called an explanation which plunged the unfortunate Fernando into ten-fold perplexity. If he might believe his eyes, he saw before him his beloved Serafina; if he might believe his ears, it was merely her hereditary form and features, perpetuated in the person of her great-granddaughter.

His brain began to spin. He sought the office of the Minister of Marine, and made a report of his expedition, and of the Island of the Seven Cities, which he had so fortunately discovered. Nobody knew anything of such an expedition, or such an island. He declared that he had undertaken the enterprise under a formal contract with the crown, and had received a regular commission, constituting him Adalantado. This must be matter of record, and he insisted loudly that the books of the department should be consulted. The wordy strife at length attracted the attention of an old gray-headed clerk, who sat perched on a high stool, at a high desk, with iron-rimmed spectacles on the top of a thin, pinched nose, copying records into an enormous folio. He had wintered and summered in the department for a great part of a century, until he had almost grown to be a piece of the desk at which he sat; his memory was a mere index of official facts and documents, and his brain was little better than red tape and parchment. After peering down for a time from his lofty perch, and ascertaining the matter in controversy, he put his pen behind his ear, and descended. He remembered to have heard something from his predecessor about an expedition of the kind in question, but then it had sailed during the reign of Don Ioam II, and he had been dead at least a hundred years. To put the matter beyond dispute, however, the archives of the Torre do Tombo, that sepulchre of old Portuguese documents, were diligently searched, and a record was found of a contract between the crown and one Fernando de Ulmo, for the discovery of the Island of the Seven Cities, and of a commission secured to him as Adalantado of the country he might discover.

"There!" cried Don Fernando, triumphantly. "There you have proof, before your own eyes, of what I have said. I am the Fernando de Ulmo specified in that record. I have discovered the Island of the Seven Cities, and am entitled to the Adalantado, according to contract."

The story of Don Fernando had certainly, what is pronounced the best of historical foundation, documentary evidence; but when a man, in the bloom of youth, talked of events that had taken place above a century previously, as having happened to himself, it is no wonder that he was set down for a madman.

The old clerk looked at him from above and below his spectacles, shrugged his shoulders, stroked his chin, reascended his lofty stool, took the pen from behind his ears, and resumed his daily and eternal task, copying records into the fiftieth volume of a series of gigantic folios. The other clerks winked at each other shrewdly, and dispersed to their several places, and poor Don Fernando, thus left to himself, flung out of the office, almost driven wild by these repeated perplexities.

In the confusion of his mind, he instinctively repaired to

the mansion of Alvarez, but it was barred against him. To break the delusion under which the youth apparently labored, and to convince him that the Serafina about whom he raved was really dead, he was conducted to her tomb. There she lay, a stately matron, cut out in alabaster; and there lay her husband beside her; a portly cavalier, in armor; and there knelt, on each side, the effigies of a numerous progeny, proving that she had been a fruitful vine. Even the very monument gave evidence of the lapse of time; the hands of her husband, folded as if in prayer, had lost their fingers, and the face of the once lovely Serafina was without a nose.

Don Fernando felt a transient glow of indignation at beholding this monumental proof of the inconstancy of his mistress; but who could expect a mistress to remain constant during a whole century of absence? And what right had he to rail about constancy, after what had passed between himself and the alcayde's daughter? The unfortunate cavalier performed one pious act of tender devotion; he had the alabaster nose of Serafina restored by a skilful statuary, and then tore himself from the tomb.

He could now no longer doubt the fact that, somehow or other, he had skipped over a whole century, during the night he had spent at the Island of the Seven Cities; and he was now as complete a stranger in his native city, as if he had never been there. A thousand times did he wish himself back to that wonderful island, with its antiquated banquet halls, where he had been so courteously received; and now that the once young and beautiful Serafina was nothing but a great-grandmother in marble, with generations of descendants, a thousand times would he recall the melting black eyes of the alcayde's daughter, who doubtless, like himself, was still flourishing in fresh juvenility, and breathe a secret wish that he was seated by her side.

He would at once have set on foot another expedition, at his own expense, to cruise in search of the sainted island, but his means were exhausted. He endeavored to rouse others to the enterprise, setting forth the certainty of profitable results, of which his own experience furnished such unquestionable proof. Alas! No one would give faith to this tale; but looked upon it as the feverish dream of a shipwrecked man. He persisted in his efforts; holding forth in all places and all companies, until he became an object of jest and jeer to the light-minded, who mistook his earnest enthusiasm for a proof of insanity; and the very children in the streets bantered him with the title of "The Adalantado of the Seven Cities."

Finding all efforts in vain, in his native city of Lisbon, he took shipping for the Canaries, as being nearer the latitude of his former cruise, and inhabited by people given to nautical adventure. Here he found ready listeners to his story; for the old pilots and mariners of those parts were notorious island-hunters, and devout believers in all the wonders of the seas. Indeed, one and all treated his adventure as a common occurrence, and turning to each other, with a sagacious nod of the head, observed, "He has been at the Island of St. Brandan."

They then went on to inform him of that great marvel and enigma of the ocean; of its repeated appearance to the inhabitants of their islands; and of the many but ineffectual expeditions that had been made in search of it. They took him to a promontory of the island of Palma, whence the shadowy St. Brandan had oftenest been descried, and they pointed out the very tract in the west where its mountains had been seen.

Don Fernando listened with rapt attention. He had no longer a doubt that this mysterious and fugacious island must be the same with that of the Seven Cities; and that some supernatural influence connected with it had operated upon himself, and made the events of a night occupy the space of a century.

He endeavored, but in vain, to rouse the islanders to another attempt at discovery; they had given up the phantom island as indeed inaccessible. Fernando, however, was not to be discouraged. The idea wore itself deeper and deeper in his mind, until it became the engrossing subject of his thoughts and object of his being. Every morning he would repair to the promontory of Palma, and sit there throughout the livelong day, in hopes of seeing the fairy mountains of St. Brandan peering above the horizon; every evening he returned to his home, a disappointed man, but ready to resume his post on the following morning.

His assiduity was all in vain. He grew gray in his ineffectual attempt; and was at length found dead at his post. His grave is still shown in the island of Palma, and a cross is erected on the spot where he used to sit and look out upon the sea, in hopes of the reappearance of the phantom island.

Note—For various particulars concerning the *Island of St. Brandan* and the *Island of the Seven Cities*, those ancient problems of the ocean, the curious reader is referred to articles under those heads in the Appendix to the *Life of Columbus*.